The Decision

A Novel of Germany

Karen A. Wyle

Oblique Angles Press

Dedication

To the brave and honest boy who became my father.

And to all those who, for one moment or for far longer, acted to save and protect Jews in Nazi-occupied Europe.

Prefatory Note

When I first considered writing this book, I thought it went without saying that my main character's statements, assumptions, and thoughts about Jews were not to be taken as valid. But since that time, we have seen hordes of people in the United States and Europe shouting their support for those who murderously attack Jews. So I guess it doesn't go without saying, after all, that what German Nazis and proto-Nazis had to say about Jews is slanderous and vile.

Introduction

Aside from a few unknown details, the incident presented at the beginning of this narrative is true. I know because the three boys with bicycles were my father and two of his brothers.

This incident cries out for explanation, but all I have — all my family has — is conjecture. So conjecture is what follows.

the bicycle accident

It was October of 1938, a cloudy day, not too warm and not too cold. A few weeks later, on November 9th and 10th, would come Kristallnacht, "the night of broken glass," when mobs — including but not limited to SS troops — rampaged through Berlin and other cities killing Jews and destroying Jewish places of worship, schools, hospitals, shops, homes, and even businesses formerly owned by Jews. Kristallnacht would mark a turning point after which anti-Jewish laws, already proliferating, multiplied greatly and violence against Jews became widespread. Already, it was increasingly difficult for Jews to leave Germany, and it would only become more so.

The street was not one of Berlin's broadest boulevards, but it had two lanes each way, with a central divider broad enough for *die Elektrische* — the electric trolley cars — to run down it. Big double-decker buses could often be seen going east and west. Those walking down the street or standing on the corner could occasionally hear the trolley conductor's bell warning pedestrians to stand clear, or the screeching noise the car made as it rounded a curve. They might see, also, the little sparks that sometimes flew from where the rods touched the power line.

On this October day, three boys sped along the avenue on what looked like brand new bicycles, the kind a Jewish family might buy with the money they would not be allowed to take out of the country. The two older boys deftly avoided all obstacles, while the youngest appeared less experienced and skilled. The older boys took turns glancing back at the youngest, but they had little attention to spare from the vehicles and the small number of pedestrians — and the youngest boy had less.

And then a wobble or a swerve brought the youngest boy's path across the path of an older man, his hair a mixture of gray and white, riding his own bicycle. The wheels entangled and brought both bicycles crashing to the ground. The clash and grinding of metal, the thud of falling bicycles and bodies, soon blended with mutters and gasps from the few onlookers as they saw that the old man's bicycle had fallen close to the path of a bus approaching from behind.

The bus driver slammed on his brakes and jerked the steering wheel to the left, away from where the old man lay entangled with his bicycle. But meanwhile, a trolley bore down on bus, bicycle, and man. For a moment, the watchers fell silent as if each of them was holding his or her breath. All that could be heard was the warning clang of the trolley, and then the squeal of its brakes as it shuddered to a stop mere inches from the old man's arm.

The few spectators became a crowd as passengers from both bus and trolley disembarked to see what had happened. Those who had seen the actual accident and the near disaster made haste to inform the newcomers in a babble of curious or excited conversations. The crowd now had leisure to look at the two older boys, who had dropped their bicycles, and the youngest boy climbing to his feet; the youngest was white and shaking. The smaller of the older boys stood straight and wide-eyed; the tallest and biggest boy looked quickly from side to side as if assessing the scene. Next to the biggest boy stood a tall man in a white raincoat, still in service among the Traffic Police after its introduction during the

1936 Olympics. The policeman wore his uniform beneath the raincoat; he had loosened the tie that came with it. Visible beneath the partly open collar of the uniform was the brown shirt of a Nazi stormtrooper.

The older boys glanced at the man and then went rigid and looked away. The biggest boy and the youngest boy could have passed for Aryans, but no one in the crowd could have missed the fact that the thin, wiry boy with the tightly curled black hair was Jewish.

The biggest boy assumed an air of conspicuous innocence as the policeman asked in a relatively quiet voice, "Did you boys have anything to do with this?"

The biggest boy opened his mouth, but the wiry boy was already saying, "*Jawohl, Offizier.*" (Yes, Officer.)

The policeman looked at all three boys in turn, studying, scrutinizing, before he said, "Are you boys Jewish?"

The biggest boy twitched, as if longing to silence the one who had already spoken, but knowing it would only make things worse. The wiry black-haired boy answered, "*Jawohl, Offizier.*"

Muttering arose from the crowd. The policeman bent closer, then stood up again. Softly, but in German's command mode, he ordered, "DISAPPEAR."

The boys' bodies jolted with the shock. Then they seized their bicycles, righted them, and rode away, the two older boys neck and neck and the youngest straggling a little behind.

They survived.

The boys never knew the policeman's name. But let's call him Hans.

PART 1

Chapter 1

Spring 1915

Mutti always started her stories from before the war with something like "You probably don't remember this, my poor Hansi. . . ." But Hansi remembered, a little.

He remembered living in a bigger flat, with more rooms and a little garden in front. His big brother Otto had his own bedroom then, instead of sharing one with Hansi and Lotte. That was back when Vati worked in a bank, before the war. They still lived in Berlin, but now they lived downstairs from Mutti's sister Gertrud, which was all right, because he got to play with Aunt Gertrud's children. Mutti said they were his cousins. Aunt Gertrud looked like Mutti if Mutti had been plump. She had a louder voice, and Mutti said it had always been loud.

He remembered Vati, a great big man with a beard Hansi could hide his hands in, and a voice even lower than Uncle Helmut upstairs. Hansi remembered curling up on the sofa between the two of them after a supper that filled his belly. And there was another time —"Mutti, did Vati take me to see a great big stone gate with horses on it?" They had taken a trolley, the air whipping past as they sat, sparks snapping and hissing from the wire overhead. He'd been afraid of the sparks, and Vati had rubbed his head and told him to be a brave little man, or they'd have to go home. And then he'd got to sit on Vati's shoulders, way up high, with Vati holding his legs tight so Hansi could look up even higher, up, up, to where the great big stones went flat and a woman made all of metal rode a metal chariot with four metal horses in front of it. Vati told him the woman and chariot and horses had been all the way to another country, Paris, when a bad man beat Germany in a war and took them away, but then the bad man had lost the war after all and the horses had come home.

He remembered, too, another day with an excited crowd filling the street, jostling him and surrounding him so he couldn't see anything but backs and shoulders and arms. And then Vati hoisting him up onto his shoulders so he could see.

He hadn't been up that high since then. Mutti couldn't lift him like that. Sometimes she'd pull him against her and hug him tight, or want him to sit on her lap even though he was too big for that sort of thing. Hansi's little sister Lotte still liked it, and if Hansi wriggled, she'd come running up and tug him away from Mutti so she could take his place.

This time Hansi didn't even pretend to mind. Instead, he asked Mutti, "Can I go play now?" Maybe his big brother Otto and the other boys would let him play soldiers this time. If he asked often enough, they might give in.

But Mutti shook her head. "First, practice your letters. You'll be starting school before you know it, and I want you to be ready. And don't pout at me like that! Remember, Vati is counting on you to make something of yourself."

Hansi planted his fists on his hips. "I am something! Aren't I something?"

Mutti stopped frowning at him and waved her fingers for him to come closer. "Of course you are, my little bear. Here, come sit next to me."

He climbed back up on the sofa and snuggled close. Lotte, still on Mutti's lap, stuck out her tongue at him, but he ignored her and said, "Would you tell us a story about Vati?"

Mutti sighed and then smiled. "Of course! Well . . . you know your Vati is a soldier, brave and strong, happy to fight for the Vaterland and the Kaiser. Oh, he looked so fine on the day he and the other soldiers marched off to war! All in their uniforms, so clean and new, marching down the street — "

Lotte jumped down from the sofa and started marching back and forth in front of it, bony knees rising as high as she could lift them. Mutti beamed and clapped. Hansi thought of sticking out his tongue the way Lotte had, but Mutti might scold him, so he just said, "Weren't they singing? Like the song Vati taught me before he left?" He might not have remembered it, he was so young when he tried to learn it, but he'd heard other boys singing it since then.

"Oh, you must mean *"Deutschland, Deutschland Über Alles"*! You remember? How clever of you!" Hansi squirmed a little as she started singing, Hansi joining in almost right away and Lotte trying to hum along.

"*Deutschland, Deutschland*, over everything
Over every other land
When for freedom and for liberty
We together always stand . . . ."

When they finished singing, Mutti lifted him down from the sofa, stood up, smoothed her apron, and said, "Why don't you go play, now, while I make some supper." Hansi's mouth watered at the thought of supper, even though he knew it wouldn't be very good or very much. He went out to look for Otto and the others, but he didn't see them. So he played soldier by himself, using a stick he found as a rifle. It wasn't much fun.

Hansi was lost.

He hadn't started out lost. He'd wanted to see the school where he'd be going when he started school, and Otto had told him where it was. Hansi had known just where to go . . . at first. But somehow he'd gotten mixed up, and now he couldn't find where he was supposed to go next. There were plenty of grownups around, but when he tried to ask one man where the school was, the man just said, "Sorry, never heard of it," and kept walking. He tried asking a woman next, but she said, "Go home, little one!" and patted him on the head. If he knew where home was from here, he probably would, but he didn't know that either.

He didn't want to cry where people could see, but no one was looking at him anyway, even when he tried to get their attention. His nose stopped up, and he looked at the ground and started to sniffle. And then a pair of big feet in shiny leather boots stopped right in front of him. He looked from the boots upward, seeing thick legs in blue trousers that bulged at the sides, and then, hanging from the belt, a big curved thing in some sort of case. His heart lurched as he remembered seeing one like it in a museum. It was a sword, a saber, and it would be sharp enough to cut off his head.

Hansi couldn't help it — he started crying harder. Could he beg the man not to cut off his head? Would it do any good? He looked up at the man's face to see if he looked angry enough to cut off heads. The man had a giant mustache with points on the ends. If Hansi had been less scared, he would have thought it looked funny. Now it just made it harder to tell what the man was thinking.

The man squatted down in front of Hansi, bringing that big face with the big moustache right down close. In a deep voice a little like Vati's, he said, "What's wrong, little one? Are you lost?"

Hansi sniffed, wiped his nose with his sleeve, and cleared his throat enough to say, "Yes, *mein Herr.*"

"I should be able to fix that! Where do you need to go?"

He didn't really need to go to the school. But he didn't want to just go home knowing he'd failed. So he mumbled, "The *Volksschule* Otto von Bismarck."

"Hmmm." The man stroked his moustache. "I think I know the way. Let's see if I'm right, shall we? Take my hand." Hansi obeyed, and they set off in a direction Hansi would never have guessed.

Ten minutes later, they were standing in front of a long building made up of yellowish bricks. "Is this it?" asked the man. Hansi looked at the sign in front of the school. Some of the letters, at least, looked right, so he nodded. The man said, "Good!" and slapped Hansi on the shoulder, not quite hard enough to hurt. "Are you going in?"

Hansi backed away, shaking his head. "No, no, I just wanted to see it . . . . Can I go home now?"

The man smiled, the smile just showing under the moustache, and said, "Certainly! Tell me your address, and I'll take you there."

As they walked to Hansi's flat, the man asked Hansi all sorts of questions, about his family and how old he was and what he liked to do. When Hansi told him about Vati, the man said, "How wonderful! We're so proud of our heroic soldiers! You know, I thought you were a soldier's boy as soon as I looked at you."

Hansi wasn't so sure about that. After all, the man had found him crying in the street. He would be braver next time. And he would stand up straight, like the man with the sword.

When they were finally standing in front of the building where Hansi's flat was, the man put out his hand to shake Hansi's. "Here we are, then! It's time to say goodbye, and I'll go about my work. I'm a policeman, you know. I catch criminals and keep people safe."

Hansi gathered his courage and said, "Before you go, could you . . . could you show me your sword?"

The policeman laughed, a big hearty laugh, and then whispered, "Just for you. It'll be our secret." He pulled the sword a little way out of its case, left it like that for long enough to give Hansi a good look, and then shoved it back in the case again, grinning. "And now, off you go inside, yes?"

Hansi nodded so hard it hurt his neck, saluted — which made the policeman smile again — and ran home. As he opened the door to his flat and looked around for Mutti, he remembered the policeman, his shiny boots and uniform and sword, and promised himself: *I'm going to grow up and be a policeman too.*

Chapter 2

Autumn 1915

Hansi's big brother Otto kept pulling on Hansi's arm. "Hurry up, or there won't be any potatoes left!"

"I'm tired of potatoes," Hansi whined, even though he knew it would make Otto angry. "We only eat potatoes these days. I want pork and cheese and buttered bread! Why can't we eat those instead?" He knew, though. Whenever he asked for the foods he liked, Mutti said no one could get them anymore, and he should be glad to have potatoes. He wasn't, but Mutti didn't want to hear about it.

Otto didn't bother to answer, tugging him through the growing crowd as they got closer to Andreas Street. One of the neighbors had told Mutti that the market there would have potatoes today. The woman must have told everyone in town. Everywhere he looked, women and children, the children almost all bigger than he was, were fighting their way forward, trying to get to the market. Mutti would have been here with Otto, only she had a cold and kept coughing and sneezing. Hansi had been jealous of Otto, getting to do something important, and then Otto had let him come, and Hansi had been so proud, but it was an awfully big crowd . . . .

Now he was starting to see people going the other way, forcing their ways through, holding bulging sacks of potatoes. The sacks looked heavy, but Otto would make Hansi carry one anyway. What if he dropped it? Maybe there were smaller sacks for children Hansi's size.

Suddenly a woman's scream, and then a girl's, came from somewhere in the crowd ahead of him. Otto kept pulling Hansi forward, but he had time to see that a woman had fallen down in the middle of the crowd. People were stepping on her, and the girl was screaming and trying to push people away so the woman — her mother, probably — could get up. The woman had blood on her face . . . and then Otto and Hansi had moved past her, with other people shoving and elbowing them so that Hansi was afraid he'd fall down too, and the crowd would step on him and squash him.

And then he heard a policeman's whistle, and a shout; "Get back! Go home! There are no more potatoes! They're all gone, get back, go home!"

He could see the policeman now. His hat was missing, and his collar was unbuttoned and didn't line up, as though someone had grabbed at it. Next to Hansi, Otto said a string of bad words, loud enough for the policeman to hear, and shook his fist. This time Hansi grabbed Otto's wrist, instead of the other way round, and pulled as hard as he could, away from the policeman, away from the crowd, away from the market that had no more potatoes. Otto resisted for a moment and then came away, saying more bad words as he went. When Otto finally went quiet, Hansi muttered, "It's all right. I didn't want any old potatoes anyway."

Otto spun around and slapped Hansi on the mouth. His face was red, and he looked like he might cry, even though Otto never cried.

Spring 1916

"Baby! Only babies drink milk!"

Hansi turned to face the older boy, clenching his fists and his teeth. School gave him new things to do during the day and got him away from his annoying little sister, but he kept stumbling on things he didn't know, saying things that made the other boys tease him or push him around. How was he to know that he shouldn't talk about liking milk? He thought most children drank milk, but not anymore, it seemed. Too late, he remembered Mutti saying how lucky he was that his father was a soldier, because it meant he could have milk to drink.

The older boy shoved him so that he almost fell backward into the playground's sand pile. "Well, baby? Want to run home to mama?"

If he did, they could kill him before he'd admit it. He remembered something else, something one of the neighbor women had said to Mutti while he was supposed to be napping. "We'd all have milk if it wasn't for the Jews! Milk, and eggs, and pork!"

Another boy, the youngest one on the playground, asked, "What do Jews have to do with it?"

Hansi hadn't heard much more. He'd have to guess. "They don't eat eggs, so they don't want anyone to have them. And . . . they drink up all the milk."

The older boy laughed, loud and mean. "You don't know anything! It's pork they don't eat. And they like money more than anything else, so they buy up all the pork and eggs and milk, and charge so much that no one can buy them."

Hansi had a vague notion that something was wrong with what the boy was saying, something about how anyone, even a Jew, could make money if no one could buy what they sold. But it was time to stop talking and nod his head.

When he got home, Mutti had a snack waiting for him, milk and bread. He almost told her milk was for babies, but then she might stop giving it to him, so he sat down and took a big gulp. He picked up the bread to dunk it in the milk, but decided to take a bite first. It tasted different. He asked Mutti, "Why does the bread taste funny?"

Mutti frowned at him. "It's perfectly good bread! It just has more potato in it, because the bakers still have potatoes and they can't get very much grain."

Potatoes again. And — "Why can't they get as much grain?"

Now she looked sad, and stroked his hair. "It's the war, Hansi. Before the war, we got plenty of grain from other countries, and also the fertilizer to make grain grow. Now we can't. There are big ships blocking the way, and our ships can't get through. Eat your bread."

Hansi dunked the bread in the milk and took another bite. The milk helped, and he finished the bread and then the milk. He wondered how long it would be before Vati got home from work, and then could have smacked himself. Of course Vati wasn't at work. He was off fighting the war. . . . "Mutti, when will the war be over? Why haven't we won it yet?"

Mutti scooped up the mug and bowl and took them to the sink. With her back to him, she said, "It can take a long time to win a war. Wars aren't so easy to win. But with brave soldiers like your father fighting every day, it won't be much longer. And I have some good news for you. Vati's coming home on leave!"

If Vati came home, he wouldn't be fighting. How could Germany win the war without Vati? Or did Mutti mean something else? "What's on-leave?"

Mutti finished with the dishes and came to sit down at the table, across from him. "It's a visit, *Liebling*. Vati's going to come home for a visit, before he goes back to the front.

We'll have to give him a wonderful welcome! Only . . . ." Mutti's voice dropped to a mumble. "Meat . . . how could I find . . . ."

Hansi wriggled in his chair. "Can I go play now?" But Mutti didn't answer. After a little while, he climbed down and ran outside.

A few days later, Hansi came home from school as excited as he'd been in months, with news he couldn't wait to tell Mutti. "Mutti, there are soup kitchens, with big dining rooms where you can get a good meal, hot! Can we go tonight? Can we?"

Mutti looked up from her mending. She didn't jump up, or even smile. "I know about those kitchens, *Bärchen*. But going to some big room full of strangers instead of eating in our own home . . . it's not right, that we should have to do that."

Hansi couldn't believe it. "Not right? We could eat! We might be able to eat until we're full, all of us! What's more right than that? Is not having enough to eat right?"

Mutti bit her lip. "I don't think your Vati would like it, our showing up at a place like that, like beggars . . . ."

Hansi bit his own lip, to stop himself from crying. Was that why Mutti was doing it? Did she want to cry? He didn't want to make her cry.

But he really, really wanted to be less hungry tonight when he tried to get to sleep.

"*Please*, Mutti?"

Mutti reached out to stroke his cheek and gave a big, big sigh. "All right," she finally said. "Just this once. Go find Otto and Lotte and let them know."

There was a line of people waiting to get into the kitchen. Most of them looked pretty much like Hansi's family, or else more ragged. The raggedy people made Hansi start to understand why Mutti hadn't wanted to come here, and why she'd made them change into their good clothes beforehand.

Once the doors opened, the pushing and shoving started. Otto had to grab Lotte's arm to keep her from falling. She whined for a moment, but then she smelled food and was ready to do her own pushing. Mutti held her back.

They found a square metal table just big enough for the four of them. And Mutti got to sit down, for a change, while someone brought food to her, instead of her having to bring everyone else's food first. She'd been looking worried, but when she saw the girl bringing her a bowl of stew, she laughed in surprise and relaxed in her chair.

Hansi had wondered if he could ever eat enough to fill up, but by the time he finished the stew and the bread people called K-Brot, he felt almost sick from eating too much. He had to make himself take the last few bites. But he wasn't going to leave any food on his plate for someone to take away.

They went back to the kitchen three days later, and a few days after that. But the next time they tried, they couldn't get past all the other people crowding in and taking the tables. And Mutti wouldn't try again.

Chapter 3

Autumn 1916 – Winter 1916-1917

A firm knock on the door, not like any knock Hansi was used to; Mutti running to answer; and then, a tall, broad figure in the doorway, a chilly breeze coming in around it. He would've been scared, if Mutti hadn't told him over and over that Vati would be home soon, home any day now.

The man who must be Vati — though he'd shaved off his beard and had only a bushy moustache — picked Mutti up and lifted her off her feet, squeezing her tight. Mutti laughed and squealed. Then Vati put her down and said, "Who's this young maiden in my arms? What happened to my plump little *hausfrau*?"

Mutti's smile dropped away before she put it back on again. "*Liebling*, when you're home to stay, I'll put on as much weight as you like. When do you think the war will be over? We hear so little, just the same confident statements over and over . . . ." Hans frowned. "Liebling" was Mutti's name for *him*.

Vati didn't answer Mutti's question, acting as if he hadn't heard it. Instead, he turned to Hansi and Otto and Lotte, all standing close together and staring up at him. Otto shoved Hansi forward, and Vati swooped down to pick him up, hoisting him much higher than he had Mutti. Vati hugged Hansi tight against the stiff, scratchy uniform he wore. His smell was almost familiar, but not quite, maybe because of how the uniform smelled, or maybe because it had been so long.

Vati put Hansi down and looked at Otto and Lotte. "Come here, the two of you!" When they shuffled forward, he picked Lotte up with his left arm and shook hands with Otto, saying, "How big you've gotten, all three of you!" But there was something strange in the way he said it, as if he wasn't sure he believed it.

Mutti fluttered around them, smiling and rubbing her hands. "Why don't you get comfortable? I'll have dinner on the table in just a little while — with meat!"

Hansi's mouth started watering, and Lotte clapped her hands. But Vati didn't look happy.

Hansi hadn't remembered how hard meat was to chew. Maybe it was his teeth — a couple of them felt a little wobbly. Or maybe meat had been different before the war, not so tough, not so dry. Vati might be thinking that, since he asked Mutti what kind of meat they were eating.

She didn't answer right away, and then she took a deep breath before she said, "It's horse, Walther. I was lucky to find it."

Vati looked down at his plate as if he was angry with it. Hansi didn't understand why — was there something wrong with horse meat? Would it make him sick? He was feeling a little sick already, but that might be because of how Mutti and Vati were acting. He put his fork down and asked, "Mutti, may I go play now?"

Mutti's eyes went wide, and she said, "Hansi! Ask your father!" Hansi turned to Vati, but Vati just nodded, his eyes still on his plate of horse. Hansi slid down from his chair and ran to get his coat. He had to push and tug to get his arms in the sleeves, but at last he had it on and could get away from the dinner table where something felt wrong, even though Vati had come home.

Hansi came inside after an hour or so, hoping there might be some milk and that Mutti would heat it up for him. He stopped when he heard Mutti and Vati talking in the kitchen. Vati was saying something about him and Otto and Lotte. "And why are the children so thin? And they've hardly grown!"

Mutti sounded as if she might cry, even though she was all grown up and his mother besides. "They have grown! Didn't you see Hansi, trying to get into that too-small coat? Maybe you just don't remember how small they were before you went away."

Vati made a noise like one of the pigs on Vati's family's farm, way out in the country. Mutti kept talking. "Anyway, things will be better when the war's over, and that can't be too much longer, can it?"

Vati made the noise again. "You mean when we win, don't you? Pretty sure of that, are you? I can imagine what the government is telling you all."

Mutti's voice got quieter, so that Hansi had to creep closer to hear. "Well, that we're winning, of course . . . though I never thought winning would take so long . . . but I always thought we could trust what they say . . . . Don't look like that! Do you mean they'd lie to us? . . . On the other hand, I do have trouble believing it when they say it doesn't matter about all the foods we can't get, because it's good for us to eat less than we used to . . . ."

"*What?*" Vati's voice was so loud, after Mutti almost whispering, that it made Hansi jump. And then came a sound he hadn't expected. Mutti and Vati were laughing, though there was something about the laughing that didn't sound right. And then came humming and lip-smacking noises he'd heard before, but not for a long time, not since Vati went away to fight.

Hansi still wanted his milk, so he snuck back toward the door and then banged it open and stumped loudly toward the kitchen. By the time he got there, Vati was sitting at the kitchen table with a glass of something clear — was it water? — and Mutti was at the stove, heating milk in a saucepan. So maybe everything was all right.

Vati had gone back to the front. The flat felt quiet and empty without him, and at the same time it felt as if Hansi had only dreamed that Vati came home at all.

A week after Vati left, during the grammar lesson, the headmaster came in and told the teacher he had something important to take care of. The teacher stepped aside, and the headmaster grabbed an empty chair, dragged it to the front of the class, and stood there. That was when Hansi realized the headmaster was carrying a cane.

The classroom was already cold, but Hansi suddenly felt colder. He held his breath until the headmaster said, "Emil Greenwald, come here!"

One of the older boys in the class walked slowly toward the headmaster. Hansi caught a glimpse of his big round face, which had gone pale. When the boy got close enough, the headmaster gripped his shoulder and turned him to face the class. In a loud voice, almost a shout, the headmaster said, "This boy has been spreading lies intended to undermine your faith in our Vaterland's coming victory. He has been claiming that our heroic soldiers are losing battles and retreating. He will be punished. Greenwald, face the chair and hold onto the back."

No one in the class made a sound as Emil bent toward the chair and held onto it. Without another word, the headmaster began beating the boy with the cane. Emil made a little squealing sound with the first blow, and then a louder noise. After ten strokes, he was whimpering and crying.

The headmaster stepped away from Emil and said, "Stand up and go stand in that corner until class is dismissed." Sniffing, wiping his nose with one hand and rubbing his bottom with the other, Emil shuffled to the corner. The headmaster looked all around the room as if he would tell someone else to come and be beaten, but instead, he said, "Our army is striding from victory to victory! Remember that!" And he walked quickly out of the room, still holding the cane.

Hansi bit his lip, and looked down to hide it. He found himself remembering that talk Mutti and Vati had had in the kitchen. He hadn't heard every word, but it had sounded a lot like what Emil must have said.

He shouldn't believe it was true. He wouldn't believe it. But he couldn't stop himself from remembering.

Fall went by, and then it was almost winter. It felt like winter already. And there was less and less to eat. Hansi loved bread with butter, but there hadn't been butter in ages, and now there was hardly any bread, and what they could get was that K-Brot stuff that smelled and tasted all wrong. Mutti said it was Romania's fault, that they had come into the war against Germany and stopped the wheat from coming in, even the wheat Germany had been able to get before. Hansi had never even heard of Romania, but now he hated them with all his might.

Still, Hansi had got used to eating potatoes. Sometimes, he could forget about all the other foods they couldn't get. Mutti would chop the potatoes into slices one day, and mash them up the next, even though mashed potatoes didn't hold together without butter or fat. But after a while, there were hardly any potatoes, in the market or anywhere else. A freezing wet cold had destroyed the fall potato crop, and even the potatoes growing in the richer people's tiny gardens. By now, almost all the potatoes people had stored were gone.

Even now with everyone struggling to find food, some decorations were going up in the streets for the Feast of Saint Nicholas — and for Christmas after. Hansi remembered a little about what Saint Nicholas' Day and Christmas should be like, and Otto remembered more and kept talking about it. On Saint Nicholas' Day, they should be leaving stockings outside their bedroom door, and finding them filled in the morning with oranges and chocolate and little toys. But it had been a long time since anyone had any fruit or any chocolate — or anything with sugar, even for Mutti's coffee — not that there was coffee anymore. And no one seemed to be selling toys. Vati would have made some, Otto said, but Vati was far away, and Mutti said he wouldn't be able to come home again any time soon.

Mutti started talking again about Christmas in the old days, before the war. "We'd have a big fat goose to eat, and cake .... You used to love cake, do you remember? And you used to make noises like a goose so Otto would chase you. Oh, those were wonderful times!" Then she wrinkled up her face in a frown. "The Jews who make everything so hard to get, they don't care — they don't celebrate Christmas at all."

Lotte, who had been playing with her old wooden doll on the floor, looked up with wide eyes and said, "Why not, Mutti?" But Mutti didn't answer.

Hansi could understand not wanting Christmas now, when nothing good could happen — it was like a promise someone would break. But before the war? It didn't make sense.

With Christmas coming, there should be an evergreen tree in the corner. If Vati were here, they would have gone to visit Vati's father's farm in the country, and Vati would have gone with Opa and Vati's brothers and cut down the prettiest trees, one for the farm and one for Mutti and Vati and all of them to take back to the city on the train. But Vati wasn't here, and there wasn't enough coal for the train they used to take. Hansi could hardly remember anything about Opa or about his uncles, and all he could remember about the farm was the smells: the animals and the barn, and then how fresh and clean the air smelled away from the barn.

Hansi was remembering the farm, and trying to remember his Opa and uncles and country cousins, when suddenly he thought he heard the wheels of their cart, and the jingle of horse bells, and then voices, many voices all mixed together outside the flat. Was he dreaming? But no, there was a knock on the door and then another, and when Mutti ran to open it, Opa and Uncle Oskar and Aunt Frieda and his cousin Kurt all tumbled in, smiling and dressed in layers and layers of clothes — and carrying sacks and baskets that smelled like food! Anyone with an arm free hugged whoever they could reach, and then they all spilled into the kitchen to watch the sacks and baskets emptied, with bread, salami, carrots, and little jars of butter and jam filling the table. Opa fished in another sack and pulled out an apple, yellow and wrinkly. He handed it to Hansi. Hansi smelled it and then tried to take a bite, but it was too hard for his teeth. Mutti wiped away tears and took the apple from him. "Never mind, *Liebchen*, I'll cut it up very small. You'll be able to eat it then."

Hansi's Uncle Oskar held up his hand and said, "There's one more thing! Wait here." He hustled out the door and came back into the living room a minute later with a fir tree on his shoulder and some sort of wood-and-metal round thing under his other arm. "For Christmas!" he called out. He dropped the whatever-it-was on the floor and tried to put the trunk of the tree inside it . . . but the tree was too tall to fit under the ceiling.

Uncle Oskar picked up the tree again and held it, looking as if he didn't know what to do. "I thought there'd be room," he muttered. "In the old flat — well, I thought there'd be more room."

Opa patted Uncle Oskar on the shoulder and said, "Don't worry, Oskar. I've got a saw in the cart. We'll cut it down a little, and it'll fit just fine."

Otto whispered to Hansi, "If they hadn't brought a tree, I was going to steal some wood and make one." It sounded like bragging, but Hansi was just as glad not to find out.

They had supper — and what a supper! — before decorating the tree. They had a few leftover ornaments that hadn't broken over the years or been left behind when they moved to the smaller flat. And there was enough paper to make paper decorations, even if it was full of printing and didn't have colors. The apples had to be saved for eating, and not even the visitors had any nuts.

Doing that was work, but they were all feeling stronger after the food. Then Mutti asked the visitors, "Would you like to go to church for the midnight service?" Hansi and Otto and Lotte all joined in saying — well, shouting — "Yes!" That meant staying up late, but Hansi didn't feel as tired as usual. Mutti wore a dress Hansi had forgotten about, dark red with red lace on it. She made Hansi and Otto and Lotte put on the best clothes they had that still fit. Lotte fell asleep hours before they had to leave, but Aunt Frieda and Uncle Oskar took turns carrying her, and Mutti let them.

Hansi thought the carol singing was wonderful, and he spent the rest of the service looking at the decorations, the green wreaths with red candles, the glass angels strung on golden ropes. But as they walked home, Hansi starting to stumble a little and drag his feet, Mutti said quietly, "The singing was different this year. The voices were thin and weak." Hansi couldn't remember whether that was true, and tried not to think about it. He would rather just remember the singing and play it over in his mind.

The visitors stayed only one more day. "We don't want to eat up everything we brought," Aunt Frieda said. "And that reminds me. It's so hard for you all here. May we take the younger children back to the farm with us? They aren't looking well, and we have enough to feed them." She said nothing about Otto, but she'd seen how much Otto ate when he had the chance. Hansi didn't blame her for not wanting Otto eating through what food they had.

Did Hansi want to go?

There would be more sausage, and probably milk and cheese, if they still had cows. They might have chickens, and he could eat eggs again. But he might end up eating too much, just like Otto would, and then what would they do? He'd be ashamed to have them bring him back home for being too much trouble.

Meanwhile, Mutti was saying, "That's so kind of you, but I don't know . . . . Hansi needs to go to school, and he'd miss his friends . . . ." She'd started crying by now. "And I'd already miss Lotte so much, I don't think I could stand to have both of them gone . . . and he's so much help to me."

So that was that, and he'd missed his chance. He felt hungrier just thinking about how he could have had enough to eat. It was too late now.

It took a week before Mutti stopped breaking into tears every time she saw something of Lotte's, or when she forgot and called Lotte as if she were still in the flat. Lotte could be a nuisance, but now Hansi wished she hadn't gone to the country, just so Mutti wouldn't be so sad. Lotte hadn't eaten that much, so her having left didn't mean that much more food for the rest of them.

And once in a while, he found himself missing his little sister, just because. Back when he was stronger, and even a couple of months ago, he used to pick Lotte up sometimes, holding her under her arms, and spin around so her legs flew out. She loved that, and Otto wouldn't do it anymore. She'd giggle and grin, and it made Hansi feel good.

He didn't tell Otto, of course. He didn't plan to tell Mutti. But one day, when Mutti looked at Lotte's little apron hanging in the kitchen, Hansi grabbed her hand before she could start crying and said, "I miss her too."

Mutti was so surprised she didn't cry after all.

Chapter 4

Winter 1917

Almost all they had to eat was turnips. Some people called them Prussian pineapples, whatever a pineapple was. Whatever you called them, they were so bitter he could hardly swallow them. His tongue would squirm as if it was trying to get away from the awful taste. Turnips might not have been so bad with sugar — Mutti said so — but there wasn't any sugar. And the turnips made his belly hurt, sometimes enough that he had trouble sleeping, more than from just being hungry. When Hansi saw Mutti writing a letter to Vati, he asked whether she was telling him about how nasty turnips without sugar were, but she said Vati didn't need to hear that sort of thing when he had fighting the war to think about.

Mutti didn't go upstairs to see Aunt Gertrud as often as she used to. Aunt Gertrud came downstairs now and then, and on one of those visits, when they didn't know Hansi was listening, Aunt Gertrud said, "Sometimes I'm almost glad our mother didn't live to see such days as these." It sounded like she started crying. Hansi couldn't quite hear what Mutti said after that.

Mutti looked tired all the time, and that's how Hansi felt too. Otto wasn't as weak, so Mutti would send him to stand in food lines or go wait at the train station for coal briquettes to fall off the trains. He was good at getting to the coal first, before the other children. He boasted that he had the strongest and sharpest elbows in all of Berlin. Hansi promised himself that he would grow up even stronger than Otto, and tougher. If there were still lines to stand in when he was older, he'd get to the front of every single one.

Otto had just got home with his small bundle of coal when Hansi heard a strange sound in the street. It was the clopping sound of horse hooves, but mixed in with wheezing and some sort of rattle. It went on for a few minutes, the clopping and then the other noises and then the clopping again. Mutti came to the front window to look and Hansi joined her. It was a horse, pulling a cart and moving slowly down the street, its sides pumping as it took those rattling breaths of the cold, cold air. It was a dull black color, and horribly thin, almost a skeleton of a horse. Hansi started to turn away.

And then the horse fell over, as much as it could fall while still fastened to the cart. It lay there, hanging from the shafts of the cart, its muzzle touching the street.

It was dead.

Hansi turned to Mutti. But Mutti had run to the kitchen, faster than he knew she could run, and came right out again carrying a butcher knife, the biggest knife she had. She ran right out the front door, without even waiting to put on her coat. By now there was a crowd in the street, a crowd of women, all with their own knives, pushing and shoving and shouting at each other, all trying to get close to the body of the horse. And there was Mutti, pushing and shouting like all the others, and waving her knife. Hansi didn't want to watch, but he couldn't look away.

In a few minutes, there was nothing left of the horse but bones dangling from the shafts of the cart. The women all disappeared into the nearby flats. Hansi heard Mutti come in the door, panting as if she'd run a long way. Then she was standing in the hall, her face red from the cold, her eyes wild, her hair falling every which way, with smears of blood on her clothes and her arms. She was holding a hunk of raw meat. She held it out toward the children and said loudly, "We'll have meat tonight!" And then, in an everyday sort of voice, as if nothing much had happened, "Otto, bring that coal to the kitchen. I'll light the stove."

It kept getting colder, and snowing. Lotte starting creeping into Hansi's bed at night to keep warm, and Hansi was glad of it. Even Otto squeezed in with them on the coldest nights.

At school, one of the boys whispered to him that his father said there should be a government department in charge of snow, because then it would disappear like so much of the food. Hansi looked around nervously and backed away. That was a few days before the school closed for the winter. There wasn't enough coal to heat it, and too many teachers and children were sick.

Being home would have been nicer if Mutti weren't so worried about everything. Her latest fear was being evicted. That meant being thrown out of the place you lived. Aunt Gertrud, Mutti's sister, didn't own the flat, she just rented it and let them stay there, even when they didn't have money to pay her. That should have made them especially safe, except that Mutti's sister wasn't married to a soldier like Mutti was. It was illegal to evict soldiers' wives, but since Mutti wasn't the one who was actually renting the flat, that didn't help. Sometimes Uncle Helmut talked about getting a better job, a job making weapons for the war, so he could make more money and keep paying the landlord, but so far that hadn't happened.

Hansi didn't know where they'd go, or where Aunt Gertrud and Uncle Helmut and his cousins would go, if they were evicted. He asked Mutti just once, and she told him to go study and stop bothering her. She cried after he left the room, and Otto cuffed him on the ear. So he didn't ask again.

The next afternoon, Aunt Gertrud came down to visit with Mutti. She did that often enough, but today she looked worried, her eyes darting from Mutti to the icebox and back again. "How are you doing lately?" she asked in a casual voice that didn't match her face. "It must be hard to make ends meet. But I have an idea that could make things a little easier." Mutti had been quiet all morning, and when Hansi looked at her, she didn't meet his eyes. She was doing the same thing with Aunt Gertrud, looking down at her lap where her fingers were fidgeting as if they needed something to do. Aunt Gertrud looked in the same direction and then went on, making her voice cheerful. "You're so good with your hands, and you sew so well. I know where you could get some sewing work — work you could do right here, while keeping an eye on the boys. You like to sew, don't you? If you'll go with me right now, I can take you to the man who's signing women up for that work. Shall we go?" Mutti looked slowly up from her lap. One of her hands moved to her hair, which looked like she hadn't combed it for days. Aunt Gertrud jumped up and said, "Here, let me take you to the bathroom and help you tidy up a bit. Then we'll go. It'll all work out, you'll see." She reached out, and Mutti took her hands. Aunt Gertrud had to give a little tug before Mutti got all the way out of the chair and followed her to the bathroom. When they came out a few minutes later, Mutti's hair was in a neat bun, and there were blotches of reddish pink on her cheeks. Aunt Gertrud fetched Mutti's coat and her own, and they put on the coats and went out the door. When Mutti came back two hours later, she had a bundle under her arm. She went to the kitchen and unwrapped it to show a stack of folded cloth, stiff and a little waxy, and a few spools of thread, all of it a dark gray-green color. Then she went into her bedroom and came back with a package of needles. She was walking with her back straight, the way she used to, and when she sat down at the table she was almost smiling. For the rest of the afternoon, and again after what passed for supper, she stitched away busily, and once in a while, she hummed a song under her breath.

Winter wasn't exactly over, but some days it seemed as though it was. It was supposed to be over later this month, but Hansi didn't know if the weather would care. It was warm enough some days that he could play outside. His suspenders were getting worn out and baggy, but that was all right, because he'd grown a little and his pants would have squeezed his crotch otherwise.

March was also the time when people marched through the streets, shouting about things that made them angry. Mutti had always kept him inside during the marches, but this year she seemed too tired to make him stay away, and he wanted to see. He tagged along behind Otto as the noise got closer.

Then Otto took a sharp breath in and backed away, saying, "Come on, Hansi, there could be trouble. We should go back inside."

Hansi stamped his foot. "I *won't*! Why should I? What's going to happen?"

"Those traitors are going to get beat up or arrested, that's what!" Otto pointed to the big banner the people in front of the march were carrying. "Can you read that, or are you too much of a stupid little baby?"

That made Hansi want to stay even more. He had to know what the banner said, and it would take him a little while to piece the letters together. He walked closer to the marchers and looked hard at the banner. "C-U-R . . . CURSE. THE. K-I-N-G. 'Curse the King! Is that what it says?"

Otto was pulling him away now. "It says 'Curse the King, the King of the Rich,' and a lot more. And here come the police! We've got to get out of here!" He yanked Hansi so hard that Hansi almost fell, but he managed to stay on his feet as Otto pulled him toward home.

When they got to the door, Hansi pulled loose and turned around. He'd never seen the police beat someone or arrest them. He wanted to know if that was really something police did. The police had caught up with the marchers and stood around them, but they weren't hitting them, or dragging them away to jail. They were just watching.

Otto hissed, "I'm going to tell Mutti how you ran toward the marchers if you don't come inside right now!" Hansi turned away and followed Otto, wishing he knew why the police just stood there, and what police were really supposed to do.

Chapter 5

Spring - Summer 1917

Hansi came into the front room and looked out the window to find little clusters of people in the street, standing in the slush in their worn-out boots and coats, acting excited — waving their arms and clutching each other's shoulders and even laughing. Otto came and stood next to him, with that smug look that said he already knew what was going on. "It's Russia," he said knowingly. "They've had a revolution."

"What's that?"

"It means the people who lived there overthrew the Tsar. A Tsar is like a Kaiser, and they just kicked him out! He isn't running things anymore."

Hansi looked back at the people. They seemed to think this was awfully important. "Why do people here care so much about the Tsar not running Russia anymore?"

Otto snorted. "You dimwit! Russia's the enemy, along with France and Italy and . . . some other countries. And the Tsar must have decided to be our enemy, and now he's gone, so maybe Russia isn't our enemy anymore, and maybe the others won't be able to keep fighting without Russia, and maybe we'll finally win the war!"

Hansi could hardly believe it. It felt as if the war had been going on forever. Could it really be over soon, and

Vati come home, and Mutti not be worried anymore, and everyone have enough to eat?

But the war didn't end. Nothing changed, except to get worse.

After a little while, people stopped talking about Russia and started talking more about profiteering. Otto said that meant buying up food and making people pay too much for it, much too much. Otto hated the profiteers, and so did everyone else, Otto said. He wanted to go out and find some profiteers and beat them up. He said he'd know who they were, because they'd be fat, or Jews, or both. But Mutti told him he couldn't beat anybody up, and even Otto still did what Mutti told him to.

Now that it was getting a little warmer, Mutti sent Hansi out sometimes to try to get food. Aunt Gertrud had heard that the Central Market near the Alexanderplatz train station might have some bread, though she didn't know where the bread or the potatoes to make bread could have come from. Mutti told Hansi to go and see and gave him a handful of ration cards. She'd saved them up, since there hadn't been any bread anywhere for so long.

He couldn't walk very fast, so it took him a long time to get there. When he'd reached the train station and was almost at the market, he smelled something bad, something rotten. He should go straight to the market, but he really wanted to know what smelled so awful, so he got closer and tried to see.

At first he didn't see anything different, but then he saw a whole lot of people standing around near some train cars, pointing and yelling. He crept up behind the people and carefully wormed his way toward the front. Then he saw that the cars were *leaking*. There was some sort of liquid coming out of them, and that's what smelled. And there were some police standing around it, standing very straight as if they were on guard, and acting like they didn't mind the smell.

He looked around for a grownup who didn't look as angry and wasn't very big. He found a woman, as thin as everyone these days, wearing an apron and wringing it in her hands but not yelling. He tapped her on the arm and said timidly, "What is that stuff that stinks so much?"

He'd thought her voice would be quiet, but it was more of a wail. "It's food! At least, it used to be food! The government found some profiteers and took the food away from them, and then they just *left* it in those cars to *rot*! It's just sitting there *rotting*, and the police just stand there as if it were still worth something and they had to keep anyone from stealing it! Why do they *bother*?" She finally shook her fist the way some of the others were doing, and then slumped her shoulders, turned, and walked away.

Hansi stared at the police. He hadn't thought for a long time about the policeman who helped him when he got lost, but now he remembered, and looked to see if he was there guarding the train cars. None of them looked familiar. Would that policeman have stood around the stinking cars like the others? He didn't want to think so.

Hansi turned and walked away, dragging his feet, until he got to the market. No one at the market had any bread. Even the feed baskets for the cart horses were empty, except for a few broken bits of brittle-looking hay. He turned around and walked home.

Mutti looked at him and sighed. She didn't seem surprised that he wasn't carrying bread. He pulled the ration cards out of his pocket and held them out for her, but she just stared at them. She stared so long it started to scare him, and he said, hearing his voice shake, "Mutti? What is it?"

Mutti spun around and ran to where she kept her purse, then ran back and stuck both hands into it. Her hands jerked around inside it before she pulled out two big handfuls of ration cards, at least twice as many as she'd given him before. And then she laughed, a crazy sort of laugh, and kept laughing, and threw all the coupons up in the air. She grabbed more coupons and threw them in the air too, laughing all the time. Hansi had seen paper confetti once, and it looked like that, except the bigger pieces of paper fell down faster, fell all over the floor.

Otto ran in to see what was going on. This time Mutti threw cards right at him. "Have some rations! Everyone, come and get some rations! There's plenty for everyone, as long as all you want is cards!" Then she scooped up one of the cards from the floor and stuffed it in her mouth, chewing at it with all her might.

Otto hurried to her and grabbed her chin, pulling it down so she couldn't keep chewing. "Spit it out, Mutti!" he begged, in a tone Hansi had never heard from him before. "Please, Mutti, spit it out!"

For a few moments, Mutti tried to keep chewing, struggling against Otto's grip. Then she stopped and let her mouth sag open. Otto reached in and pulled the wad of paper out of her mouth, once and again, until he'd gotten all of it that he could reach.

Mutti walked slowly to the sofa and sat down all at once, as if she were falling instead of sitting. Otto walked over, slowly, as if afraid of what might happen next, and sat down beside her. Hansi came last, sitting as close to her as he could on her other side, burrowing against her as if he could hide there. They sat like that for a long time.

School reopened, though not everyone, student or teacher, came back to it. Hansi tried to do his work, but he kept almost falling asleep in class. The first time the teacher caught him, he thought he'd get a whipping, but the teacher looked at him almost the way an uncle would and just told him to try to stay awake.

At home, even turnips were hard to find. What food they could get hold of got stranger. Shops sold what was supposed to be butter, but it wasn't. Mutti said she'd heard it was made of washing soda, and that the "coffee" was really ground-up walnut shells or corn powder. She didn't say what the "dried egg" might be, but it didn't taste or feel like eggs.

One morning, Mutti had been talking to a neighbor on the stairway and came back in stomping her feet and clenching her fists. "Those rich people in Wilmersdorf have plenty of bread! There's a baker there that has so much bread, he can hardly fit it in his shop! And we're trying to eat sawdust and corn powder baked into loaves as hard as a brick! Well, we're not going to just sit here and starve! Hansi, you stay here until I get back." And she grabbed her worn-out spring coat and rushed out the door. He looked out the window and saw her with Aunt Gertrud and a lot of other women from their building and the one next door. They milled around talking for a minute, acting all excited, and then they started marching together toward Wilmersdorf, Mutti trying to keep up with the others. Hansi looked around the flat, and at the closed door, and then he opened the door and crept out. He got to the street just as the crowd of women were getting near the corner. He ran as quietly as he could to follow them.

He was out of breath and lagging behind by the time they got where they were going. The women didn't even stop to rest. They rushed right up to the door of a bakery and started pounding on the door, and then pulled it open and shoved their way inside, some of them getting in each other's way. He couldn't see Mutti or Aunt Gertrud, but they must be in the bakery — doing what?

Only then did Hansi notice the three policemen coming closer.

One of them, fatter than anyone Hansi had seen in years, stood just outside the bakery and shouted, "You women! For shame! Come out of there at once! Go to your homes!"

From inside the bakery, Hansi could hear women shouting and laughing. Was it Aunt Gertrud he heard, yelling back, "Look at all that fat on him! I wish I could carve some of it off and take it home for cooking! Waddle away now before you get hurt!"

The fat policeman looked at the other two, as if for help, but they were looking away from the bakery full of angry women. One was even whistling. Just then, a shriek came from inside the bakery. It sounded like Mutti's voice. It reminded him of that time years ago when he and Otto tried to get potatoes, and a woman fell to the ground in a crowd like this. Another shriek came, this one muffled as if many bodies were in the way. Hansi needed to do something! He should charge into the bakery and rescue Mutti . . . but could he even get to her? And what would happen to him?

He was trying to work up his courage when one of the policemen who had been ignoring everything came running past, pushing his way through the women near the door and disappearing inside. Hansi ran behind him, trying to see. It helped that the women in the way were trying to get to one side or the other as the policeman shoved farther in. And then he saw the man bending down and lifting something — someone — Mutti! She tried to stand up, staggered, started to fall again, but he pulled her back up, using his broad back as a shield against anyone bumping into her.

Hansi stepped quickly backward as the policeman tugged Mutti toward the bakery door and then through it. The policeman looked at Hansi and winked. Then he gave Mutti a polite little push toward Hansi and walked away as if he hadn't done anything, hadn't seen anything, hadn't saved anyone.

Mutti was breathing in great gulps of air. Her hair had been pulled out of its bun and was sticking out all over. She was holding a long loaf of bread. When she saw Hansi, she didn't scold him for leaving the house, or say anything — she just held up the bread with both hands and shook it like a fighter who'd won a prize.

Hansi could feel his eyes going as wide as they could. He was shaking. Mutti let her arms drop, turned her face away, and started to cry, clutching the bread to her chest. Then she walked away, stumbling. Hansi caught up with her, took her hand, and led her home.

That day, Mutti and Otto and Hansi sat down to something like a real dinner. Mutti gave both boys three thick slices of bread. She only ate one herself. Otto told her she should have another, but she just smiled and shook her head. Hansi should have tried too, but there was only the one loaf, and he just couldn't make himself say that she should leave less of it for him.

The bread gave them enough energy that they went outside after dinner to play. So did children from other families whose mothers had gone to the bakery. Hansi looked around and saw that not as many of the boys as before were bigger than he was. He said boldly, "Let's play soldiers!"

A couple of the boys looked interested, but not many. Cousin Rudolf from upstairs looked sour; another boy spat on the ground and said, "What would we do, take turns running away?"

Hansi clenched his fists and got ready to fight, but the boy next to the one who had said it turned and cuffed him on the shoulder. That boy looked back at Hansi and said, in a friendly voice, "What else would you like to play?"

Hansi remembered the policeman who had helped Mutti when she fell, and the other who had let the women take the bread without stopping them, and the one who had helped him so long ago when he got lost. "Can we play police? With the sabers? We can make our own." He pointed to a cardboard box someone had thrown into the street.

The boys ran to the box, took out their pocket knives, and cut some sabers. Hansi almost told them how he'd seen a saber up close, but he didn't want to explain about getting lost. He just made sure the saber he cut was as big as any of the others, and looked as sharp.

Then they went looking for profiteers. Some of the girls were playing jacks farther down the street, and the boys marched over to arrest them. A few of the girls yelled insults at the boys or threw jacks at them, but two of them agreed to be arrested. The boys surrounded them and marched them back to Hansi's building, the girls bragging about all the different food they'd been selling to the rich people. That made all of them hungry, and they went to their flats, where the lucky ones without too many brothers and sisters still had some bread left for supper.

Eating his bread and pretending his hot water was milk, Hansi wondered what Lotte was having for supper. She probably had more than bread, but the bread was still good. It had ended up being a good day, the best in a long, long time.

Chapter 6

Winter 1917-1918 – Late Autumn 1918

Hansi was old enough to know what year it was, and he knew it was 1917, but only for a little while longer. It was Christmas Eve, and the year would last only another week.

This year, Mutti had told him about the Christkindl, a sort of angel with wings and golden hair, who brought people gifts. And tonight, Mutti told the two boys to stay with her in the front room and wait.

Otto was getting restless. "I don't believe in angels, anyway," he grumbled, "and I'm sick of sitting here." He was about to say more when suddenly, there came a knocking at the door, two knocks and then two more. Mutti jumped up, saying, "There she is!" and ran to open the door. There, right in their doorway, stood a lady in a long white dress, with gold-colored hair that looked somehow stiff. She had big wings, almost as long as her arms, attached to the shoulders of the dress. She looked a little like Aunt Gertrud. Did his aunt know that she looked like an angel?

"Boys," she said in a sort of whisper, "I've come to give you something special for Christmas. Stand right there, and I'll bring it inside." Then she moved to the outside steps, and Hansi heard the sound of wheels whirring, and then the chime of some sort of bell.

Otto understood first. "That's a bicycle bell!" He turned to Mutti and grabbed her arm. "Did the Christkindl bring us a bicycle? Did she?"

Mutti had tears in her eyes, but she was smiling. "Yes, my dears! She brought a bicycle for you to share. And if you're careful and don't damage it, Lotte might get to ride it when you're too big."

Otto and Hansi stood with Mutti as the Christkindl wheeled the bicycle inside. It was mostly blue, with dirt here and there and a few rusty spots. Maybe even an angel had trouble finding anything new in the angel shops.

Otto walked up to the Christkindl and put his hand out to shake hers, saying, "Thank you, angel! I never thought to get such a gift!" Hansi nodded vigorously.

The angel smiled and said, "You're most welcome. But you must also thank your mother. She and I worked together. She's a very special lady."

Mutti had hung back, but Hansi turned and ran to her, hugging her around the knees. "Thank you too! It's the best gift ever!"

For some reason, that seemed to make Mutti sad. She kissed the top of his head, lifted her apron to her eyes, and hurried into the kitchen.

Otto, it turned out, had learned to ride a friend's bicycle, and even though he complained and made faces about it, he taught Hansi. Once Hansi got past wobbling and falling down, it was almost like having wings. When either boy went to look for loose coals fallen off the freight cars, or to stand in line in case the rumors of bread or coffee or whatever food turned out to be true, they could get there so much faster, with the wind blowing past them! The only problems were having to keep track of the bicycle and finding a way to carry things home. Aunt Gertrud, who seemed to know a lot about bicycles, made them a reed basket to hang on the handlebars.

But even his aunt didn't know how to fix bicycles when something broke. And for a present from an angel, the bicycle seemed to be in pretty bad shape. First it was the wheel that got bent, when Hansi hit a rock a couple of months into the new year. Otto managed to bend it almost back where it should be, but the bicycle still ended up harder to steer. Then one of the handlebars somehow worked itself loose. Luckily Mutti had some glue that more or less put it back together, but it fell off every couple of weeks from then on.

It wasn't until summer that the chain broke. Otto was riding when that happened, and he went flying off the front and chipped a tooth. There was no way to fix the tooth, and no way to fix the chain. The dream was over.

Mutti and Otto carried the bicycle to the storage shed that all the flats shared. The shed, like so many buildings, needed repair, and the roof leaked. What was left of the bicycle would be sure to rust. Hansi followed along, and when Mutti and Otto had left, he went up to the bicycle, put his hand on the glued-on handlebar, and whispered, "Thank you for being ours for a little while." He stayed in the shed until he thought his eyes would no longer show he'd been crying.

Back to walking everywhere. At least his feet still worked.

Now that Hansi was older, he had learned something important: people lied. Even the Kaiser. Or at least whoever the Kaiser ordered to tell the people what was going on.

And not just about the war going well, or that it was good for people not to get enough to eat. There was the jam.

In October, they said some fruit had turned and was going to be given out to people as jam. Jam would be better if there was bread to put on it, but you could still eat it with a spoon or your fingers. But then nothing happened, and nothing kept happening. The jam hadn't come. He didn't think it ever would.

Then it was herring. The people in charge announced that there would soon be plenty of herring. But Hansi knew better. There would never be herring. There would never be anything worth eating. Things would always be like this.

So the next month, when everyone started saying the war was over, he didn't believe them. Even when Mutti and Aunt Gertrud joined hands and danced around the kitchen, he thought they must have it wrong, and was sorry for how sad they'd be when they found out.

But then the signs started going up along the biggest streets. He could read them well enough by himself, now. They weren't like the banners in spring of last year, when the angry people were marching. They said things like "Welcome, heroes!" and "A Grateful Heimat Greets You" and more. And policemen were tying flowers to the lamp-posts, and smiling when they saw the children watching, and throwing flowers down to the prettiest girls.

If something was going to happen, it would have to happen soon, or the flowers would lose petals and wilt.

When Hansi showed up at school the next morning, the headmaster was standing in front of the school — and he was smiling. Hansi couldn't remember him ever smiling before. "Go home, all of you!" He said. "Today is a special day! Go home and be with your families."

Hansi ran all the way home, or as much of it as he could before he got out of breath. When he got there, Mutti was standing in the street. She hadn't been going outside much, too tired to go to the markets and join the protests there, but now she was standing up straight and even going up on her toes, trying to see to the end of the street.

And then Hansi heard trumpets.

The air was fresh and cold, and the sun was shining, and the breeze was rippling the banners and the flower petals and the few leaves that hadn't fallen from the trees. The trumpets were coming closer. And there was another sound, like thunder if thunder came over and over, or like drums, if many people were playing drums all at once. And then he could see people, but marching, not drumming — hundreds of them, so their marching sounded like drums.

It was soldiers, hundreds of soldiers, all marching together.

The people lining the street started waving and cheering. For years, Hansi had only heard so many voices together when they were shouting and angry. Even the Christmas when the country family came and they all went to sing in church — the Christmas Lotte left — hadn't had so many people all together.

As if the thought had somehow jumped from Hansi to Mutti, she stopped waving for a moment and clasped her hands, saying under her breath, "If only Lotte were here with us, to see her Vati come home!" But then she pulled Hansi close and hugged him with one arm. "But my boys, my big boys, at least *you're* here. Can you see Vati anywhere?"

Hansi looked at the soldiers. They all looked so — not fat, but not thin, not like almost everyone he was used to seeing. Among all those big strong men, could he find the father he hadn't seen in so long?

It was Otto who saw him first, coming closer on their side of the street. There were two men next to him in the way, but Otto and Hansi waved and screamed at him, and he turned toward them, staring with the stern look most of the soldiers wore and then breaking into a broad smile.

Before they could do anything else, one of the soldiers next to him pointed at the banners and said something. He must not have liked the banners, and Vati must have felt the same way, because his smile went away and it looked as if he growled something to the soldier who'd pointed. The soldier muttered something back and laughed. Hansi couldn't hear the laugh, what with the trumpets and the marching feet and all the people cheering and calling out, but it didn't look like a happy laugh.

The line of soldiers was moving away now. Mutti tapped Hansi on the shoulder, and then Otto. "Vati will be done marching and come home soon. We have to go get ready!"

Mutti made Hansi and Otto scrub themselves clean, even though the water was awfully cold with winter getting close. While they were washing, she found and set out the clothes that had the fewest patches on them. She didn't change her own clothes, but she put on her best apron, the one with flowers on it.

A knock on the door! But it didn't sound like Vati's knock. Mutti hurried to open it, and Aunt Gertrud walked in with a big smile, carrying a loaf of bread — fresh bread, and not even from potatoes! Hansi could smell it. Aunt Gertrud said, "I saw Walther come marching in! Please, take this for his first supper at home." And then, at Mutti's shocked expression, she said with a grimace: "Don't ask me how — where I got it. We'll see Walther soon, but you can have him to yourselves tonight."

She gave Mutti a hug and went back upstairs. And then they waited, looking at the bread, smelling it, waiting for Vati.

Finally, a loud, firm knock, high up on the door, let them know he was home. Otto rushed toward the door, but Mutti got there ahead of him and flung it open, breathing hard from the effort of moving that fast for even a little way.

She gazed up at Vati, standing there in his uniform, almost filling the doorway, and she seemed to Hansi to have somehow become younger, years younger, if only for a minute. Vati stepped across the threshold and picked her up, holding her tight in his arms.

Even Otto stopped and gave them their moment, a wife welcoming her husband home from the war. Then Otto, and Hansi close behind him, ran forward and grabbed whatever part of Vati they could reach. Vati kissed Mutti's cheek, put her down, and went to one knee, his arms open. "Come and give me a real hug, you two!"

They crowded into his arms. Hansi hadn't cried since the bicycle chain broke, but he was crying now, and he thought he heard sniffs from Otto that said Otto was crying too.

Vati let go of them and looked at them sternly. "Act like men, now. None of these woman's tears. Tell me, now: have you been good, strong boys, and helped your mother every day?"

Hansi couldn't remember all those days. He couldn't remember whether he'd helped her or not, except when she told him to do something. He heard Otto clear his throat awkwardly. Mutti rescued them, saying firmly, "They've been such a help! I'd never have made it through without them. You can be proud of them, really, Walther." She had gone tense, and waited now for Vati to tell her whether she'd said enough. Vati smiled at her and nodded; she relaxed and said, "I'll have supper on the table in just a minute! Boys, go with your father and sit down." She bustled back to the kitchen, and Hansi heard her opening a drawer and closing it again.

Hansi wriggled in his chair. The trousers Mutti had made him wear might not be patched, but they were too small. Otto, watching him, punched his arm, and then stretched against his own too-small shirt. Hansi took a quick look at Vati to see if they were in trouble for fighting, but Vati was watching Mutti come out of the kitchen, carrying the bread. She had already put small plates on the table. Small plates would make pieces of bread look bigger.

"Gertrud brought us this. We can go see her tomorrow and thank her. And wait just a minute — I have something else!" She walked quickly back to the kitchen and then out again, carrying a bottle and a small tin, the colors in the picture on its lid still bright. "Look — sardines! and beer!"

"*Sardines?*" said Otto loudly, while Hansi stared at the tin. "Where — how — "

Mutti turned a little red. "I saved them! When food started getting scarce, I saved them for this day, for welcoming Vati home. They'd have been gone in no time if we'd eaten them, and now they can be part of our celebration."

She put the sardines on the table and held the beer out to Vati. He took it, looking confused, and said, "You saved *sardines* for a *celebration?*"

Mutti looked down at the table. Otto bristled and said, almost angrily, "We haven't had sardines in *years*! And I want mine!"

Mutti looked slowly up again. She reached for the sardine tin and turned the key to open it. It took her two tries, because her hands were shaking. She looked inside and said to Hansi, her voice hoarse, "Darling, would you go get some forks? Somehow I forgot."

Hansi jumped up, ran to the kitchen, and yanked a drawer open so far it came loose and fell to the floor. He jumped at the noise, but grabbed four forks and ran back to the table, handing one to Mutti. Vati was frowning toward the kitchen, but Mutti just took a deep breath and used the fork to fish out a sardine. She put it on Vati's plate, and then did the same with a second before going on to serve one sardine each to Hansi, Otto, and last to herself. Then she tore the bread in half, tore one half into pieces, and put the pieces on the plates.

Mutti looked sharply at Hansi and Otto when they started to reach for the food. "Walther, do you want to say *Tischgebet?*"

Vati sat up very straight, looked at the plates and then at each of them. In a firm voice, he said, "We thank God that we are all together. In spite of all that has happened, we hope for better days, and trust in Your power. Amen."

Hansi didn't understand. In spite of? Wasn't this a happy day, with the war over and Vati home? But it wasn't the time to think about that. He picked up his fork and speared the sardine, biting off half of it. And oh, the feel of the oil, and the taste of salt, and feeling of the fish against his teeth! . . . He knew he should eat more slowly to make it last, but he shoved the other half in his mouth almost before he'd finished chewing the first.

And then there was the bread. Mutti wouldn't make him use a fork for that. He picked it up and took as big a bite as he could, feeling the corners of his mouth stretch. Bread, bread, real bread! He had missed real bread so much!

Mutti made a strange noise, the noise Hansi would have made if he stepped on something sharp with his feet bare. He looked at her. She was holding bread too, and she had her other hand against her cheek. Vati said, "*Liebchen*, what is it?"

Mutti dropped her hand and tried to smile, but the smile was crooked. "It's nothing, *Liebling*. It was just my tooth. I bit too hard on the crust. I'm fine now." She opened her mouth to try another bite, and then put her hand quickly to her mouth as something fell out of it.

The tooth.

The tooth lay in Mutti's hand with hardly any blood on it, as if it had barely been in Mutti's mouth to begin with. Mutti closed her hand over it and got up from the table. "Excuse me — I'll be right back." She walked to the bathroom as if nothing much was the matter, and came back a few minutes later, looking around the table. "Boys, are you done? You can take the plates to the kitchen. Walther, you haven't finished your beer. Shall I sit with you, or would you rather take it to the other room and read the paper with it?"

Vati was drinking his beer and reading the paper. When he finished the beer, he looked at it as if he'd have liked another and put it down on the side table next to his armchair. It was the best armchair they had, and Hansi and Lotte had sat there together sometimes. Then Otto had claimed it. But now it was Vati's again. Hansi sat on the floor next to it. Otto had gone out, the way he did more and more these days. Mutti used to try to stop him, but she didn't anymore. Maybe Vati would make him stay home.

Vati picked the paper back up, turned a page — and then threw it down on the side table, almost knocking the bottle over. Mutti heard the noise from the kitchen and ran in, looking at Hansi as though he must have caused it. Hansi shook his head and looked toward Vati. Mutti looked too, but there was nothing much for her to see. She tiptoed forward, kissed the top of Vati's head, and was leaving the room when Vati picked the newspaper back up and shook it at her. "The traitors! They've dragged the Kaiser off the throne and sent him out of the *Vaterland*! To the Netherlands — they've cut out the heart of this country and sent it to the Netherlands! And now all they can do is talk, talk, talk, instead of finding a way to save the country and bring back our honor! Those cowards, those—"

Mutti knelt down next to Vati and took his hands. He stopped talking and took a deep breath. "Ah, *Liebling*, here you are, after all I've seen, my angel, waiting for me . . . ." Then, for the first time since before supper, he smiled, running a finger along her cheek. "Are you ready to welcome your man home? Shall we go to our room?"

Mutti smiled back at him, looking shy. "Hansi," she said, "go study for a while, and then you can read or play until time to bed. Come here and get a kiss." She climbed to her feet as he got near, kissed him, and then stood there waiting. He couldn't figure out for what, at first, and then he remembered. His father was home, and Hansi should kiss him too. He edged over to Vati. Vati stood up too — still so tall, even though Hansi was so much older! — and bent down to kiss Hansi and be kissed. Then he put an arm around Mutti's waist, and they left the room.

Hansi looked after them, feeling strange. He was used to spending the evening with Mutti unless he was busy playing, and she always put him to bed. But he went to his and Otto's room. He didn't do any studying. Instead, he picked up one of his favorite books, a book about brave German knights fighting the Hussites, and read until he fell asleep.

Chapter 7

Winter – Summer 1919

Surely life would finally be better now, with Vati home and the war over. Now the new government, the Weimar Republic, could make sure there was enough food, and more kinds of food, butter and pork fat and pork and bread, and coffee, and sugar for it.

And Mutti would get stronger, going shopping for all that food, climbing the stairs to visit Aunt Gertrud, even playing games with him.

But none of that had happened yet. He tried asking Mutti when it would. At first, Mutti would say, "Soon, darling." Then she started acting like she hadn't heard him, telling him to do some chore or go do schoolwork. The day she cried, a few weeks after Vati came home, Hansi stopped asking. A couple of days later he went to Vati, who was standing in front of the icebox and looking inside as if searching for more food than was in it. Hansi said, standing very straight, "Now that I'm a big boy, Vati, could you tell me —" He almost said, "when things will get better," but instead he gulped and said, "whether things will get better — whether we'll have more food soon?"

Vati turned away from the icebox, letting it close behind him, and put his hands on Hansi's shoulders. He looked in Hansi's eyes and spoke to him solemnly, man to man, the way no one ever had before. It was a moment Hansi was sure he would remember for the rest of his life.

"The war is not over," he said. "We were forced to sign an armistice, but our enemies are still blocking our ports, trying to starve us. They were not content with driving our Kaiser from his throne — the crowd in England are baying for his blood. The Allies want to cripple Germany, to weaken it and keep it weak forever. I don't know when we will have the chance to fight again, to protect our country, to restore our *Vaterland*. I may be too old when the time comes. It may be your task, and Otto's, to fight that battle."

Hansi could hardly breathe, but he managed to say, "Should I become a soldier like you, Vati?"

Then he heard footsteps behind him, Mutti's footsteps. Vati looked up, over Hansi's head, as if looking at Mutti. Mutti said softly, "Hansi admires policemen. He saw a policeman save me, when I was — in trouble, in danger, once." Vati frowned, in a worried way, as Mutti added, "And another time, a policeman brought him home when he was lost."

How had she known? Had she been watching from the window?

Vati still held Hansi's shoulders. He gripped them tight and said, "That's a good ambition, my son. We face a bad time now. With the Kaiser gone, Germany will be in disarray, and Bolsheviks will run wild. We will need the police more than ever, until the time to fight comes again."

When Vati let go of his shoulders, Hansi hugged him round the waist and then hurried to his room to hide the tears in his eyes.

That night, Vati went out to meet some friends. They weren't people Hansi knew, Vati said, but people he'd met in the army, soldiers like him. They would find some supper, so Mutti needn't make supper for him. Whatever supper might turn out to be. Hansi hoped Vati would find something better, and wished he could go along too.

Vati didn't come home before Mutti sent Hansi off to bed. He lay there, awake, listening, for what felt like hours, and finally he heard the front door open and then heavy footsteps. They didn't sound like Vati's footsteps usually did — they were uneven, as if he was stumbling. But it was Vati's voice he heard next, calling for Mutti, slurring her name. Then Hansi heard lighter steps coming out of his parents' bedroom. Mutti must have been sleeping, or trying to.

He could hear them talking, but not what they were saying. Then Vati's voice got louder. "They all abandoned us! Bulgaria, Turkey, Austria-Hungary — cowards! Traitors!" And then, after Mutti said something: "It was the Jews! They wanted Palestine turned over to them, and in return they brought America into the war to destroy us! In spite of everything, we could have won the war, if not for the damned, Christ-killing Jews! The Jews and the Bolsheviks, the November criminals who signed that cursed paper, they stabbed us in the back!"

More murmuring from Mutti, and then, "So I wake the boys! They should hear! They should know! It'll be their job to avenge us! They'll take the battle to the communists and the Jews . . . ." And then, after more murmuring, "All right, all right, I'm coming."

When nothing else happened, Hansi rolled over and finally fell asleep.

Now that the war was over, if it was over, Mutti didn't have anymore sewing work. Sometimes, when Vati wasn't around, she sat in a chair looking restless, her hands even twitching now and then as if they wanted to be busy.

Vati had gone back to the bank where he'd worked before the war, but some nights he came home complaining about what they had him doing. "It's busywork. This 'republic' of theirs —" He stopped and made a face, then went on. " — promised to give the soldiers their jobs back, but I'm an office manager, and lately I've been put to cleaning the floors and windows!"

Mutti opened her mouth and shut it again. Vati looked at her and added, "Yes, at least they're paying me. It could be worse. If we couldn't pay them any rent, Helmut and Gertrud might throw us out in the street. We're lucky." And then, angry again: "This is what Germany has come to, that we're lucky to have a roof over our heads, after all the good men who died. . . ."

Was Hansi supposed to be happy or sad, angry or not? Somehow, life had gotten even more confusing since Vati came home.

At least there was a little more food now. It wasn't enough to keep Hansi and Otto from being hungry, or Vati from grumbling, or Mutti from moving slowly and sitting down a lot, but Hansi told himself that more food was better than less.

The dustmen went out on strike, and the streets got dirtier and dirtier — "filthy," said Vati. Mutti wrung her hands at how dirty all their clothes got — except hers, because she hardly ever went outside anymore. Hansi and Otto went to the market and stood in the lines, and sometimes Vati went with Hansi to keep him safe. It felt strange, but good, to have someone bigger and stronger looking out for him. It reminded him of the policeman who helped him so long ago. But then one of the other children in school said there had been a big fight between police and protesters on the east side of the city. The other boy didn't know what or who started it.

Spring came, and Mutti seemed a little stronger. Vati took her for a walk to see the new leaves, Mutti leaning on his arm. She was smiling when they came back.

One evening in late June, Hansi was reading Grimm's book of tales when the front door slammed open and Vati burst in. His face was red and veins were bulging in his neck, and he shouted for Mutti. Before she could even get to the front room, he yelled, "Those traitors! How could they sign a treaty like this? Our army cut down to a size that couldn't fight a kindergarten! A navy that could barely fill a puddle! No air force, no tanks, no armor, no submarines, no dirigibles, no heavy guns, fortifications to be destroyed! Railroad cars turned over to the enemy! Our police not allowed to hire enough men! Even our children, my God! The boys not to be cadets when they reach high school!"

Mutti had reached the front room in the middle of all this, and was standing and staring at Vati. Her face looked hard, somehow, especially her jaw. It had been so long that it took Hansi a minute to remember: that was how Mutti looked when she was angry. Ever since life became so hard, with the food worse and hard to find and people rioting, she'd stopped getting angry even though she had good reasons. Maybe she'd been saving her strength. But she was angry now.

"The Saar coal mines turned over to the French! The Rhineland occupied for the next fifteen years! And— " He stopped, his fists clenched, and looked as if he might break into tears. Hansi held his breath and stared. Finally Vati said, his voice breaking, "And the war trophies our victorious soldiers brought home in better days, like the flags we took from the cursed bastard French almost fifty years ago — we have to give them back, as if we'd never won those battles at all! The soldiers who brought them home in triumph must be rising from their graves!"

Vati stumbled to his chair and fell into it, his head hanging down. Mutti came to stand behind the chair and rubbed Vati's shoulders, saying in a high tight voice, "What are we going to *do*?"

Vati grabbed one of Mutti's hands and pulled her onto his lap. Holding her tight, he growled, "We have to find a leader, someone who can show us how to fight back! Someone who'll bring the country together to wipe out this shame and set us on the path back to German greatness!"

Hansi moved closer and asked, "Couldn't that leader be you, Vati?"

Mutti went stiff, and Vati looked at Hansi, very sad, and shook his head. "No, my son. For that, we need a better leader than I. There's an art to bringing people together and filling them with strength, inspiring them to take on hardship and put aside fear. I don't have that." He smiled in a way that looked forced. "Maybe you will. But God willing, we won't have to wait that long. We must keep our eyes open, so we can recognize our leader when he appears." He gave Mutti a kiss and sat back in his chair.

Hans crept quietly away and went to his room, dreaming of the leader to come.

Chapter 8

Autumn 1919 – Winter 1919-1920

Every once in a while, Vati took to grumbling about the Jews again — that they had betrayed Germany, that no true German should trust them, that they were sneaky and sly, that they ran shops and cheated their customers. But how could Hansi recognize a Jew, so he would know to be careful? No one had explained that.

So he asked Vati.

Vati smiled and said, "That's good, Hansi, that you want to know. There might even be Jewish students at your school, and you need to know that." He stopped and stroked his chin. Hansi had the feeling Vati would have liked to puff on his pipe, if he could still afford to smoke. "There are a few ways to spot a Jew. To start with, there's how they look. They have big, hooked noses — a little like the number 6, except backwards." Vati showed Hansi with his finger how long and hooked a Jew's nose would be. "And they have dark, beady eyes — with their eyelids half closed, to make it harder for you to look them in the eye or read their expressions."

Hansi nodded, hoping he could remember all these details.

"Their skin is darker, like the Italians. Usually they have black, curly hair, greasy, or else all curled up tight, almost like the Africans you've seen in pictures. But sometimes they have red hair. It might mean that someone in their family, generations ago, betrayed his race and married a Jew. Or it might be something they do to try to disguise what they are.

"I should have told you all this before, my son. Now you are armed with information, and can spot these enemies before they can weaken you or do you harm."

At school the next day, Hansi studied his fellow students. None of them had red hair. Some had darker hair and some lighter. None of them had a big hooked nose, but Samuel's nose stuck out more than some, and he had curly hair that was darker than Hansi's. Hansi waited until school was dismissed for the day and went up to Samuel before Samuel could run home to some Jewish hideaway. He marched right up to him and asked, "Are you a Jew?"

Samuel stared at him as if puzzled. "*Ja.* So?"

Now what? Hansi couldn't kick him out of the school. He settled on, "I just wanted to know, so I can . . . can keep an eye on you. In case you start any Jew trouble."

Samuel grabbed Hansi's arm and pulled him aside from the stream of students leaving the school. "That's enough, you *Ignorantin!* I'll fight you here and now!" He put up his fists.

Hansi looked at his own hands and back at Samuel's. "You'd fight me? But Jews are cowards!"

Samuel spat at Hansi. Some of the spit touched Hansi's hands, and he wiped them on his pants as hard as he could. Meanwhile, Samuel was shouting, "My father is a war hero! He won a medal! You should be such a coward!"

A medal? Not even Vati had won a medal — or had he, and just not wanted to brag about it? Meanwhile, the two of them were attracting attention. So far it was only other boys, but a teacher or even the headmaster could show up any minute. Samuel looked around as if he were thinking the same thing, Jew or no. He turned back to Hansi, shook one fist at him and said, "We can finish this around the corner, if you're not a *coward*." He pointed in the direction of the nearest intersection.

Hansi squared his shoulders and said, "Sure." He tried to think as Samuel stalked off toward the corner. Vati would want him to fight, and be proud of him for doing it. Mutti, though, might cry or scold or both, even if she hated Jews as much as Vati did. Did she? Hansi didn't even know.

He trudged to the corner, wondering if he had any way out of a fight he didn't much want. It was a hot day, especially for October — that must be why he was sweating.

Samuel was waiting. He didn't look scared, which would have helped . . . but he didn't look as mad as he had before. As Hansi walked up, Samuel said, "I'm ready to fight if you are. But if you don't want to, I won't make you."

Hansi didn't want to. He should want to, but he didn't. It wasn't just that he'd probably get hurt, and that Mutti would fuss. Samuel seemed like a good enough fellow. And there must be something wrong with how he'd understood Vati . . . or even, little as he wanted to think it, with how Vati understood Jews, because Samuel didn't look that much like what Vati had said he should, and he didn't seem sneaky. And if he was a coward, what did that make Hansi?

Vati would want him to fight. But if he didn't tell Vati about the Jew at school, Hansi wouldn't have to disappoint him or get in trouble about it. Hansi shifted his weight and said, "I won't make you, either."

Samuel stuck out his hand and said, "Shake on it?"

It would be rude to say no. Touching a Jew couldn't be that much worse than talking to one and deciding not to fight him. Hansi shook hands, and then turned and ran home through the heat.

It was just an ordinary day. Vati had come home from work and was asking Hansi about school when Mutti called him aside. Hansi would have liked to pout, but that was for little children. Instead, he shrugged and went back outside to play.

Only a few minutes later, Vati called him in again. Instead of the genial expression he had shown Hansi a few minutes ago, his face was grim. He led the way to Hansi's bedroom, closed the door, and stood looming over Hansi. "I hear you told Mutti that you would put the dishes away, but then as soon as she left the room, she saw you go outside."

Hansi looked down at his feet. "I didn't know she saw me."

"That isn't the point." This, Hansi realized, was what a stern father sounded like. "You broke a promise. And it happened so soon after you promised that I don't think you meant to keep your promise. Making a promise without intending to keep it is a type of lie. And men in this family must not lie."

Vati unbuckled his belt and pulled it loose. "Bring your desk chair and put it down in front of me," he ordered. And when Hansi froze in place, he snapped, "Now." Hansi walked shakily over and got the chair, setting it down at Vati's feet. He knew what would happen next. But it had never happened before, not to him.

"Bend over the back of the chair with your hands on the seat."

Hansi could hardly breathe, but he did as he was told, and waited.

"You have, so far, grown up without a father, and your mother has been too overwhelmed by carrying on alone to instruct you as you needed. Let this be a lesson, then, a very important lesson, that you must not treat your solemn word as a plaything. You must not tell lies." And the belt smacked down against his bottom, once, and again, and then twice more, the blows falling quickly one after the other.

Hansi had fallen and skinned his knees or hurt his wrist often enough, but he had never felt this type of pain. He was too stunned to cry out at first, and then, when he would have yelled, it was over, and Vati's hands were on his shoulders, helping him stand up. Vati stood close to him and put his fingers under Hansi's chin, lifting his face up to look in his eyes. "You didn't make any noise. That's good. I'm glad my son is brave. You've learned courage, it seems, even without my teaching it to you, or else you were born with it like a proper German boy."

That meant Hansi couldn't cry, not now. Maybe when Mutti put him to bed that night, he could cry into her lap. But for now, he just said, trying not to let his voice shake, "I'm sorry, Vati. I won't lie again."

Vati pressed lightly on his shoulder and let go again. "That's a good boy. Now, it's time for supper. It may hurt to sit still, but my brave boy can do that, can't you?"

Hansi's heart sank. He didn't want to be brave again this soon. But he said, "Yes, sir," and followed Vati to the table.

For the first time in three years, their family in the country came for a Christmas visit. They brought a tree, the way they had before, and some nuts, and a salami. And of course, they brought Lotte with them.

Mutti ran to Lotte and knelt down to squeeze her tight. Hansi thought Lotte might cry to see her mother again, but she just babbled about the trip, and the tree, and what she'd been doing back at the farm. It was Mutti who cried, and she did it so quietly Hansi wouldn't have known if he hadn't been looking.

Vati squatted down and held out his arms. Mutti turned Lotte to see him as he said, "Lotte, little one, do you remember me? Will you come kiss your Vati?"

She didn't hang onto Mutti, or turn away. But she didn't run into Vati's arms. Instead, she marched toward him, stopped a little ways away, and looked him over from head to foot. Then she nodded firmly as if he'd done something right, marched the rest of the way, leaned on his leg, and gave him a smacking kiss on the cheek before sitting cross-legged on the floor in front of him. "I'm Lotte!" she announced, in the tone of a teacher lecturing a student. "I'm almost seven years old!" Then she walked back over to stand between Opa and Aunt Frieda, grabbing their hands.

She looked healthy and strong, at least compared to most of the people Hansi saw in Berlin. Including Mutti and Otto, and Aunt Gertrud and Uncle Helmut upstairs. And Vati, even, now that he'd been home for a year, eating the food you could get in Berlin instead of what they gave the soldiers.

Watching Lotte with the visitors, looking more like them, a stranger could have thought she belonged with them instead of with her own parents, with him. Hansi felt his face get hot. She was *his* sister!

And then, three days later on the last night of the visit, Hansi was coming back from the bathroom and heard the grownups talking. Opa was saying in his rumbly voice, "We love her like our own. But you must have heard how bad the harvest was. We took her because we could feed her better than her mother could, but I'm afraid that won't be true this winter. So shouldn't she be with her parents?"

No one said anything for a little while. Then came Vati's voice, hard and sharp, biting off the words: "I can feed my family. I wasn't here when Lotte went with you, I wasn't part of that decision, but I'm here now, and Lotte will stay."

When the relatives got ready to leave, Lotte trotted up to Opa with her little bag of clothes, her face bright with excitement. "Will we see more bridges on this trip? How many?"

Uncle Oskar knelt down in front of her. "Wouldn't you rather stay here, *Schatzi*? With your Mutti and Vati and your brothers?"

Lotte looked at him wide-eyed with confusion. "Stay?" she asked. "But I live with you now." Hansi saw Vati, standing to one side, clench his jaw, and Mutti, next to him, put her apron to her eyes.

"You did live with us, Lotte, and we loved having you visit." Uncle Oskar stressed the word. "But now it's time for you to come home. Your Vati is back from his honorable service to our country, and he deserves to have his children with him. And now that you're so big, you can be a help to your mother."

Lotte seemed to like that idea. She stood up very straight and then walked over to Mutti. "How can I help?"

Mutti looked over at Uncle Oskar as if trying to figure out what to say. "Well. What did you do to help Aunt Frieda while you were staying with her?"

"I hunted for eggs in the chicken coop! I got good at that! And I was learning to milk the cows." She looked around the flat. "I don't think . . . you don't have chickens or cows, do you." She sighed, then perked up again. "And I dried the dishes, and I hardly broke any! You have dishes, don't you?"

Mutti ran to Lotte and hugged her. "Yes, yes, my darling, we have dishes! And you'll help me so much by drying them, and maybe washing them too."

Uncle Oskar and Aunt Frieda smiled at each other, but the smiles didn't last, and Aunt Freida blinked hard twice before she said, "We'll be going, then. May God keep you all well and safe until we see you again. Maybe there will be enough railroad cars, and coal, to bring you to visit us next time."

"And I could show them around, so they can meet the cows and chickens!" Lotte said as she waved goodbye.

Lotte had been home for three weeks, by Hansi's count. He'd expected Mutti to give Lotte as much food as she could, to keep her as healthy as she'd been when she came home from the country. But instead, Mutti seemed to be giving Otto and Hansi more food, and making up for it by eating less herself. He waited a few days after he noticed, and then asked Vati what Mutti was doing and why. But Vati acted as if Hansi might be wrong, or even making it up. Hansi watched for a few more days, and once he was absolutely sure, he asked Vati again.

"Still going on about this nonsense?" Vati lowered his newspaper and frowned at Hansi. "That's quite enough. You're imagining things. And I don't want you bothering your mother about it."

Hansi never disobeyed Vati. A good German boy obeyed his father. And boys who disobeyed their fathers got a whipping.

But Lotte looked thinner to him. And she didn't bounce around the house as much as when she first came home.

He was going to be a soldier or a policeman someday. That meant being brave, but also knowing how to obey orders. . . . Maybe, sometimes, once in a long while, when something was very important, being brave might come first, and might even mean making trouble and being punished.

He waited until the next morning, after Vati left for work and Mutti and Lotte finished with the breakfast dishes. He waited some more until Lotte went out to play, pretending to find chicken eggs in the patch of dirt and weeds behind the building. Then he read one of his books about heroic soldiers to help him work up his courage, and went to Mutti where she was mending one of Otto's shirts. He stood next to her until she looked up and asked, "What is it, Hansi? Do you need something?"

Just the idea seemed to make her more tired. "No, nothing," he said quickly — and then contradicted himself by saying, "I just want to know something."

Now that the time came, his voice stuck in his throat. But he made himself go on. "Why are you giving Otto and me some of your food? And not Lotte?"

Mutti's eyes went wide, and her mouth hung open. But she pulled herself together and said, "I didn't mean you to notice. Have Otto or — or Lotte?"

Hansi shrugged. "I don't know. But I did."

Mutti took a deep breath, looked him in the eye, and said, "You are the future. All you children are, but you and Otto are boys and will be men. Men who can fight. Men who can defend Germany against those who want to destroy it. Men who can take *back* what was taken from us — our land, our resources, our honor. You must grow up strong, so you can do such things." Her voice cracked. "Poor little Lotte . . . she will be like me, a woman who waits."

At dinner that night, Hansi waited until Mutti turned to talk to Vati and snuck some of his potatoes onto Lotte's plate. She opened her mouth to say something, but he held his finger to his lips and then made eating motions. Her face showed when she understood. She looked at him gratefully and shoveled the extra food into her mouth before Mutti could turn back and notice.

Hansi couldn't do the same at every meal, but he kept doing it almost as often as he could. Sometimes, he was just too hungry. But then he would feel ashamed, afterward, and try again the next time.

Chapter 9

Spring 1920

Hansi had turned ten years old, so it was time to leave primary school and go to middle school. He didn't know as many students there, and felt a little lost. Samuel, the Jew, was at the new school, and Hansi was glad to see a familiar face, and also ashamed of actually wanting to see the face of a Jew, even if he didn't look that much like one.

Hansi wouldn't have gone out of his way to spend time with Samuel. But they were given seats near each other, and sometimes it made sense for them to work together on an assignment. Samuel turned out to be good at history, while Hansi was better at mathematics. So they got better marks when they worked together.

A few weeks after Hansi started at the middle school, Vati sat him down before supper and asked, "Are you getting along all right in the new school? I remember how strange it was, changing schools at that age, being around strangers after years of seeing all the same children every day." He leaned toward Hansi and whispered, "I'll tell you a secret. You won't believe it, but when I first started middle school, there were mornings I didn't want to go. Your Opa had to force me, tell me I could stay home and get a whipping or go to school and learn something to fill my empty head."

Hansi swallowed. "I don't mind going, Vati. And there are a few boys from my old school."

Vati leaned back and smiled. "That's good. Friends you know from your early years and manage not to lose, they can be friends for life. Make new friends, by all means! — they may be the ones to help you in your career, even introduce you to the right sort of girls! But don't drift away from the old ones."

"Yes, Vati," Hansi mumbled. He couldn't tell Vati he'd been thinking mainly of Samuel. He never would.

Hansi had been playing with some friends after school, but now he was ready to go home — or at least, he knew Mutti would be expecting him. As he got near the steps, he saw his cousin Rudolf coming the other way. He was hunched over, and he seemed to have something in his coat, something big enough to shove the cloth out.

Was it a book that Rudolf didn't want his parents to see? There were some books and cards in the shop windows lately showing women with almost no clothes on. It made Hansi feel funny to see them, partly ashamed and partly uncomfortable, as if he were overheated. Did he dare ask Rudolf to let him borrow one?

But as Rudolf squeezed by him on his way up the stairs, Hansi smelled something he hadn't smelled since the last time the country family had come to visit. He smelled sausage. And fresh bread.

He grabbed Rudolf's arm and said, "What's that? Where did you get it?" Rudolf squirmed to get away. But as he pulled loose from Hansi's grip, something fell out of his coat onto the step. Rudolf froze for a moment and then ran up the stairs.

Hansi squatted down and stared at the sausage lying there, next to him, right within his reach.

Hansi looked every which way. No one was watching. He grabbed the sausage, tucked it under his coat with his arm clamped down to hold it, and ran back outside. He looked around again, seeing other children playing or heading for their flats. Where could he go? Trying to act natural, he walked to the patch of dirt where Lotte sometimes played her farm games. No one was near. As fast as he could, he pulled out the sausage, tore it into three pieces, and stuffed one after another in his mouth, chewing just enough to get them down. He almost choked on the third.

Then he walked casually back to his flat and went inside.

His stomach hurt that night, and Mutti looked at him, worried. "Are you sick? Did some friend of yours give you something bad to eat?"

Hansi didn't know whether to laugh or cry, but of course he couldn't do either. Yes, a friend of his. No, he hadn't given Hansi anything on purpose. And yes, it had been something bad.

Hansi wasn't as hungry as usual the next day. But by the day after that, he was as hungry as ever. He cornered Rudolf on the school playground and said, "Tell me where you got it, and how you can get more, or else." He hoped Rudolf wouldn't ask "or else what," because he didn't know. If they fought Hansi might end up with bruises or a black eye, and would have to explain somehow. And he didn't think he could tell on Rudolf even if he wanted to, not after eating that sausage himself.

Rudolf blustered, "I don't have to tell you anything! But — " He looked up at Hansi. Hansi used to be the shorter one, but he'd grown more. "But you could come along next time. I don't know if we'll find anything good, but you could come and see."

Hansi and Rudolf met after school. It turned out Rudolf was bringing his sister Maria along. Hansi couldn't imagine letting Lotte do anything of the kind, but Maria was only a year younger than Rudolf and tougher than Lotte as well.

They made their way a long way across the city, to a fancy district full of people wearing the kind of clothes Hansi had forgotten even existed. The smells from the food shops — and candy shops! — they passed made his mouth water, and there were shops for all sorts of other things — furniture, books, paintings, even toys. Rudolf led the way through so many right and left turns that Hansi would have had no idea how to get home — and he could hardly wish for a policeman to help him, when he was here to commit a crime. He felt as if the word THIEF was written in big red letters on his back, and would stay there no matter what he wore and where he went.

His stomach twisted and then growled, and he followed Rudolf farther into the maze.

They finally came to a shop with a storage shed in the alley behind it, locked with a big rusty padlock. Rudolf leaned on it and took a handful of keys, all different shapes and sizes, out of his pocket. "My father used to make locks for people. He keeps the extra locks and keys in a chest in the attic." Rudolf sorted through the keys, found the one he was looking for, and put the rest away. "I just have to wiggle it the right way, and the lock'll open."

The wiggling took forever. Hansi kept looking around until Maria hissed at him to keep still before his moving around made someone notice them. Finally the lock opened, and Rudolf unhooked it and laid it on the ground. Grinning, he opened the door of the shed and swept his arm out toward Hansi and Maria like a host inviting his guests inside.

Hansi couldn't see or smell any sausage, this time. But there were tins of sardines, and round tins that had a picture of a different fish on the lid, and a whole row of round, wax-covered cheeses bigger than both Hansi's hands held together. Rudolf grabbed a cheese and some sardines, handing the sardines to his sister, and got out of the way so Hansi could take what he wanted. Hansi took a cheese, a tin of sardines, and one of the round tins. He stuffed the tins in his pockets. He had brought his school knapsack and tucked the cheese on top of his books, closing it up again tighter than before.

Suddenly the back door of the shop started to open. The boys and Maria ran around behind the shed and held their breath. Then Hansi saw the open lock, lying on the ground right where anyone could see it.

They were doomed. They would all be arrested, and a policeman would bring Hansi home and tell Mutti and Vati what he had done. And the policeman would tell all the other police, and they would never let Hansi become a policeman . . . . But the shopkeeper just yawned, rubbed his eyes — had he just taken a nap? — peed in the dirt of the alley, and went back inside.

Rudolf darted out and shoved the lock back in place, locking it with shaking hands. They ran out of the alley and then skidded to a walk, ambling down the shop-lined streets back toward their own part of town.

Mutti stopped Hansi as he was heading for his room to hide the food. "Where have you been, *Liebling*, since school let out? Otto was home more than an hour ago."

Hansi stood up straight and tried to act angry. "Why the questions? I went for a walk with Rudolf and Maria, around the city. Shouldn't I?"

Mutti wrinkled her forehead. "Aunt Gertrud is worried that Rudolf might be getting into mischief. She didn't say what kind before your uncle called her and we stopped talking. You'll be a good boy, won't you?"

He couldn't answer her, except with a nod.

"Do you want a snack? Aunt Gertrud found some crackers that aren't too stale, and she gave me some, the darling."

Where had the crackers really come from? Hansi's throat was too tight for him to eat. He kissed Mutti on the cheek and then ran upstairs. He made sure Otto wasn't around and then locked the bedroom door. After he let himself cry for a few minutes, he took the cheese out and hid it in his chest of drawers under his shirts, then put the sardines alongside it. He sat down with the round tin, which he now saw had the word Kaviar on it. He'd never heard of Kaviar, but it must have something to do with a fish. He opened it and saw little round black balls of something. When he picked one up, it felt a little like a marble, but not as hard. He put it in his mouth and bit down. It popped when he bit it. It tasted salty, and a little like fish, and a little oily, and just a little like butter. He brought the tin to his mouth and scooped out a quarter of it.

The door knob rattled, and Otto called from the hall, "What's going on? Let me in, pipsqueak!" Hansi jumped, put the lid back on the tin, shoved it in the drawer, and pushed it shut. Then he ran to open the door and tried to breathe as if he hadn't been running and everything was normal.

"You look funny." Otto peered at him. "You've been up to something, haven't you? Talk, or I'll tell Vati!"

It was an empty threat, or Hansi hoped so. The boys didn't tell on each other. He opened his mouth and couldn't think of anything to say. Otto leaned closer. "You've been eating something! Your breath smells funny!" Otto glared at him. Hansi might have grown, but Otto was still taller than he was. And meaner. Hansi gave up and opened the drawer, pulling out the Kaviar tin and handing it to Otto. Otto opened it eagerly, and then poked at the little round balls less eagerly. "What *is* this stuff?"

Hansi shrugged. "Something to do with fish. It tastes all right." And then, struggling with and giving in to the inevitable: "You can have some."

Otto upended the tin over his mouth, gulped, and closed it again. From what Hansi could see, there were only a few balls left. "Not bad." He turned away, and Hansi held his breath. Otto paused. He turned back, slowly. Hansi bit his lip hard, sure he was going to cry again, and that Otto would tease him about it for the rest of his life.

Otto looked at his face, snorted, and said, "I'll let you know when I get hungry again." Then he left the room.

How could Otto not be hungry? A few fish balls wouldn't fill him up. They were always hungry, all of them.

He thought about starting on the cheese. But for some reason, he still wanted to cry. He'd save the cheese for later.

A couple of hours later, Hansi heard a faint howling from upstairs. It sounded as if Rudolf were getting a whipping. Hansi crawled into bed and put his pillow over his ears.

Vati and Mutti weren't quite arguing, but they were talking loudly in their bedroom. Hansi heard Aunt Gertrud's name, and Uncle Helmut's, and then Rudolf's. And then he heard the word "thief."

Rudolf might tell on him. If that happened, he'd know soon enough. But if it didn't happen, he should confess. Confess and take his punishment.

But — what would Vati do with the cheese, and the sardines? He might throw them away, to punish Hansi more and to show that stealing never got you what you wanted. And then he and Otto and Lotte — he had to give some to Lotte — would be just as hungry as ever.

But if he said nothing and shared the food with his brother and sister, Vati and Mutti wouldn't get anything. And Mutti was so weak . . . .

The next morning, he called Lotte into his room before he left for school. He had already cut a wedge of cheese for her. He held it behind his back and said, "I've got something secret to show you. Can you keep a secret? Even — even from Mutti and Vati?"

Lotte's little nose twitched. She must have smelled the cheese. She nodded, her eyes big as mill-wheels, and he brought the wedge of cheese out and gave it to her. She grabbed it and took a bite so big he was afraid she would choke, but she got it down. Hansi pushed her arm down when she went to take another. "No. Take it to your room — put it in your pocket until you get there — and hide it. You can eat a little more of it every day until it's gone. All right?"

Without saying a word, she stuck the cheese in her pocket and ran out.

Hansi couldn't pay attention in school that day. When he was called up to do a mathematics problem on the board, he made two mistakes. After the second, the teacher made him stick out his palm and gave him three whacks with a ruler. Hansi was almost glad. It was like being punished for his crime without having to confess it.

When he got home, he went to his room, locked the door, and cut himself another wedge of cheese, eating it slowly to make it last. Then he cut the rest into two pieces he could just barely fit in his pockets and went into the kitchen. Mutti was there sewing at the table. He asked, "May I look in the pantry for something to eat?"

Mutti sighed. "I don't know what you can find there. But maybe I missed something. Go ahead."

Hansi went to the pantry, opened it, and carefully slipped the cheese out of his pockets and put it in the very back. There was an extra apron on the next shelf, and he moved it to cover most of the cheese. Then he threw the door open wide and said, his voice as excited as he could make it, "Look, Mutti! Look! I found some cheese!" He pulled the pieces back out and showed them to her.

Mutti put her sewing down and stared at him. "There can't be cheese there. We haven't had cheese in years. Who has cheese anymore? Rich people have cheese! And farmers . . . ." She stopped, and her mouth dropped open. "Aunt Frieda must have brought it and put it there the last time she came to visit. But why put it there, instead of handing it to me?"

Hansi could hardly believe it. Mutti had made up an excuse for him! or most of one. He mumbled, "Maybe she wanted it to be a surprise."

Mutti's eyes teared up. "Maybe she wanted us to find it when we needed it most. Was it tucked in the back, where we might miss it unless we were looking hard?"

Hansi swallowed and answered, "At the very back, and partly under an apron."

Mutti came to him and took the cheese, hugging it to her breast. "Cheese! I can't believe it! I'll tell Vati when he comes home, and we'll have it at supper. And I'll write to Aunt Frieda right away, thanking her for being so kind to us!"

Hansi tried to think through sudden panic. "I, I . . . I can take the letter to mail, when you're done. You can keep sewing, or rest."

Mutti smiled at him with wet cheeks. "My good boy. My dear, good boy. Thank you, *Liebling*."

Hansi tried to smile back at her as if he weren't the lowest worm crawling in the yard.

Chapter 10

Summer 1920 – Spring 1924

After a while, there was more food around. Shops might have pork fat, or something shaped like bread that didn't make you sick, even if it still didn't taste like real bread. Once, Mutti sent Hansi to a shop that even had eggs. But the eggs came three at a time, and cost too much. Everything cost so much.

Hansi couldn't remember what things cost before the war. He had probably never known. But now Mutti, and especially Aunt Gertrud, talked about how much prices had gone up. "It takes sixteen times as much to pay for anything!" she moaned. It was hard for Hansi to believe that, but Mutti nodded agreement.

And then everything started costing even more, and more, and more again.

Vati said the government had done it on purpose, so the money Germany had to pay the Allies after the war was worth less. He said it with a smirk, as if the government had been clever. And his job paid him more, to make up for it. But his pay didn't go up as fast as the money got worth less. Then Vati's daily newspaper cost too much for the family to afford, and he started complaining. The last paper he bought said something about the central bank printing a *one million mark* bill. And even that bill bought less and less.

Cousin Rudolf still wandered around the expensive parts of the city. Hansi didn't know if he kept stealing food, in spite of the whipping, but he did come back with stories. When he watched people eating in cafés, he said, sometimes the prices of the food went up while they were sitting there!

Vati met with other war veterans once a week, but they had to buy a single beer and pass it around. The veterans who used to get money for their war injuries weren't getting enough to keep up with prices, or even come close. Vati would come home shouting and cursing. Mutti tried to calm him down by reminding him, "At least rent, ours and theirs, doesn't go up. There's still rent control, so Helmut and Gertrud can let us stay here."

"Yes, how lovely," Vati snarled. "They can, and we can, starve in our own homes. When I die in my favorite chair, you can bury me in it. And burn down the flat for my funeral pyre!"

"Oh, how sad!"

Hansi was sitting in the front room studying his mathematics book, but he looked up to see what Mutti was sad about. She had gone to the window and was looking down at the street. He put his book down and joined her. At first he wasn't sure what had gotten her attention, but then he saw a man in a faded army jacket sitting on the sidewalk on the far side, leaning on the building behind him, almost blending into it on this gray day. He had a straggly beard that looked as if it had run out of strength to grow. His legs were stretched out — no, his leg, only one, because his right leg ended in a stump above where his knee should have been, and his pants leg was folded underneath. He had a cup next to him, and a handwritten cardboard sign next to that, though Hansi couldn't read what the sign said.

Would the man still be there when Vati got home from work? Vati would probably fly into another rage. But where else would the man go? And how? Looking harder, Hansi could see some wooden pieces behind him that might have been crutches.

Mutti had left the window and was making her slow way to the kitchen. In a minute she came back out, holding a couple of coins. "Here, Hansi. Please go down and put these in the man's cup. And tell him we hope things get better for him."

Hansi would rather have kept studying his mathematics. The man might glare at him, or ask how things could possibly get better. But he took the coins and headed down the stairs.

He'd almost reached ground level when it occurred to him that the man had no way of knowing how many coins Mutti had given him. Mutti would never know if he kept one. He took a quick look at the coins. Was there anything that one of those coins could still buy? He could stop at a shop on the way home from school tomorrow and check. Vati would never find out. And even if Mutti somehow guessed, she wasn't likely to punish him. Or at least, if she tried to whip him, she wasn't strong enough for it to hurt much. . . .

And he was a dirty, horrible sinner to even think about doing such a thing. God would punish him, even if Mutti and Vati didn't.

He trudged on down the stairs and out the door. He couldn't look the man in the eye. He just dropped the coins in the cup and ran back across the street.

The kitchen faucet had been leaking for weeks. A plumber would charge too much to fix it. Vati tried to do it himself, and it got better for a couple of days and then worse again.

Money kept being worth even less. Shops sold eggs one at a time, and by the winter of 1923, people were using double handfuls of the new *one billion mark* bills to pay for one. Those who could afford to buy a newspaper had to bring the bills in a sack, and then in a wheelbarrow. Then there were no more eggs in the shops, or meat, or fat, or bread, or potatoes, because the farmers wouldn't sell their food for worthless money. "We should have let Lotte stay in the country," Vati growled.

"Your family told us they couldn't keep her anymore," Mutti said, wiping her eyes.

"I should have made them keep her! What will we feed her, and the boys?"

The next day, Hansi found Rudolf on the playground and whispered, "Are you still going to the shed?"

"Not in a long time," Rudolf whispered back. "I've been other places. But they're getting harder to find. It might be worth trying the shed again."

Hansi took a deep breath and said, "I'll go with you."

Rudolf looked ready to refuse. He must not want to share whatever food he found. But Hansi stretched to his tallest and clenched his fists, and Rudolf finally said yes.

But when they got to the shed, the door was hanging open, and it was empty. Rudolf and Hansi tore some boards loose from it for firewood and ran away before anyone could stop them.

It was late in 1923, and Hansi couldn't really remember when paper money had been worth anything. One day, Lotte and her friends found some that people had thrown out or tossed into the street. They tried making kites out of it, but it was too little for a good kite. Then they turned it into confetti and played at having celebrations; or they pretended to be soldiers coming home from the war and tossed confetti at each other.

Vati kept talking about how his family should have kept Lotte with them, and even about finding a way to take her back there, until the day they got a letter from Opa. Mutti, reading it, gasped and turned toward Vati, looking shocked. "They've been robbed, and threatened!"

"*What?*" Vati stared and gripped the arms of his chair.

"A mob from the city! They marched into the country and went from one farm to another, stealing their cattle, their chickens, even the carrots and potatoes in the root cellar! They're left with hardly enough to eat! And — " Her hand shook as she held the letter, making it rattle. "Oskar was hurt, trying to hold them off. He took a blow to the head. And he injured one of the looters, who had to be carried away, and he's afraid something bad will come of it."

Hansi thought Vati would start shouting. But Vati slumped back in his chair and put his head in his hands. Somehow, that scared Hansi more than shouting would have done.

A few days later, though, the headmaster called all the students in the school together in the auditorium. "We have new currency!" he announced. "The new president of the Reichsbank has made it happen. The new currency is called the Rentenmark, and it's based on real, solid things like factories and land, so it can't keep losing value. This is a new beginning for Germany!"

Someone started cheering, and a few other children joined in. Hansi wanted to, but he was afraid nothing would come of it and he'd have cheered for nothing.

After school, he hurried home and told Mutti and Vati about it. Vati had already heard, and knew more than Hansi did. "Backed up by factories and land, did he say? What about the American gold? That's what's really behind this — the damned Americans!"

But people started using the Rentenmark. A loaf of bread that had cost billions of marks only cost a handful of Rentenmarks. And the farmers must have thought it was worth something, because there started being food in the shops again. When Vati, and then Uncle Helmut upstairs, started being paid in Rentenmarks, Mutti and Aunt Gertrud went out together to buy a loaf of bread and share it between them.

But even with prices now in Rentenmarks, they were still too high for either family to eat well. Hansi and Otto were thin, but at least they were growing. Lotte wasn't, much. And Mutti had been weak for so long that Hansi almost forgot she had ever been strong. She spent hours on the sofa, holding a book but hardly ever reading it. She always smiled at Hansi when he came home, asking how his day had been, whether he'd studied hard . . . except when she was asleep and didn't wake up even as he closed the door or rummaged in the pantry.

The first time Hansi saw Vati making dinner, he stopped and stared. Vati just grunted and said, "Any good soldier knows how to put a meal together. I'll teach you." After a couple of weeks, Hansi got used to that too.

Only once in a while, something Hansi saw, like a dish towel, or smelled, like the far-away hint of meat with spices, reminded him of how busy Mutti used to be in the kitchen, and how she used to be the one to stand in lines and even fight for their food.

Vati had been talking for years about the new National Socialist German Workers Party, which he sometimes called the Nazis. Its leader was someone called Adolf Hitler, and Vati mentioned him more and more often. He even went to a meeting where Herr Hitler spoke, and came home saying Hitler was the most inspiring speaker he'd ever heard. When Aunt Gertrud told Mutti about Hitler's Storm Section, the S.A., who hired men to go around in their brown shirts and attack people who didn't like Hitler or his party, Mutti asked Vati what he thought. If he saw anything wrong with it, he wouldn't admit it, calling Mutti a weak-minded woman who couldn't see the danger Germany was in and what had to be done to protect it. Then, just as the new money was used more and more and Hansi was hoping things would get better, Hitler was arrested for trying to take over the government. Vati didn't talk about him as much for a while, but he still grumbled to Mutti about him.

Then one day in early spring, Vati came home even angrier than he had been when he heard about some veterans losing their disability payments. It took Hansi a while to figure out what Vati was so mad about — he kept yelling about "treason! They're the traitors!" and "why can't they see that the Party could save us!" But finally, Mutti got him to explain. Herr Hitler had been convicted of high treason.

At first Hansi assumed that Hitler would be shot. Would it be out where people could see? Did he want to go? Would Vati go? Would the S.A. rescue Hitler? But then Vati said Hitler would be locked up, not shot. He was supposed to be locked up for five years, but they might let him out earlier. It didn't make sense — weren't traitors the worst criminals of all? But at least Vati wouldn't go with the S.A. to try to save him, and maybe get shot himself.

Hansi lay awake that night wishing he understood what was going on. If Otto had been there, he'd have asked him what he thought about Hitler and the Nazis, but Otto was out somewhere. He was spending more and more time away. He didn't say much about what he was doing in the evenings, but once in a while he would come in wobbly and loud and smelling of something that must be liquor, though it didn't smell like beer. If Mutti asked questions or got upset, Otto would just walk out on her. And he somehow stayed out of Vati's way.

Just as he was thinking that, Hansi heard heavy footsteps and then the door slamming open, and someone singing. Otto had come home, hours after Hansi had gone to bed, and was singing a song Hansi didn't know. He couldn't hear all the words, but some of the words he could hear were the vulgar words Otto seemed so fond of these days.

More footsteps, Vati's now, and then Vati's rumbling voice, stern, commanding. And Otto's, disrespectful, even mocking. As both voices got louder, Hansi could hear almost everything. Vati, shouting: "Germany is going to the dogs, with its young people caring nothing for morality, modesty, dignity — disgracing yourself, disgracing your heritage!" And Otto, bitterly: "What difference does it make? The world's going to hell — what should we be waiting for or working for? At least we're enjoying life while we can, before you old people finish ruining it!"

"Why, you little . . ." and then, a sharp, echoing slap.

And then the impossible — another slap, as loud as the first, and a gasp that didn't come from Otto. And then the door slamming again, as Mutti, her voice high and frightened, called out Otto's name.

Hansi pulled the covers over his head and curled up in a ball, shaking. Was Vati all right? Where was Otto going? Would he ever come back?

It was a long time before Hansi could sleep, and in the morning, Mutti looked even more fragile than before, and her eyes were red.

Chapter 11

Spring 1924 – Winter 1924-1925

A few things were changing in the world around him. After always seeing the same bus stops and trolley stops and subway entrances, Hansi now noticed workmen building something new, digging down under the street for what must be a new subway station. He would have liked to go explore the diggings, but not by himself – and Otto was pretending not to care about such things, probably to show off how much older he was.

The other change made him nervous. Mutti always seemed to feel cold these days. At least, when Vati helped her get dressed, he would choose her warmest winter things. She used to care what colors she wore and take trouble to fix her hair just right, but no longer.

Sometimes she would wear her winter coat inside. Or she wouldn't get dressed at all, but would wear one night-gown over another, and her coat over that. She was thin enough now that she didn't look fat no matter how many layers of clothes she wore.

Then came a day that finally felt like spring. When Hansi came home from school, the stuffy air in the flat, after the soft fresh breeze outside, almost choked him. He went right to the window and opened it. Mutti stirred on the coach. "Oh . . . what a lovely smell. What is it?"

Hansi went over and squatted next to the sofa. "It's the air, Mutti," he said, fighting tears. "It's the fresh air outside. It's spring starting."

Mutti struggled to sit up. Hansi got up to help her, and then sat next to her. She said softly, "I did hope I would see spring again. Thank you, *Liebling*." She hesitated. "Would you help me get up, so I can walk to the window?"

Hansi bit his lip and put his hands under her arms. Leaning back for leverage, he tried to lift her. He couldn't quite, the first time, and she fell back onto the sofa with a little gasp. But the second time, he got her to her feet. He held her around the waist, pulled her against his side, and moved very slowly toward the window. She wobbled, and he had to grip her so tight he was afraid he was hurting her, would even leave bruises. But she looked eagerly toward the window, and he kept going.

Finally he reached it. Slowly, carefully, he stopped next to the window and leaned forward so she could put her hands on the window frame. He stepped behind her, keeping his hands ready in case she started to fall sideways or backwards. But she stayed where he'd put her, and took a long, deep breath. She even hummed a few notes of a tune, one she used to sing to him and Lotte about flowers waking up in springtime. He looked at her cheeks to see if any color would come into them. But none did.

She turned her head a little, looking up and down the street. "I don't see any flowers yet. Are there any flowers?"

Hansi swallowed hard and said hoarsely, "A few, here and there." It might be true, though he hadn't seen any. "I'll look for some tomorrow and bring them home."

Mutti smiled. "Thank you, sweetheart. Now I think I'd better sit down again. Will you . . ." She let out a breathy little laugh. "Will you escort me, good knight?"

Hansi grinned. He hadn't heard her joke in so long! "With a good will, my queen." He took her back to the sofa and helped her sit down, and then lie down. Then he went to Mutti's and Vati's bedroom, gathered up the quilt on the bed, and brought it to the sofa, covering her up. Vati could bring it back to the bedroom when they went to bed.

Mutti gave him another little smile, and then she was asleep.

The next day was Sunday. The family hadn't gone to church for at least a year, but Hansi might have gone, to see if praying for Mutti would do any good, if he didn't have more urgent business. He walked all over the city, looking for a flower, any flower, to pick for Mutti. He stopped home in midday to rest a little, and Lotte came to ask him, "Where have you been? Are you going out again?" At his nod, she clutched his sleeve and said, "Please let me come too! I won't be any trouble, I promise!" And then, with a dramatic sigh, "I want somewhere to *go!*"

He hadn't spent much time with Lotte lately — or in a long time, really. She could use as much fresh air as he could give her. And she was still somewhat lower to the ground, so maybe she'd have more luck finding flowers. "All right. Get your jacket — it's chilly outside."

They ended up stopping often, of course. And Hansi let Lotte snuggle up to him when she got cold, which made things take even longer. But as the sun was setting, Lotte found a flower. He carried it home, but when they got there, he let Lotte be the one to give it to Mutti. At least Lotte was nice enough to say, "Look what Hansi and I found! Look, Mutti!"

Mutti reached out for the flower. Her hand shook, and Hansi hurriedly stepped in to guide Lotte's and Mutti's hands toward each other. Mutti took the flower and brought it up to her nose. Hansi hadn't thought to sniff it, so he didn't know whether Mutti was telling the truth when she murmured,

"How nice it smells! Thank you, darlings." Whether that was true or not, Hansi had done his best.

April became May. Mutti didn't make it to the window again, but every day when Hansi got home from school, she asked him to open it. Hansi would open the window and then fetch the quilt to cover her. And he made sure to get home as fast as he could, even if another boy wanted him to come over or go somewhere.

Neighbors knew, by now, that Mutti was ailing. Sometimes they would drop by with a bit of food they'd been able to buy, or had been given themselves. Through the spring and into the summer, hardly a week went by that Mutti didn't receive a carrot or a parsnip or some green beans, or whatever else was coming from the farms. In summer, the neighbors sometimes brought fruit. Her teeth weren't good enough to bite an apple, or even a slice of one, but Vati showed Lotte how to smash up bits of apple into applesauce. When Aunt Gertrud heard what they were doing, she showed up with a little sugar to sweeten it.

When autumn came and the weather turned colder, Hansi stopped opening the window. Instead, he would haunt the train stations, collecting bits of coal — when there were coal cars. There weren't that many. Otto, still taller and stronger than Hansi, searched the city for abandoned wooden outbuildings and tore them apart, bringing home the wood. Between them, they managed to keep the flat from being as cold as outside. And a neighbor Hansi didn't even know came over one day with a blanket. "I made it for when my daughter gets married," she said, waving off their thanks. "But with all her wild living these days, I don't know if anyone will be willing to marry her, or if she'll even want to marry. You can give it back to me if that ever happens."

"So kind . . ." Mutti whispered. Even after the neighbor left, she kept whispering "so kind . . . so kind . . ." as she stroked the blanket.

Saint Nicholas Day came and went. Hansi didn't call it the Feast of Saint Nicolas anymore, when a feast should mean plenty of food for everyone, possibly even with leftovers. But they went upstairs to join his aunt and uncle, and everyone got a couple of shreds of chicken and a slice of egg, plus some mashed turnips with almost enough sugar. The children didn't bring their stockings upstairs. Vati said that would look like begging. Looking at his face when he said it, Hansi guessed it might be better not to hang the stockings up even at home.

When they got back downstairs, Hansi counted days in his head. He was old enough to go to the Christmas Eve midnight service by himself. Maybe he'd try praying for Mutti to be healthy and strong again.

Four days before Christmas, Hansi came home hours after school let out. He'd been waiting for any coal cars to arrive at the train station, and one had come just when he was about to give up. He'd been able to grab two full handfuls, now that he was bigger than some of the other boys who were waiting too. He was eager to show Mutti, but when he came home she was curled up on the sofa under her blankets, looking like she was asleep. Instead, he walked softly over to the coal scuttle and gently put the coal there.

Before he had time to do anything else, Vati burst through the door, not even trying to be quiet. The door banged against the wall. Hansi glanced over at Mutti, but she didn't stir. Vati looked happier and more excited than Hansi could remember seeing him. "Anna!" he shouted. "Hans, my son! He's free! Our leader, Herr Hitler, is free! They released him today!" He threw his head back and laughed joyfully, then, to Hansi's astonishment, did some sort of dance step over to the sofa. "Anna, my love, come waltz with me. The future begins today! The future belongs to us, and Herr Hitler will lead us there!" He dropped to his knees beside the sofa, pulled back the blankets, and lifted Mutti's hand toward his lips. Then he dropped it as if it was burning hot. Had Mutti come down with fever?

But . . . "Cold . . ." Vati said slowly, slow and halting, as if something made no sense, as if he didn't understand. "Anna, your hand . . . why is it so cold?" He threw the rest of the covers off the sofa in one violent movement, bent over her, and kissed her on the lips. Then he jumped to his feet and backed away as if from some dreadful thing, shouting, "Cold! Cold! Cold!"

Hansi squeezed between Vati and the sofa, kneeling where Vati had knelt. His hand shaking, he touched Mutti's cheek. Cold, yes, almost as cold as ice. Nothing living could feel like that.

Mutti was dead.

She might have been dead when he'd come home with his coal. He could have brought all the coal in the train, and it would never have warmed her, would never warm her again.

Someone was coming to the door, and whistling. The cheerful sound was so wrong that Hansi jumped up and ran to the door, pushing on it to keep the sound out. The doorknob rattled, and a fist pounded on the door, saying, "What the hell? Let me in!" It was Otto. Hansi stumbled back, and Otto came in, whistling again — until he saw Hansi's and Vati's faces. His face went white, and suddenly he looked like the child he used to be. He tried to speak, cleared his throat, tried again, and finally said in a harsh whisper, "Is it Mutti?"

Vati, by now, was standing in the farthest corner, arms wrapped around himself, staring. Hansi nodded and pointed at the sofa. Otto slowly approached it, crouched down, and stroked Mutti's hair. He leaned into the sofa to give her a kiss on her cold, cold cheek. Then he stood up without a word and walked out the door.

Hansi looked after him, looked at Vati, looked at Mutti, and walked to the kitchen. Feeling the way a sleepwalker might feel, he opened the pantry and then the icebox for what food might be there. Of what he found, he took as much as Mutti might have had for supper, if she'd been alive and well. He carried the food out the door, not looking at anything but the door, and sat on the step. He ate it all up before he went upstairs to tell the family there that Mutti was dead.

The next days passed in a blur. Four men in some kind of uniform came and took Mutti's body away. Vati spent his time in a chair, wrapped in the quilt, saying nothing. Hansi didn't go to school, from some vague fear of what might happen while he was gone. Aunt Gertrud came downstairs once a day bringing what food she could. She tried to talk to Vati the first two times and then gave up. She hugged Hansi, and he let her, but didn't hug her back. Lotte, on the other hand, clung to Gertrud's legs until Gertrud had to pry Lotte's hands loose.

Otto came home so late at night that it was more like morning, and fell into his bed without talking to Hansi. When Hansi got up in the morning, Otto was either asleep or already gone. Lotte spoke little during the day, but at night she woke up screaming from nightmares. Sometimes she would climb into Hansi's bed. He let her.

The funeral was on Christmas Eve. Instead of going to the midnight service and praying, Hans went to the church wearing the black suit Aunt Gertrud brought him that morning. It looked as if it had been worn before, but he didn't ask whose suit it used to be. Instead of praying for Mutti to recover, he was supposed to pray for her soul, and to sing a hymn. He didn't have any prayers in his heart, and he couldn't sing. Afterward, some of the people came to Aunt Gertrud and Uncle Helmut's flat, maybe because Vati had stayed in their own flat staring at the sofa instead of coming to the funeral. Aunt Gertrud served bread and pretzels, and a single sausage that not everyone got to eat.

Now that it was too late to pray at the funeral, Hansi felt bad about it, and even frightened, as if Mutti might not go to heaven if her own son hadn't prayed. So that evening, he tucked Lotte into bed and told her he would be going to church. He thought she might want to go too, or try to get him to stay home, but she just curled up in a tight ball under the covers. He struggled into his too-small coat and headed out, joining the streams of people heading to the church, feeling a bit of comfort in their company. When the time came to pray, though, he still didn't know what to say. What could he beg for? What could make things better? In the end, he just prayed for something better to happen, and left it up to God to decide what. Even though God had let Mutti die. He listened to the carols the other people sang and imagined Mutti's voice joining in.

When he got home, he let himself in as quietly as he could and went straight to bed. Lotte was lying in his bed, in the center, curled up tight again. He moved her enough to make room and squeezed himself in next to her, remembering the carols as he fell asleep.

The next morning, Hansi woke up to snoring and found that Otto had come home and joined Hansi and Lotte in the bed. Hansi and Lotte got up and got dressed. Next, Hansi went with Lotte to the front room and looked around to see if anything was different. There weren't any presents, which didn't surprise him even if he'd hoped just a little that somehow there would be.

He started and jumped back when he saw a large blanket-covered bundle on the sofa. It was just Mutti's size. He looked around wildly and saw Vati, sitting in his chair, holding his finger to his lips. "Let her sleep," he whispered, pointing at the sofa. "She'll get better if she sleeps."

Lotte grabbed Hansi's hand and pulled him toward the sofa. Hansi resisted, staring at the bundle. Could God have given them a miracle? Was Mutti really lying there, sleeping, maybe even well instead of sick? He was afraid to go closer in case it wasn't true. But Lotte kept tugging, and finally he followed her. Then it was Lotte's turn to hang back. She poked him and said, "*You* look."

Hansi gulped, said one more prayer to himself, and then touched the top blanket, the same quilt as before. He felt along it, trying to feel what was under the blanket. It felt soft, softer than Mutti's thin body had felt. Slowly, he lifted the blanket at the end where Mutti had always rested her head.

There was nothing there, nothing but more blankets. He lifted it more, looking underneath. Blankets, blankets rolled up tight, and nothing else.

"That's enough," came Vati's voice, sounding perfectly normal. "You'll wake her up. Just let her sleep."

"Yes, Vati," Hansi said as he backed away, and ran to wake up Otto.

Otto was not happy to be disturbed. "Go 'way, pip-squeak," he growled. And when Hansi shook him again, he made a fist and added, "If I get up, it'll be to clobber you. Go 'way and let me sleep!"

Hansi used both hands to shake him harder, shouting, "It's important! Vati — " Realizing too late that Vati might hear him, he lowered his voice and said, "Vati's gone crazy! I don't know what to do!"

Otto groaned, stretched, and sat up in bed. Lotte had followed Hans and now climbed up on the foot of Otto's bed. Otto gave her a half-hearted shove with his foot and then ignored her as Hansi told him what had happened, his words rushing out and tripping over each other. Otto's face went very serious as he listened. When Hansi finished, Otto didn't say anything right away. But Lotte did. Even though she'd been right there, she said in a small voice, "You looked all through the blankets?"

Hansi half expected Otto to say something nasty, but he left it to Hansi to answer. Hansi said simply, "I looked. Mutti wasn't there."

"There wasn't — was there some other lady lying there?" Otto let out a little snort of surprise, or maybe laughter. Hansi shook his head.

Lotte clenched her fists and asked, very quietly, "Is there another lady anywhere? To take care of us?" Left unspoken was that Vati was in no condition to take care of anyone.

Otto said, surprisingly gently, "Not that we know about, little mouse. Only Aunt Gertrud upstairs, if she can and if she will. I think we should take you there. Maybe you can stay there until Vati . . . is feeling better. Get dressed, now, so we can go upstairs."

When Hansi knocked on the door upstairs, Lotte holding his left hand and Otto right behind, it was Uncle Helmut who answered the door. He looked worried and nervous when he saw them, asking, "Has something else happened?"

Otto explained this time, beckoning Lotte forward. Uncle Helmut went from worried to confused to horrified. When Otto put his hand on Lotte's shoulder and started to ask about her, Uncle Helmut interrupted to say, "Of course Lotte must stay here! Poor child, poor girl . . . ." Then he hesitated a moment and said, "And the two of you, too — we could fit you in somehow."

It would be so much easier to stay with them, even if he had to sleep on the floor and go out to find his own food. He'd have to find food no matter where he stayed. Vati couldn't go to work like this, or to the shops. But Hansi would be near people who were still normal, in their right minds, in a place where no one had just died.

But Vati would be alone. Anything could happen to him. He might go out and start raving in public, or not know where he was and start taking things that weren't his, or just sit down in the street and stare until . . . . "Thank you for the offer," he choked out. "But I'd better stay with Vati. Until he gets better, like Otto told Lotte."

Otto looked hard at Hansi. "Are you sure? How can you handle him, if he gets worse?" Plainly, Otto had no intention of staying with him and helping.

Hansi straightened up and said proudly, "I can manage. You do what you want."

Otto flinched and turned away, saying, "Well, I can find better places to stay!" He turned back just long enough to say, "I'll see you around. Lotte, be a good girl and don't make trouble." And then he was clattering down the stairs and on out into the street. Lotte stood looking after him, standing very still.

Aunt Gertrud came over, knelt down, and gave Lotte a big hug. "Come with me, *Liebchen*. You can help me make breakfast."

Lotte looked at her with wide eyes. "You have breakfast? Every day, or it just today, because – because our mother died?"

Aunt Gertrud hugged her again and stood up, not answering, and led her into the kitchen. Hansi shifted from foot to foot. He would not invite himself to breakfast, whatever Uncle Helmut had said; and his uncle did not repeat the offer. So Hansi just said, "Thank you for taking care of Lotte. Let me know when I should come get her, if I don't come for her first."

Uncle Helmut put out his hand. "You're a good, brave lad, Hansi. God bless you, and keep you and Walther safe." Hansi shook his hand, took a deep breath, and went downstairs.

For the next six days, Vati kept acting as if the bundle of blankets were Mutti. At night, he picked it up and carried it to their bedroom. Hansi didn't look inside to see whether Vati took the quilt off to cover both Vati and the rest of the blankets, but that's what he imagined. And dreamed. He dreamed, night after night, that the bundle of blankets sat up in bed and called to him. "Hansi, Hansi, come kiss your mother! Where are you, Hansi?" The first two nights he woke up panting, his own blanket soaked in sweat. For the next four nights, he still woke up sitting bolt upright, but then he lay down and went back to sleep.

The next day was New Year's Day. When Hansi came out of his bedroom that morning, he knew something was different, but it took him a minute or so to figure out what. Vati was sitting in his chair, the way he'd been doing every day, but he was reading a book. And there were no blankets on the sofa, none at all.

Hansi walked slowly into the room, not sure what to do next. He looked at the sofa. Did he dare to sit on it? Would he ever? Then, behind him, he heard Vati say, "It's the New Year, my son. A new year for all of us, for Germany."

Hansi swallowed and said, "Happy New Year, Vati." Vati smiled at him, clumsily, as if trying to remember how, and got up, walking over to the sofa. He sat on it and patted the cushion next to him. "Come sit, Hans. Let's talk."

Hansi sat, looking down at his hands, waiting for whatever Vati wanted to say.

"The Communists and Socialists have had everything their own way since they made us lose the war. Yes, we lost, whatever the weasels in the government say! And we lost because traitors undermined us. But as we go forward into this new year, this new beginning, everything will change." He gripped Hansi's shoulder and shook it. "Strong young men like you, and even old, worn-out men like me, we'll make it change. And Herr Hitler will lead the way. Next time he speaks, you'll come with me and hear him. You'll see he's the leader we've been waiting for, the leader who will save Germany."

Maybe he was. Hansi would go listen, and see what he thought. But it was hard to find room for such thoughts now, sitting on the sofa where Mutti had spent so many days.

As if hearing what Hansi didn't say, Vati sighed and said, "If only your mother could see the new day dawn! If only she could go with us to hear Hitler speak! But they killed her, starved and weakened and killed her. We'll avenge her, you and I."

That was an idea worth thinking about. If there was nothing else he could do for Mutti, he could look forward to that day. Hansi turned to face Vati and said solemnly, "I will."

PART 2

Chapter 12

Autumn 1926 – Spring 1927

Hans should know, by now, to be careful about looking forward to things. He had looked forward to the end of the war, and he'd been a fool to do it -- almost everything had gotten worse after the war instead of better, for years. But the past two years had been different. Prices weren't crazy anymore, and there was enough food, and there were enough jobs to go around. He was almost ready to let himself hope for things again. Like the Great Police Exhibition of 1926.

He'd started hearing rumors about it back in March, just when he was getting impatient waiting for spring weather. So he'd had two things to wait for. Spring had come on schedule, and now, in mid-September, the Exhibition was supposed to open in little more than a week.

All three of them would be going, Hans and Lotte and Vati. It had been years since they went anywhere as a family, not since before Mutti got sick. (He could think about her now without wanting to cry. At least when he had something else to think about.)

There were only nine days to wait. And then eight, and then seven . . . and finally it was September 24th, and the exhibition opened tomorrow. Vati had talked of waiting a few days for the crowds to thin out, but then he looked at

Hans and chuckled. "Such despair! All right, all right, we'll go tomorrow."

Hans had forgotten how crowds felt — at least peaceful ones, with people happy and eager instead of desperate and enraged. Maybe the people watching the soldiers come home had been happy, at least for those few moments, but they had just gone through the hunger and sickness of the war years. This crowd looked well fed and healthy. They were squeezing together, the way the mobs had, but once they entered the large Exhibition Hall they spread out again. Vati grabbed his and Lotte's hands and said hurriedly, "If we get separated, meet next to the big car!"

A big car sounded intriguing. But what Hans saw first was a row of policemen, smiling and calling out greetings. He was a little sorry that they weren't wearing sabers, even though he knew the police force had abandoned sabers years before. He looked at their faces, wondering if any of them might be the policeman who had helped him when he was lost or the one who had rescued Mutti from being trampled, but none of them looked familiar.

Vati was striding through quickly, for no good reason Hans could see. Hans wanted to take it all in. And Vati had told him what to do if they were separated . . . so he let go. Lotte noticed and looked back at him, startled, but he smiled and winked at her. Her eyes went wide for an instant before she nodded, smiling and holding a finger to her lips.

After Vati and Lotte disappeared into the crowd, he felt a sudden qualm: what if Lotte let go, by accident, and got lost? But it was too late now, and if he did manage to catch up, Vati might even think he'd been afraid to be on his own. So he squared his shoulders and prepared to explore.

Another policeman caught his eye — or was it a policeman? The man had a helmet and a saber. Except it wasn't a man. It was a mannequin, posed in a setting like a stage set, with a cardboard city street behind it. And Hans had managed to walk by a similar setting without noticing, because the mannequin wore the same uniform as all the real policemen he'd passed and was holding a radio. On the other side of the mannequin with the saber, he saw a long row of similar scenes. Walking along the row, he soon realized that the scenes were designed to take the viewer back into the past, like some sort of time machine: first settings and uniforms not very different from the one he'd noticed first, and then more and more strange, the cardboard cities getting smaller and the shapes of the buildings changing. The very last scene showed a man in a knee-length tunic and a short robe over it, standing in what looked like an ancient Roman city, and holding a short sword.

Hans stopped to get his bearings, turning around in a circle, and realized that across from the Roman policeman stood another scene that looked like the inside of a laboratory. The laboratory table was built of something sturdier than cardboard, with glass beakers full of colored liquids scattered along it. One even had something like steam rising from behind it. At one end of the table stood yet another mannequin, but this one wearing the white coat of a scientist and bending over a beaker of lime green liquid with bubbles in it. Someone had even painted the face to look as if the scientist was studying the liquid with great intensity.

Next to the laboratory scene was a large space empty except for a marvelous silver aeroplane, just big enough to carry one man, with huge propellers at the front. A man in a soldier's uniform and a leather jacket over it stood beside the plane, answering eager questions from the people admiring it. Hans squirmed through to the front and asked, "Can you turn the propellers on ?"

The man smiled and shook his head. "I'd love to, but they're afraid some fool will get too close and end up with his head cut off." Hans sighed and moved on.

And then he saw a long black car, polished to almost a mirror shine, with the doors and trunk open. Vati and Lotte stood looking at it, Lotte pointing inside at things Hans couldn't yet see and bouncing on her toes. Vati was beaming, obviously pleased with her excitement. Hans joined them and looked inside.

The car was a traveling criminal detection laboratory. The main compartment had a table with a typewriter, and a mannequin seated at it as if typing. Another table had all sorts of equipment: a steel post marked with numbers for measuring, a slim sharp knife, a magnifying glass Hans longed to try out for himself, and even an axe. Mounted on the hood was a gigantic searchlight, and behind it a painted board showed a nighttime scene and the beam of the light lancing through it.

"Isn't it marvelous?" Vati exclaimed, his hand sweeping from one end to the other. "All the most modern equipment! They may have made us shrink our police force, but our detectives still do Germany proud! How'd you like to be riding along in that car someday, Hans, swooping down on a nest of criminals?"

Hans had no words, but he knew his desire for that imagined future must be shining in his eyes.

Vati took Hans' and Lotte's hands. "Let's go on — together, now — and see what else there is to see." Off they went, delving into every corner and cranny of the exhibit. By the time they left, Lotte was dragging her feet as if she wished she were still small enough to carry. But Hans felt as if he could walk forever, or as if the wonders he had seen had given him wings.

The Exhibition was such a success that by December, toy shops had dolls in police uniforms. If Hans hadn't been a boy, almost a man, he might have wanted one for himself. He made sure Vati saw them in the shop windows, and sure enough, Lotte got one for Christmas. She clutched it tight and hugged it everywhere she went for the rest of the day, and Hans felt as proud as if he'd bought it himself.

Vati always kept Hans up to date on Herr Hitler and the Nazis. Nothing much had happened after Hitler got out of prison, with Hitler living up in the mountains in some village, forbidden to make public speeches, but Vati made sure Hans knew this wasn't Hitler's fault. Vati swung back and forth between fuming at the authorities for keeping Hitler muzzled and faith that when he was free to act, he would sweep all before him. Vati chuckled at reports of a conference Hitler held in February, calling together a few dozen Nazi leaders and, as Vati put it, "whipping them into shape." "None of this endless voting and squabbling and haggling and talking things to death! The *Führerprinzip*, that's what Germany needs! One strong man giving the orders and showing the way, and the rest making it happen!" He also gave Hans a leaflet — printed up in the mountains, or secretly in Berlin? — with the Nazis' new Twenty-Five Point Platform listing the things they would do once they took over. "There *is* a way for us to save ourselves, for our youth to have a future worth living for — worth fighting for! Read it!"

Hans read the leaflet. He didn't understand it all — what did "self-determination" mean, and "annulment," and "confiscation," and "nationalization," and "expropriation"? He asked Vati, who beamed at him and patted his shoulder. "I'm proud of you, boy, for taking such an interest!" He explained the words Hans hadn't known, though he hesitated over some of them, and sent Hans off to read the leaflet again.

Hans liked some of what he read. The Nazis wanted more farmland for growing food, and room for people to live. They wanted to "annul" the terrible treaty Germany had been forced to sign. They wanted officials to get their jobs by character and ability. They wanted enough jobs for all the Germans. They intended to punish profiteers and take away what they'd squeezed out of the people. They would make sure all the old people got pensions, so they wouldn't starve. They'd pay for children with poor parents to go to school, at least some of them. They would teach even the younger children about Germany's glorious history.

The part he didn't understand, and was afraid to think he didn't like, was about the Jews. Somehow, no Jew could be a "national" or a citizen, and citizens had more rights than other people. As two of the few students who had gone to Hans' old primary school, he and Samuel had become friendly, and he couldn't see how it made sense or would help Germany if Samuel and his family weren't allowed to be Germans anymore. Did Samuel know anything about the Nazis? Was he afraid of what they would do about Jews, or did he think the good things they planned, if he knew about those, were more important?

Samuel's sister Grete was about Lotte's age and went to Lotte's school. When Lotte came home from school and said that Grete had asked her to come over after school the next day, Hans saw his chance. "Do you think she'd mind if I came over too?" he asked her. "If her brother's going to be around, that is." He didn't dare mention Samuel's name in case Vati should come home early and walk in at that moment. Hans knew by now that Samuel was a Jewish name.

"Why would she? Anyway, she said you could come."

So Hans mentioned casually over breakfast, "Lotte's been invited to play with her friend Grete, and the friend has a brother in my school, so I thought I'd go with her. May we? We'll be home for supper."

Vati, chewing, nodded, swallowed, and said heartily, "Good, good! You children should be more social, go out, make friends." He smiled benevolently. "Have a good time."

Hans took the leaflet with the Twenty-Five Point Platform with him. As he and Samuel walked to the girls' school to pick up their sisters, he asked, "Do you know who Herr Hitler is?"

Samuel snorted. "He's just a blowhard. A thug with his own little army of thugs. He likes to make trouble, but there's only so much of his nonsense people will put up with."

Hansi pulled out the leaflet. "This says what they want to do. Some of it makes sense, would help people. But . . . there's parts you may not like. Do you want to see? Be careful with it — it's my father's."

Samuel shrugged and took the leaflet, sitting down on one of the stones lining the front walk. He read it quickly, Hansi noticed with envy. As Samuel read, his jaw went hard, and he started breathing more loudly. When he'd finished it, he waved it in Hans's face. "This is crazy stuff! I'm not German? My parents and sisters aren't German? We were all born here! My father fought for Germany, bled for Germany, and he's somehow not a German any longer, if these lunatics get their way? You think *that* makes sense?"

Hansi shuffled his feet. "No, not that part. Just some of the rest."

Samuel scowled. "My father should see this. Can I borrow it?"

Hansi wanted to say no. Vati might not like it. But he said slowly, "All right."

Samuel's and Grete's mother greeted them in a distracted sort of way, as though she had three things to do and this was one of them, and set out some sausage and nuts for them to snack on. The girls ran off to play whatever girls played, and the boys played chess. Hans hadn't known how, but Samuel was teaching him, and he was getting pretty good, though not good enough yet to beat Samuel. They stayed until the father came home. The mother was cooking something for supper, and it smelled good, but when the mother invited them to stay and help eat it, Hans regretfully declined for both of them. Vati was expecting them, he said. And, he didn't say, if Vati somehow found out that they'd been visiting a Jewish family, he'd be even more upset if they'd eaten Jewish food.

The next morning, Samuel was waiting for Hans in front of the school. He held out his hand with the leaflet crumpled into a tight little ball. "I'm sorry. As soon as my father read it, he did this and then threw it across the room. I don't know where to get another one. And he told me not to go near any Nazis, no matter what." He looked Hans in the eye. "Are you a Nazi?"

Hans didn't know what he was. But he'd never been to one of their meetings, and besides, he was too young. So he held out his hand for the crumpled leaflet and said, "No, I'm not."

"That's all right, then. I'm sorry about your father."

Hans wanted to protest that Samuel had no right to insult Vati, and that he hadn't meant to say anything bad about him. But he just followed Samuel into the building.

When he came home, he tried to straighten out the leaflet and press away the wrinkles. It didn't work very well. He found the biggest, heaviest book in his bedroom bookcase and laid the book on top of the leaflet, where it might make the paper flatter, and Vati wouldn't see what had happened to it. And he made sure not to ask Vati anymore questions about the Nazis.

Chapter 13

Spring - Summer 1927

Vati had gotten more and more impatient about going to see Hitler speak and taking Hans along. Hitler spoke in Berlin in May, but since he still wasn't allowed to speak in public, they had a "private" meeting of five thousand people and he spoke there. Vati might be a fervent supporter of the National Socialists, but he wasn't one of those high up enough in the Party to get an invitation. But then he found out about a big Party rally in Nuremberg, scheduled for August. There would be a march from Berlin to the rally, starting in July, even though the march was prohibited by law. At first, Vati talked of joining the march, all 300 miles of it. But he couldn't take the time off work, even if the family could afford to do without his salary for that long. So Vati hatched a new plan.

"We'll take the train, you and I! Some of the marchers are scheduled to arrive on Saturday evening, and Herr Hitler is speaking on Sunday. We'll ride down on Friday — you can leave school early or even take the day off, and I'll do the same. We'll find an inn to stay at, and come back Sunday after the speech. An adventure!"

And so it was decided. Lotte would stay with the relatives upstairs. "I'd rather go stay with Grete," she murmured while Vati was out of the room, "but at least I don't have to go listen to some old speech."

Hans, on the other hand, was almost as excited as Vati — not so much about the rally and the speech, but about the trip itself. He hadn't been on a train since before the war, and he'd been too little to remember anything except the rumble and the speed, which had first frightened him and then thrilled him. To take a train again! And to travel with his father, just the two of them, two men on an adventure together! To be with Vati when Vati was happy, not angry or sunk in gloom, but looking forward to the future, making the future seem like something to look forward to . . . . Hans could hardly wait.

Once they were on the train and Hans could look out the window, he realized that not only had he not been on a train for many years, he also hadn't been out of Berlin. His memories of countryside, from long-ago visits to Opa's farm, were as old and piecemeal as his memories of the train. There were fields of grain, some still green and some going yellow, with horses pulling plows or more mysterious equipment; and cows grazing or drinking from ponds, and villages where the houses were tiny and had thatched or tiled roofs. And after hours of that, they went up into hills with mountains staring down at them, the train going through a forest, as many trees as soldiers in a mighty army, pressed close together and thick with dark green leaves.

And then, as the light was going golden with early evening, they pulled into Nuremberg.

Even Nuremberg had something new to show him — or rather, to show his feet. The streets were made of rounded stones close together. Vati said the streets were "cobbled," and that more and more Berlin streets were getting cobblestones too, little as that made sense to Hans. It was harder to walk on a cobbled street. If you weren't careful — say, if you were too busy looking at the buildings, older and prettier than buildings in Berlin — you could step wrong and twist your ankle. Hans' ankles were sore by the time they found an inn where they could get a room for the night. And he had never been in an inn, either, except when a few of the boys from school went into one for a glass of beer. He'd certainly never spent the night in one.

Nor had he ever shared a room, let alone a bed, with Vati before, only with his siblings. But travelers did, sometimes even with strangers. It was all part of the adventure. And tomorrow they would see the marchers enter Nuremberg, and see the rally, and on Sunday he would finally hear Herr Hitler speak.

They spent Saturday walking around the city. Hans got better at keeping his balance on the cobblestones. The streets of Nuremberg tended to have flower boxes outside their second and third story windows. Flags with swastikas, the National Socialist symbol, hung from some of them. The policemen he saw all seemed to be in a good mood, smiling at the people walking by. One of them even waved at Hans. Hans happily waved back. It was like seeing a friend.

Just then, though, there was some sort of commotion in the street. Three men came out of an alley carrying signs and shouting something Hans couldn't hear. He saw the word "Hitler" on one of the signs and "Traitor!" on another before the police surrounded the men and hauled them away.

By evening, they found places in the crowd lining the street where the marchers from Berlin would appear. None of them had arrived yet when Hans saw an open car with a man standing up in it, a man with an Iron Cross on his uniform, smiling and giving the straight-arm salute. Of course, Hans had never seen Herr Hitler in the flesh, but he had seen pictures, and that had to be Hitler. People all around, including a few policemen, started cheering, and people in the windows threw flowers down, covering the car and the street.

Hitler got out and stood in front of a big hotel. As the sound of music and marching feet got nearer and nearer, people looked out of more windows, not only the ones with swastika flags. Then the marchers appeared, masses of brown-shirted storm troopers right behind them carrying flaming torches. The people standing nearby and in the windows above started cheering, and Vati did too. Hans might not have cheered just because of the parade, but he had to cheer the torches, so many of them, blazing in the darkening street. With a great shout of "HEIL!", the torchbearers raised the torches high toward Herr Hitler in a great salute. Vati clapped him on the shoulder.

Another group – miners, Vati whispered to him – carried lanterns instead of torches, lanterns they must use to find their way in the darkness of the mines. They raised the lanterns just as the torchbearers had raised their torches. Then came one group after another with big banners at the front of each, the first showing a shield – a coat of arms, Hans thought it might be – with a crown on top and lions on each side. Most groups of marchers also came with their own bands playing at top volume, the different tunes adding up to a clashing confusion of sound.

Some of the groups were around Hans' age, from the Hitler Youth. Vati called out to them: "Hooray, lads! You are the hope of our future!" He gave Hans a look and said, "Someday soon, you'll be joining them, won't you?" Hans made a point of watching the marchers to postpone an answer.

When the last of the marchers had passed, Hitler saluted the crowd, which responded with one more ground-shaking shout of "HEIL!", and then went inside the hotel. Vati sighed and said, "That's it for now, then. Let's seek our bed and be well rested for the speeches tomorrow."

In the morning, they learned that Hitler would actually speak twice, first in the morning at an outdoor dedication of the regional banners, and then again in a great hall. "I'll get us into that hall somehow," Vati promised. "But it should be easy to go see the morning ceremony."

They arrived early, though not as early as some, in the hope of finding a good place to stand. Hans had almost caught up with Vati in height, but he was still afraid he might not be able to see the speakers. They could stand in the upper portion of the terraced field, but then they'd be farther away from the stand at the front. They compromised on a terrace around halfway up and picked a spot on the side where they could see at least part of the speakers' area over the closer rows. That area was already set up, a short slope leading to a row of posts with swastika signs on them, looking something like medals hanging from a uniform. Off to the sides, there were a host of flagpoles bearing flags from the different regions that had gathered for the rally. Hans, and then Vati, sat down to wait.

Soon, uniformed men started showing up and filling the slope in straight rows. And then more marchers arrived, and Vati poked Hans' arm and whispered excitedly, "There, now, are the marchers from Berlin!" The marchers were shown to the front terraces, and Hans could hardly begrudge them the prime spots after they'd walked so far and so long.

Up at the front now stood more musicians, some of them trumpeters with bright-colored cloths hanging from their instruments, white and green on one side, red with the black swastika on the other. If only it had been sunny out, the trumpets and the cloths would have been a sight to see.

Hitler and some men who must have been his staff appeared, and the trumpets played a fanfare as the thousands of people crammed onto the terrace shouted, *"Heil! Heil!"* And then Hitler spoke. Hans could tell at once that he was a fine speaker, though what he actually said was mostly about flags and banners: the battle flags they had lost to the Allies when the war ended, the Republic flag forced upon them, and all the new flags the National Socialists had come up with since, including some introduced that very day. When Hitler mentioned the battle flags, Vati let out a gasp that might have been a sob.

Hans' attention wandered this way and that, to the younger and older people in the crowd, and the different colors of the banners. Vati tapped his shoulder and gestured toward Herr Hitler, whispering, "This is a rare chance — don't waste it!"

Hans looked away from his stern gaze. "This isn't what I thought he'd be talking about."

Vati said nothing for a few seconds, and then, in the tone of a solemn vow, said under his breath, "I'll get us into that meeting hall. You'll see."

After all the banners were "consecrated," the ceremony closed with a song. Hans hadn't heard it before, but Vati and most of the people around them seemed to know it and sang along lustily. Hans wasn't sure he was hearing the words properly with so many people singing, not always keeping good time or singing in tune, but it sounded like, "Germany awake from your nightmares, give foreign Jews no room in your country!"

He had been planning to hum along, if he could pick up the tune, but the last few words startled him. He shouldn't be surprised – he knew how Vati and lots of other people felt about Jews. But he had a hard time concentrating on picking out the rest of the words.

The terraces emptied out, and Hans and Vati followed the people to a square at the center of the city. There they found more swastika banners and flowers and a big platform, and two bands, and Hitler and the other party leaders, there to watch the marchers from all the different regions march back out of town. More cheerful police were keeping traffic orderly. The sun came out, and sparkling band instruments and the colors and the music and shouts of "Heil!" combined to make Hans almost dizzy. The marchers left the square to go through the city and then came back, thousands of them rushing toward the stage and stretching out their hands toward Hitler. Hans would never forget it all, but he was glad when the square grew quiet again and they could go back to the inn for a meal and a rest.

That evening, they joined the people streaming toward the entrance to the hall. "Stay with me," Vati ordered, and started squirming through the crowd, asking questions. He must be trying to find someone he knew, someone with the power to help them. Finally he uttered a bark of satisfaction and closed in on a man who saw him coming and called out a greeting. Vati returned it and said to Hans, "This man is a party official in Berlin! Now we're all set."

And indeed, they entered the hall with the man and his group, finding seats together about two-thirds of the way toward the front. Large swastika banners hung on each side of the stage, and a giant one, flanked by almost as big banners with much smaller swastikas, stood in the center.

Finally, it was time for Hitler to give his second speech, the climax, Vati proclaimed, of the entire event.

Hitler's voice rang out in the crowded hall even more than on the terrace earlier. The crowd kept interrupting him to cheer, but his voice rose above them all.

He started out by talking about territory, how Germany needed more for how many people it had, and that farmers, agricultural production, mattered even more than the technological wonders and industries that had impressed Hans up to now. But the foundation of all of it, Hitler said, was power. He went on to explain different kinds of power, starting with territory and population. Then, with even more energy, he moved on to other kinds. There was a people's "intrinsic value in its race," having purity of blood, and understanding that they had it. "The purity of blood means nothing if the nation can be persuaded of the absurdity that its blood is worthless!"

Next came the ability to produce and recognize great minds. "If a nation has the ability to produce great minds a thousand times over, but has no appreciation for the value of these minds and excludes them from its political life, these great men are of no use!"

Then came the drive to self-assertion, "the eternal striving to rise higher." And this had something to do with pacifism, not wanting to fight no matter who, no matter what.

Pacifism is the clearest form of cowardice, possessing no willingness to fight for anything at all. . . .

A people that limits the number of its children cannot demand of fate that it give it great minds from the few children who are born. More likely, such a people will hatch the most unworthy offspring and will attempt to preserve them at any price. Such a nation has first born, but no longer any great men.

He went back to race.

Today one places no value on our blood, on the intrinsic value of our race, rather apostles proclaim that it is completely irrelevant whether one is Chinese, Kaffir or Indian. If a nation internalizes such thinking, its own values are of no use. It has renounced the protection of its values. . . .

But Germany still had something to be proud of.

We have our blood-building value, the best proof of which is the great men of world history over the millennia. We have this value of race and personality. We have a third value: a sense of battle. It is there, it is only buried under a pile of foreign doctrines. A large and strong party is attempting to prove the opposite, until suddenly an ordinary military band begins to play. Then the sleeper awakes from his dreams and begins to feel himself a member of a people that is on the march, and he marches along. That is how it is today. We only need to show our people the better way. They see: we are marching already!

The cheers from the crowd made Hans' ears ring. The air was growing stifling, with so many people standing near, but he disregarded it.

Hitler went on some more about the international powers, and the pacifists, and cowardice. And then, finally, he mentioned "the international Jew" that stood behind it all.

Were there really so many Jews, and so powerful, and none of them loyal to Germany? What about Jews like Samuel's father, who fought in the war and won medals? Did Hitler think they were all just pretending to love Germany, even when they shed blood for it? That would make them a fearful enemy indeed.

Next, Hitler talked about leadership. People didn't really want democracy, no matter how often the enemies inside Germany talked about it. They just wanted leadership they could believe in, leadership that would make great plans and carry them out. Here, he was interrupted by shouts from the crowd, shouts of "Our Führer! Heil, Führer!"

Hitler smiled broadly and went on, talking about the war, the men at the front, and how united they were because they knew the enemy, how they'd been aghast to see what was going on at home. How important it was that they'd felt a "holy solidarity" with "members of their own blood." Again, Hansi thought of Samuel's father. Had he and the soldiers around them known the same enemy? Was his blood truly different?

Hitler warned the people not to squander their energies or their blood on "nonsense." Instead, they must all ask themselves, especially if accused of being imperialists: did they want their children to starve? He went back to Germany's need for more territory to feed its people, and thundered,

If someone says to you that you are an imperialist, ask him: You do not want to be one? If you say no, then you may never be a father, for he who has a child must always worry about his

daily bread. But if you provide his daily bread, then you are an imperialist.

Our goal must be to form a kernel that will steadily grow, winning energy and strength for the great goal. To whom heaven has given the majority of decisiveness, it has also given the right to rule.

The cheering rose higher again, so that even Hitler had to shout over it. He blasted the flag of the Republic, praising the new symbol the Party had chosen:

The symbol of the coming new German Reich: a symbol of national strength and power joined with the purity of the blood. . . .

May these colors be a witness of how the German people broke its chains of slavery and won freedom. On that day this flag will be the German national flag.

Today you see thousands behind this flag. Seven years ago there was no one. All these people marched past us today under this flag with enthusiasm and glowing eyes because they see in these colors the struggle for the freedom of our people.

And with that, the speech came to an end. With another deafening roar of cheers, the crowd rose to its feet and thrust its thousands of arms forward in salute.

Vati and his father headed back to the inn, neither saying much to the other. From Vati's occasional muttering, he was remembering, reliving, Hitler's final speech. Hans was doing the same, and asking himself questions he knew Vati would not want to hear, let alone answer. At the inn, they retrieved their bags and moved on to the train station, where special trains had brought many of the people who came to the rally and were now ready to take them home again. There was no scenery to look at on this ride, only occasional dark outlines of buildings showing against the dark sky, and now and then a star glimmering above.

When they got home, they grabbed a quick snack of pretzels and cheese, and then fell into bed.

Being back at school Monday morning, just like every Monday morning except for less sleep, felt odd simply because it felt so normal. His travels must have broadened him, and yet he felt unchanged. He hung onto the trip by telling some of the other students, who gratified him with their interest, even if not all of them seemed impressed by his account of the rally. Then a couple of them started glancing to one side, or making a point of not looking there, and he saw Samuel, his shoulders thrown back and his nose wrinkled as if Hans had come home with some foul smell lingering on him. Hans paused, preparing something to say, but Samuel walked away.

When school was dismissed for the midday meal, Samuel came up to him and said stiffly, "I'm glad you got to take a train trip, anyway." A pause, and then: "We might get to take a train trip ourselves sometime soon."

"It was wonderful! And making the trip with Vati . . . ." He had told his friend enough, over the years, that he could say, "It's getting easier, spending time with my father. So that didn't stop me enjoying it."

But Samuel had that disgusted look again. "It must be hard enough, though, having a Nazi for a father."

Hans gritted his teeth and held back the obvious retort about what sort of father Samuel had. Samuel flushed as if he'd heard it anyway, and said hotly, "You know, they're only letting your precious Hitler give speeches again because the Nazis did so badly in the last election. He's a loser, wasting his time with a bunch of losers."

Hans clenched his fists. "There sure were a lot of those losers, marching and lining the streets and waving and then cheering at what Hitler said." At everything he said, even the parts Hans hadn't much agreed with, but this was no time to mention that.

"Is he crazy, or just ignorant? Doesn't he know everything Jews have done for Germany? I'm not just talking about fighting for Germany or even winning medals, like my father. Do you know how many doctors are Jews? And scientists? Albert Einstein, a Jew, won the 1921 Nobel Prize for Physics. Does your precious Hitler even know what the Nobel Prize is? Or what physics is?"

Herr Hitler probably knew about physics, and Hans didn't know what a Nobel Prize was. But he didn't want to keep fighting with Samuel about it. Samuel, though, kept going. Hans had the feeling he'd been storing up things he wanted to say until he couldn't bottle them up any longer.

"There's a film your father and his precious Nazis should see. Or they could read the book, if Hitler knows how to read —"

"Wait a minute!"

"All right, he can probably read and write. Though who knows if he wrote his own book. Anyway, the book and the movie are called *A City Without Jews*. It's about how a city in Austria has problems, like Berlin does, and a fellow a lot like Hitler gets them all to blame everything on the Jews. So they drive all the Jews away. And guess how it turns out?"

It could only turn out one way, or Samuel wouldn't be going on about it. "It turns out bad?"

"You bet it does! And it'd be just the same here, without all our doctors and scientists and soldiers and all!"

Vati would call that nonsense. Hans didn't know, and didn't see how he could know. But it sounded awfully one-sided. "What about all the merchants who cheat people, and the spies, and all of those?"

Samuel was on his feet now, with his own fists clenched, ready for battle. "It's a lot of lies! Jews, the rabbis who know all about everything, spend their whole lives figuring out how to be honest and just and treat everyone fairly, even when they want different things! It's the Nazis who are a lot of criminals!"

They'd never got this close to fighting before, or not since the day they met. And Hans didn't want to, not when Samuel was so sure, and Hans seemed to know less than Samuel did. But Vati *couldn't* be as wrong as Samuel said.

Samuel must have been waiting for Hans to say something, to admit Samuel was right and Vati was wrong. When that didn't happen, he looked as angry and miserable as Hans felt. He let his hands drop and slowly walked away.

Samuel wasn't at school on Tuesday. And Lotte came home with red eyes, sniffling and wiping her nose on Mutti's old handkerchief that she liked to carry. "Grete's leaving! They're moving *away*! I might never *see* her again!"

So that explained Samuel's absence, most likely. Hans might not even get a chance to say goodbye.

Lotte would miss her friend, at least for a while. Coming on top of losing Mutti, it might be hard for her. Hans would have to give her extra attention to make up for it. As for himself, he might miss Samuel at least a little. He would have liked to talk to him about the questions that puzzled him, even though he could guess what Samuel would have said. But it was probably for the best. Maybe they were leaving the country. It might be a good thing for Jews like Samuel and his family to leave.

Chapter 14

Winter – Early Spring 1928

Hans was still not sure what he would do once he graduated from secondary school. Should he become a policeman, as he had dreamed in his childhood? He was good at mathematics — what jobs and professions required that skill? For now, he let himself put such questions aside, telling himself he needed his full attention to complete this final school year successfully.

Walking home from school one day, he heard the clip-clop of horses' hooves and saw a milk wagon coming down the street. People were emerging from their houses with jugs to fetch their milk, including a smiling young mother, with the sort of shape he had recently started to notice and a plump young boy tagging along behind her. How different from the hardships of the war years! He started to smile and then stopped short, ambushed by a sudden memory: himself, running behind Mutti as a milk wagon came closer. He must have been very small, with how big Mutti seemed to him. And she looked as rosy and healthy as the woman in front of him.

The little boy was staring at him. Hans realized, shocked, that he had tears on his cheeks. He turned away and rushed down the street toward home, trying not to think of how empty it would be.

Walking, walking fast, felt good. It felt better than reading or cleaning the flat or staring at the walls would. Abruptly he changed direction and headed downtown, toward gleaming shop windows and busy streets. Weaving his way through crowds – when had people started wearing so much white, even shoeshine boys? – and around bustling sidewalk cafés, he paused only to watch the occasional animated display. A mechanical shoe-shining mannequin; a comical little man with a bulging sore on his waving foot; a mechanical chef with his mouth moving as if listing the day's menu and his spoon going up and down . . .

He did a double-take at the window where a mannequin drove a wind machine with his feet to ruffle the skirt of a female mannequin. He stared for a moment, then hurried on – only to come to a shop that apparently sold flimsy, silky garments held up by almost invisible straps. They couldn't be dresses, could they? They must be some kind of undergarment. He could almost see through them, as they hung on a whole rank of slender, sculpted women showing long sculpted legs. . . .

Hans turned around and walked home even faster than before.

Hans' route to and from school took him past the flat where Samuel's family had lived. It was easy enough not to look in that direction. But one day, movement drew his eye to the building, and he saw men carrying boxes and furniture into it. Someone might be moving into Samuel's old flat. Not that it made any difference he could see.

Would it be a Jewish family? As far as he knew, the building wasn't especially full of Jews, though they might have some Jewish-only network steering its members to particular housing. He kept an eye out for the actual new residents, and finally, a week or so after the movers carried in the last box, saw an unfamiliar girl sitting on the steps. He knew by now that he couldn't reliably detect Jews by appearance — Grete and Samuel's mother had both had lighter hair than Samuel, though the father had the tightly curled black hair about which Vati had warned him — but the girl was so blonde and fresh-faced, with light blue eyes, that he'd have bet she bore no Jewish blood.

Could he introduce himself? He stood there, staring like a fool, for a couple of minutes before she saw him and gave him a friendly wave. He gathered his courage and walked over. With a little bow that probably looked ridiculous, he said, "I'm Hans Schäfer. I walk by here every day on my way home from school. Are you going to the Lyzeum nearby? My little sister Lotte goes there."

She smiled, dazzling him, and said, "It's good to meet you! I'm Klara Bauer. Yes, I've just started there. I wonder if I've seen your sister. Does she look rather like you, except smaller of course, and with brown hair instead of blond?"

Hans would not normally have welcomed the suggestion that he looked at all like Lotte, but at least Klara was looking closely enough at him to have an opinion. She cheered him further by adding, "She's such a pretty little girl!" and then blushing at having implied a compliment to Hans himself.

And now Hans was entirely out of ideas for conversation. He escaped by telling her, "I should be getting home. I hope I see you again soon."

Klara stood up and dropped a little curtsy. "I hope the same. Until then!" And she went up the stairs, her movements almost like dancing.

Hans hurried home, to make his excuse closer to true, and also to question Lotte. He found her playing hopscotch where some younger children had drawn the game and abandoned it. He stood nearby, shifting from foot to foot, and asked as casually as he could, "Have you noticed anyone new at your school lately?"

Lotte looked over at him slyly and took her time answering. Just as he was about to repeat the question, she replied, "I wonder if you're talking about that pretty blonde girl your age, who started two days ago. No, it couldn't be. Why would you care about her? You must have some other reason for asking."

Hans ground his teeth, wishing he was still young enough to pinch Lotte when she annoyed him. "I hope you're being nice to her. It can be hard to be the new student."

Lotte stared at him. "What would a girl so much older care about how I acted? The girls that age ignore all of us younger girls. But she seems to be getting on all right with the others her age."

He could think of nothing else to ask her, even if he wanted to give her more opportunities to make fun of him. He left her to her solitary game and went inside.

The next day, a chilly and drizzly one, Hans glanced over at the new girl's building as he walked by. He was almost sure he saw a curtain twitch on the floor where Samuel had lived. And the day after that, Klara was sitting on the steps again, wearing a lightweight flowered jacket and reading a letter. She laid down the letter and smiled at him as he approached. "It's lovely to see the sun again, isn't it?" she said cheerfully. He'd barely noticed the sunshine, but now, seeing it reflected off her gleaming blonde hair, he appreciated it more. Holding his breath, he sat down on the step beneath hers, gazing up at her. He had to say something. He settled on, "Is that a letter from one of your friends back where you used to live? Where did you live, anyway?"

She petted the letter and said, "Yes, it's from my best friend back in Leipzig." She sighed. "I hated to leave my friends there, and everything I was used to. But I'm trying to think of Berlin as a place to discover, full of new sights . . . and new friends." She glanced at him and turned away. Was that a faint blush on her cheek?

"There really is a lot to see," he assured her. "Maybe, sometime, when you're not busy, I could show you around."

She beamed at him. "Oh, I'd like that! I'm a little nervous about wandering around by myself. It's such a big city, and I hear some parts of town are a little . . . wild. An escort who knows his way around, what's safe and suitable and what isn't, would be such a help!"

Hans gulped and said, "I'll start thinking of the best places to show you." But even a sunny day would be too cold for sitting outside for long, especially on stone steps. Time to be brave! "Could we go get some coffee sometime soon, after both our schools let out? Then I could tell you what I've come up with."

Her eager expression was his reward. "Let's set a day and time, in case I'm not out here the next time you walk by. Could we meet on Friday at 16:30? But you'd better choose the place, and tell me how to get there."

Hans stood up very straight. "I know a café that should be suitable. It's not far, but I'd better show you the way. May I pick you up at 16:30, instead of meeting you then?"

Klara stood up. "That would be lovely. And you can meet my parents, too. They can get away from work early, to meet my new friend."

Her parents must be important enough to have such freedom. . . . More courage would, it seemed, be needed for this enterprise. But he had until Friday to work up to it.

When he got home, Otto was there. That rarely happened these days. More unusual yet, he looked happy and at ease, rather than belligerently pretending to be carefree. And he was well groomed, his hair somehow shaped, and with a strange sort of beard, only on his chin and combined with a moustache so that his mouth was circled with hair and his cheeks were clean-shaven. Hans must have shown his surprise, because Otto grinned and then bowed with a flourish. "The new and improved Otto, actor, at your service! I have a speaking part in a play starting next week."

Otto had been good at memorizing, back when he paid attention to school, and he'd sometimes entertained the family reciting speeches famous people had given, or from plays. (Mutti had been proud . . . .) And since Mutti died, Otto had been spending his time anywhere that people drank and danced and lived as if life was a party that might end before they got there. Some of the places where that went on could have been theatres, or claimed to be. But this sounded like a real play in a real theatre. "What theatre? Where in town?"

Otto gave a name Hans didn't know, not that he knew many — well, hardly any. "It's on a respectable stretch of Friedrichstrasse. I can even obtain tickets for, ah, one or two of you."

A dutiful son would make sure Vati knew of this opportunity. A kind brother would attend and take Lotte. Hans mumbled, "If you could give me two tickets, I know someone who might like the second."

Hans stayed up late on Thursday night deciding whether to get up early on Friday morning. Should he wear his best clothes? But he had a whole school day to get through before he picked Klara up, and the other boys would be likely to tease him if he dressed up. He could think of two who might even make a point of spoiling his outfit. Was there a middle ground? Or he could just take extra care when washing his face and combing his hair . . . . In the end, he wore a particularly clean shirt, pressed his pants, and hoped for the best.

He'd feared he wouldn't be able to concentrate on his schoolwork, with any of several unpleasant results, but he was nervous enough about meeting Klara that lectures and exercises were a welcome distraction. When school let out, it was like being thrust out of a shelter into the cold, or toward a battle. He tried to stretch away the tension and marched toward Klara's building.

Klara opened the door of the building as he mounted the steps. She must have been standing there waiting for him. She wore a dress that showed most of her legs below the knee, made of some deep blue fabric that brought out her eyes, with a silky yellow lining peeking out like a sunset around clouds. If she'd worn that dress to school, then girls must treat each other very differently than boys, at least when the girl had dressed with a boy in mind.

"Come on in and meet my parents!"

Hans hadn't intended to hesitate, but he must have, because Klara chuckled and patted his hand. "They're not too monstrous. Really. You're quite likely to get out alive. I certainly hope so, or I won't get my coffee."

Hans laughed outright and followed her with hardly a qualm.

Klara's parents were almost as blond as she was, though her mother had green eyes and her father hazel. Hans' last trace of fear that this flat was somehow reserved for Jews faded away. He shook hands with the father and bowed to the mother before they pointed him at an armchair. Herr Bauer said genially, "So you're going to be Klara's guide around Berlin?"

"Yes, sir. At least a little. I don't know that much about some parts of town, the, ah, more modern ones. But I know where they are, so I can stay clear of them." At least, he hoped he knew where all of them were. If in doubt, he'd better not venture into them. At least not with Klara. With Otto, now . . . maybe.

Herr Bauer appeared satisfied; Frau Bauer, less so. "You'll be careful? We're from Leipzig. It's hardly a village, but it's nowhere near the size of Berlin."

"Mama!" cried Klara indignantly. "Leipzig is a very long way from a village! We have — they have the Court of Justice, and the National Library, and lots of big publishers, and so many railroads passing through! And the big cotton mill!"

"Yes, dear," Frau Bauer said mildly, while Hans marveled at both parents' tolerance of Klara's tone. "But we didn't have the . . . cultural extremes that have developed here."

Hans stalled for time to come up with a reassuring response. "I'll make sure to tell you about the places I'll be showing Klara. Right now, we're only going to Café Josty. It's been around for many years." Matching Klara for daring, he stood up. "It isn't far, so we should be back in an hour."

That was good enough to get them out of the flat. Coming from school, Hans had no hat, and the stylishly trim little straw hat Klara took from the rack had him just as glad his secondhand fedora remained at home. When they got to the street Klara stopped, smiled at him, and said, "Lead on!"

Was it too soon to take her hand? There was brave and then there was careless. Touching her too soon could make things enough worse that he refrained.

The outdoor terrace of the Café Josty had a terrific view of Potsdamer Platz's hustle and bustle. But it was also too chilly, so Hans just pointed out the busy square as he led Klara inside. There was an empty table toward the middle of the room, and the two of them squeezed through the crowded space to claim it. While they waited to order, Hans told her a little more about the place. "All sorts of artists — the modern kind, Expressionists and such — come here. Sometimes you can see them painting, though mostly at night. And a poet, Paul Boldt, wrote a poem about it."

Klara looked around and then let out a little gasp of excitement. "Oh, look, there's a man sketching!"

"They have all sorts of sweets here, and good ones." No need to mention, this early in their getting to know each other, how rarely he could afford to order any.

The waiter came by and took their orders – an éclair for Klara, bread pudding for Hans. That left a silence that Hans did not want to leave hanging for long. He had asked Otto what girls like to talk about, and Otto had laughed and said, "Like anyone else, they like to talk about themselves! Oh, she'll be polite and ask about you, but unless she's coming from some traumatic past, she'll want to tell you about where she comes from, what she likes to do, and so forth. You might not have to say a thing besides 'oh, really?' and 'how fascinating!' and the like."

Hoping fervently that Otto knew as much as he claimed, Hans asked, "Did you always live in Leipzig before coming here? How did you like it?"

Klara sighed. "Oh, it was lovely! We lived by the bay, and I loved to sit and watch the boats come and go, or to walk along one of the rivers. And there's so much music in Leipzig, you can almost count on hearing someone play, or a whole ensemble practicing together, when you walk down the street and it's warm enough for open windows . . . ."

By the time she finished telling him about the ring of parks around the city, and the ancient roads that used to run through town, and the famous battle fought there against France, it was almost time to go, and he'd hardly had to say anything, just as Otto had predicted. But just as Hans was checking the clock and planning the route back to Klara's flat, she put her hand to her mouth and said, "Oh, but I've been running on so long, and I've hardly asked you anything! Have you always lived in Berlin? Do you like it?"

So much of his time in this city had been miserable, he was hard put to answer truthfully. But he said something general and then shifted the conversation to his trip to Nuremberg and everything he'd seen on the way. Before he knew it, they were turning onto Klara's street. And Hans suddenly realized they hadn't talked about what sights he was going to show her. Quickly he said, "Would you like to go to the theatre? My brother's an actor and he's in a play starting next week. I don't know much about it — " What an idiot he'd been, not to ask Otto for details. "Or we could go to the Clärchen ballroom."

"I'd love to see your brother's play!" Klara said brightly. "Is your brother anything like you?"

Hans barely stopped himself from laughing. "Not very much, I don't think. But you can decide that once you meet him."

Hans collected Klara the following Saturday as dusk was falling, and they made their way on foot and by trolley to the small theatre. Illuminated by the old-fashioned hanging street lights nearby, it stood out from the neighboring buildings with its two Romanesque columns on either side of the black-painted door and the black sign with somewhat shakily painted white letters above the door. A girl around Otto's age, dressed in a shorter version of a maid's uniform, took their tickets and handed them programs as they passed through. Inside, it was almost too dark to see. He almost missed the cloakroom off to one side, but saw it in time to hand over his jacket and Klara's wrap. Now Hans had a good excuse to take Klara's hand as he did his best to guide them toward the closely packed plush seats.

Klara held up her program and tried to read it. "I can't read in this light," she murmured. "Do you know the name of the play?"

Hans knew only because Otto had made a point of telling him. "It's *A Respectable Wedding*, by a man named Bertolt Brecht. Otto plays the bridegroom's friend."

The curtain rose almost right away, showing a largish room with three different doors, decorated for a wedding celebration. At first, the play seemed remarkably tame for anything in which Otto took an interest. But soon, one accident after another turned the room into a landscape of broken furniture and then a battlefield of quarreling people, from the guests and family members to the bride and groom themselves. It must have taken careful planning to keep such a disaster from making the audience sad, but the comic timing of the dialogue and the calamities, and the way the script constantly made fun of the characters, left them laughing instead. Klara went from tittering behind her hand to sitting back in her seat and laughing full out with tears on her cheeks. Otto's part was small, but he seemed to know what he was doing.

When the curtain finally fell, the crowd added applause to their laughter and the actors came out for a bow. Then the lights went up and Hans took Klara's hand again, this time to make his way to the front to find Otto. As he spotted Otto in a group of laughing actors passing a flask around, he slowed down and imagined saying that he couldn't find Otto, that Otto must have left already. After all, he and Otto didn't look that much alike, and Klara probably wouldn't know . . . . . But Otto spotted him and came toward them, fortunately handing the flask off to another actor first.

Otto did smell of Schnaps. Hans was afraid Klara would notice, but she smiled sweetly at Otto and said, "Congratulations on a fine performance! And the play was so entertaining. Your brother can tell you how hard I laughed!"

Otto gave her a deep bow, complete with flourish. "This humble player thanks you." And then, in a more natural tone, "I'll admit to some stage fright beforehand, but as soon as the stage lights came on, I felt . . . I felt I was finally where I belonged." He was looking at Hans now, intently, as if conveying some important message.

A message for Vati, perhaps? Hans had no desire to act as messenger. He said their goodbyes as quickly as he could, retrieved their outer garments from the cloakroom, and led Klara out of the theatre. As they walked toward the trolley stop, Hans looked around at the bustling people, the brightly lit shop windows, the neon signs of every size, the lit entrances to cafés and cabarets, and felt as proud as if he had conjured it all himself. Klara's lips parted as if drinking it all in before she turned toward him and said, "Thank you so much for this evening! I feel quite like a Berliner, going to the theatre and coming out again to see the nightlife all around. I wish we could make a wild night of it . . . ." His breath caught, and he had just time to wonder if he dared before she sighed and added, "But we'd best be getting home."

What would Hans say if he were more like Otto, older, sophisticated? He took her arm, this time, and said, "Another night, perhaps."

They chatted about the play, and the sights, and (leaning close together so as not to be heard) the other people on the trolley. He wished it could go on forever, but all too soon they had reached Klara's building. As he stood there wondering how best to say goodnight, Klara stood on her tiptoes and kissed his cheek. "I had a wonderful time, Hans. Thank you for everything."

It was too soon to give her a real kiss. Remembering Otto's show of gallantry, he took her hand instead, kissed it, and said, "It was my pleasure, Fräulein Bauer. Goodnight."

It was hard to tell in the light of the street lamps, but he thought she blushed before she ran lightly up the steps.

Hans hadn't sung in years. But now, as he made his way home, he hummed and then sang *"Der Mond ist aufgegangen."* Yes, he thought, the moon must be beaming and the stars gleaming, even if the bright city lights made them hard to see.

Chapter 15

When Hans finished with his schooling, he found work restocking the shelves of a cheese shop. The place would have seemed like heaven to the ravenously hungry boy he had once been. But he thought of those days as little as possible; and after years of having enough to eat, a shop like this was just a place to earn some money while he was waiting.

At twenty, he would be able to apply to the *Schutzpolizei*. He was reminded of his goal more vividly as street battles between the National Socialists and the Communists broke out more often and got larger. One of them almost swept over him as he was simply walking home from the shop. He had to jump up on the central divider where the trolley tracks ran, looking frantically in both directions to make sure no trolley was bearing down on him. Amid the chanting of slogans and the yelling of insults, and then the grunts and cries as men began hitting each other with the signs they carried, he heard the steady approach of marching booted feet, and then the shouted orders and the thuds and smacking sounds of truncheons striking cloth and flesh. Could he imagine being one of the policemen behind those blows? Yes, to keep the streets safe for bystanders like him, and girls like Klara, and children such as he and Lotte had been!

On long walks and over many cups of coffee, he explained to Klara about the policeman who had helped him when he was lost, and the policeman who had saved his mother in the riot. Hearing himself, it struck him how rare it had been, to have someone help him. Outside his family, he could think of no one else who had. (Except Samuel, with some of his schoolwork. He generally tried not to think about Samuel either.)

Klara would put her hand over his, if they were in a café, or move closer to him, if they were walking, and say with reassuring certainty, "They'll be lucky to have you! You're the tallest man I know — except your father, and he stoops — and . . . you have such strong hands. And you care about it so much — that must matter to them."

"I hope so." But he was almost sure she was right. He didn't know any of the boys he'd gone to school with who had grown up taller or stronger than he had.

One day, Klara met him at their latest favorite café looking somehow both excited and nervous. When they had their orders and Klara was scooping up whipped cream with a spoon, Hans blew on his too-hot coffee and asked her, as casually as he could, "What's up? Do you have some sort of news?"

Klara put down her spoon and said, "How clever of you to find me out! I . . . I saw a traffic policeman outside our flat when there wasn't much traffic, looking bored, and I . . . went down to talk to him. He seemed glad for something to do. I asked him a few questions."

A traffic policeman? It wasn't much of a job, not what he hoped to do, but he must know more than Hans did about what real police did. Hans took a sip of the coffee and regretted it — it was still too hot. He swallowed it anyway and motioned for her to go on.

"I wanted to know what it's like, being a policeman just starting out. Because once you get in, that'll be how it is for you. He told me a lot I hadn't known. Like about the barracks. Did you know the new recruits live in barracks for six years, in dormitories?"

The question Hans wanted to ask seemed to burn on his tongue, though that was probably just the effect of the coffee. He worked his way up to it. "All of them, even the older ones?" She nodded.

"No matter what their . . . family situations?"

Klara blushed, which always showed so prettily on her fair skin, and said with her eyes on her cake, "They don't have family situations, really. Because they aren't allowed to marry until they move out of the barracks and get assigned to precincts."

Had Klara been so bold as to ask about married police? Or had she somehow led the man in that direction? If he thought long about what questions she might have used, he would be the one blushing, and that would be less than manly.

Once he was sure he wouldn't blush, he looked at Klara until she looked back at him, and asked gently, "What did you think about all that?"

She took another spoonful of whipped cream, put her spoon down, and said frankly, "It bothered me, to think about all the young men who might want to get married and would have to wait. And about the girls who had to wait along with them." A pause, that stretched until Hans was ready to say almost anything to break it; and then, "But I think that if the man was really the right man, then the right girl would wait for him."

And that was all Hans could hope for, so far.

And then, in late 1929, things started to fall apart again. Hadn't Germany been through enough? Was it too much to ask for enough food, and a job to pay for it? But somehow, because of what other countries were doing, nothing could be counted on. Bread lines. Gangs breaking into shops and stealing their wares. It was like waking from a nightmare and then looking out the window to see the nightmare come to life.

Klara's father lost his job, and there was no question of her mother finding one, not like during the war when women could work to keep arms and supplies flowing to the front. The family was lucky, luckier than many, to have savings to fall back on. If the money became worthless again, what would happen to them? And what if Hans lost his own job? He didn't dare look for higher-paying work, when there were fewer and fewer jobs to be had. He worked late and took on extra tasks, trying to make himself too valuable to lose.

Hans and Klara stopped meeting at cafés and going to the theater. Theaters were going bankrupt anyway, and whatever Otto was doing now, it probably wasn't acting. Hans and Klara went for walks instead, or simply sat and talked, or listened to music on Klara's family's gramophone. They made an exception for Klara's nineteenth birthday, planning to meet at their old favorite café to celebrate. But when Klara came in, she was pale and shaking. He jumped up to meet her and put an arm around her, steering her to the table he had found — all too easy, these days — and asking, "Darling! What's wrong? Has something happened?"

Klara fell into her chair, tried to smile, failed, and bit her lip. Hans waved vigorously to get the waiter's attention, and instead of her usual coffee with steamed milk, he ordered her a vodka soda with lime, something he had seen ladies drink there. Only when she had taken a sip did she say apologetically, "I'm sorry to make such a fuss. It was nothing, really, only a beggar following me in the street. He was dirty, and he kept saying, 'Lady, lady, I'm hungry, give me something, anything," over and over until I ran to get away from him." She put her drink down and buried her face in her hands.

Hans emptied his pockets to buy her a piece of black forest cake piled high with whipped cream, and she at least pretended to cheer up. And when he gave her the music box he'd saved up to buy her, she seemed genuinely delighted. He insisted on escorting her home.

After that, he escorted her whenever he could. But working long hours, there were so many hours he couldn't be with her. Without saying much about it, Klara stopped going places by herself. She became as house-bound as an invalid. Hans watched her light dim and cursed the foreigners, the old enemies, who had somehow contrived to ruin Germany once again.

All he could do was support those like the National Socialists who dedicated themselves to restoring Germany to glory — and wait to turn twenty, when he could apply to the police.

The morning of his birthday, he was at police head-quarters the minute they opened. He had to ask around to find the recruiting office. And as he knocked here and there and talked to this and that official, he started to notice the young men he passed, doing military-looking exercises in a large room on his left, or bustling through the hallway past him with crisp sheafs of documents in their hands.

Many of them were his height. And almost all of them were broader in the chest, the sleeves of their blue uniforms packed with muscle. He had forgotten that men could look like that. That men did, were supposed to, look like that. Yes, he had remembered the policemen from his past as gloriously big and strong, but he'd been a child. In the back of his mind, he had supposed that if that child saw what Hans had become, he would have regarded him with the same awe.

When he finally found the recruiting office, they sent him to a waiting room with a dozen others his age, where one by one they were summoned to examination cubicles. They were all in ordinary clothes, with about half of them wearing clothes one wore in the city. The rest looked like farm boys, with overalls and coarse linen shirts and boots that could stomp through mud.

His own turn came and he was ordered to strip. The doctor looked him up and down, shook his head, and said, "Spent the war years in Berlin, did you? Not much to eat, I suppose."

"No, *Herr Doktor*. Not back then."

The doctor sighed and asked, "Do you really want to take the fitness tests?"

Hans threw his head back and said, "Of course!" He would show that doctor how tough the men in his family were, not soft like boys who had enough to eat almost all the way through the war . . . .

He couldn't help but see he was doing poorly. But maybe it would only be the worst of the group who would be excluded.

When the tests were done, and about a third of the men were led away by an officer, he knew he'd been right to hope. Though the men walking out the door looked fit, just like the ones he'd seen when he first arrived.

Another officer came in to address the ones who remained. At first, Hans had trouble understanding him. His tone was kind, consoling. "Those of you from the cities, without the access to food that farm boys had, suffer from a disadvantage that very few can overcome . . . . You can be proud of your ambition and determination, which I am confident will be rewarded in whatever endeavors you undertake . . . ."

As he stumbled out the door, the midday sun making him all too visible, he was finally coming to grips with what had happened. He had failed. His lifelong dream had led him to that humiliating room full of failures, failures like him. He would have to go home and figure out what to do with the rest of his life.

And somehow, he would have to tell Klara.

He was supposed to see Klara the very next day. He could almost wish that someone else would tell her. If she didn't know, she'd be full of hope and expectation, and he would have to destroy all that. But if she already knew, would she meet him at the door looking disappointed, or even scornful? Or would her eyes show only sympathy?

Standing at her door, he heard approaching footsteps and looked up, suspense tightening his throat. Klara opened the door — but her face showed neither the feelings he had hoped for nor those he had feared. She looked — shocked? embarrassed? frightened? As soon as they sat down on the sofa, he reached for her hand and said, "What's wrong, *Elfchen?*"

She tried to wave away his question, saying, "We should talk about yesterday, not my silly troubles . . . ."

No, they shouldn't. It would be better to talk about anything else. "That can wait. What's happened?"

Her eyes looked haunted as she said, "I just found out that there were *Jews* living in here, in this very flat, before we got there!"

Hans almost laughed. Was that all? Was she afraid of Samuel, of little Grete? True, their parents were full-grown Jews and might have been up to some mischief . . . . He shouldn't find that hard to believe.

What would comfort her? "Please don't be upset, my angel. They weren't so bad — "

"You mean you *knew*?"

Oh-oh. "I knew the people living there were Jews, yes. But I didn't see the point in telling you when you'd already moved in. And I never saw them doing anything awful."

She gave him a skeptical look. "You never *saw* anything awful. But how much did you have the chance to see, really?"

Hans gulped, and hoped Klara didn't notice. If he told her that he'd been a frequent guest in that very flat, treated as a friend by the Jews living there, how would she react? . . . Maybe at a better time, on a day when he hadn't suffered such a crushing blow, he could confess such things. But today, when she had enough reason to be disappointed in him, he couldn't do it. He evaded the question, though his answer was hardly an evasion, really. "Of course I wasn't living there and seeing everything they did." The words seemed to linger on the air.

As Klara calmed down, he could see her curiosity reviving. "Did you ever get a peek inside? Did they have lots of gaudy, expensive things?"

"Ah . . . not that I noticed. Except they didn't look as hungry as we were, somehow. Other than that, they looked pretty much like anyone else, though the boy had curly hair."

Too late, he realized that had been a misstep. Klara's face clouded over again. "If you couldn't tell what they were by looking at them, they could be *anywhere*. . . . Did — did you ever see one of them carrying a *baby* into the flat? Or hear a baby cry as you walked by?"

That, he could answer straight out. "No, I never saw or heard anything like that." Nor did he know just why she had asked. There must be something she'd heard about Jews that he'd missed. He would have to ask Vati about it.

Klara still looked nervous. And he had waited long enough to tell her his own bad news. At least it would act as a distraction from her fears. But it was still very hard to begin. "I haven't told you what happened at the recruitment office."

Her face lit up, eager, trusting. He couldn't stand it; he closed his eyes and said bluntly: "I failed."

He heard a soft indrawn breath, and made himself open his eyes. She looked more confused than anything. "What? How?"

"I couldn't do the tests well enough. I'm not fit."

"But — "

"It's because I spent the war here, where there wasn't enough to eat for so long. They mainly take farm boys who didn't go hungry so much."

Klara shook her head in indignation, vigorously enough to make her hair fly back and forth. "Well, that's hardly your fault! It's not fair!"

Her passion on his behalf warmed him in spite of everything. "It's not about what's fair, Klara. It's about who can do the job. The police have to be the strongest, the best, especially now that we don't have a real army anymore."

Klara reached out and laced her fingers into his. "You can get stronger. I know you can. So you'll do something else for a while, and work your hardest, and later you can try again."

As he sat there trying to draw some comfort from her words, she startled him by smiling, with a sort of shy mischief in her face. "And there's something else you should remember."

Hans wrinkled his forehead, resisting the impulse to frown. "What else could there be, after this?"

Klara lifted his hand and kissed it. "My dear one, now that you won't be spending the next six years in barracks and following all those rules, you could get married." She put his hand down again and dropped her gaze, suddenly shy. "If you wanted to."

Had the sun come out, pouring down radiant light all the way into Klara's front room? No, but it might just as well have. Hans leaped to his feet, grabbed Klara out of her chair, and whirled her around, laughing with delight. Klara's mother came running in from the kitchen, holding an empty tray on which she must have been planning to put cakes. Hans set Klara on her feet, clasped both her hands, and looked into her eyes. "Klara Bauer, kindest and sweetest and loveliest of women, will you marry me?"

Klara looked back at him, eyes shining. "Yes, Hans Schäfer, kindest and bravest and best of men, I would be honored."

Now he could kiss her. And did. Klara's mother ran back to the kitchen and came back without the tray but waving a dish towel like a flag. She tried to take both of them in her arms, but she was too small and had to settle, laughing, for hugging each of them in turn. Klara's father came out of his little office, shook Hans' hand over and over, and then embraced Klara and her mother together. The women started talking like a tumbling waterfall, talking over each other, about wedding plans. Klara looked as if she had never been afraid, whether of beggars or long-gone Jews.

Hans might not be the man Klara thought him. But he would try his best to deserve her.

To hell with the police and what they thought of him. He and Klara had seized the day and turned it around.

Chapter 16

Summer – Autumn 1930

Hans still struggled with how to tell his family about the recruitment tests. In the end, he simply told them his other news instead, and he did it with Klara at his side.

Lotte jumped up and down like the little girl she used to be and ran to give each of them a hug. Klara squeezed her tight and said, "I've always wanted a sister! Will you be my sister?"

Lotte beamed and said, "*I've* always wanted a sister *too*!" Meanwhile, Vati stood looking at Hans. He must know that police recruits didn't marry, that Hans was not going to be a policeman after all. But Hans didn't have to tell him why. Let him think it was only for love of Klara, that Hans had had a choice and changed his mind.

Vati would question him later, about how he would support a wife if nothing else. But for now, with Klara here and Lotte so happy, he refrained, and Hans was grateful.

He should be more grateful to his father, about so many things. About enduring all those years at the front, and helping Mutti as she got sicker, and working for so long to keep the family afloat. And if there was any chance that he and Klara would at some point need a loan, or even shelter, he needed to be man enough to let Vati ask his questions. So after he walked Klara home, he came straight back and sat across from the armchair where his father read newspapers, asking, "Is this a good time to talk?"

Vati let *Der Angriff* fall to his lap and said, "We may as well." Not the most encouraging response, but enough.

Hans took a deep breath and began by saying, "The police didn't want me." He hadn't planned to say it, had decided just the opposite, but sitting there he realized that letting his father assume he'd thrown that chance away would . . . would hurt too much. It would make him look like someone he didn't want to be. It would give his father a reason to be ashamed of him.

Vati's jaw dropped, and then his face slowly went red. "The fools! What, are they too busy taking in Communists and Jews? Is a good German boy not what they want out there on the streets?" By now he was shouting. "Do they plan to fight the criminal gangs and the Communists, or join them?"

Glad as Hans was to be defended, and angry as he was — though at what, he wasn't sure — he could not simply agree. "It wasn't like that, Vati. I couldn't do the physical tests well enough, not like the men who spent the war on farms and got enough to eat." If Hans' fuzzy memories of Herr Hitler's Nuremberg speech were accurate, he'd talked about how important farmers were, so that should calm Vati down." I did better on tests that were just about strength, but not the ones that needed endurance. I ran out of strength too quickly."

Vati perked up at once. "Then you can apply again! You just need to build up your abilities. Have you considered joining the Amateur Boxing Association?"

With the work schedule he'd been keeping, Hans had barely had time to look right and left, let alone to consider activities that required so much time as sports. He said as much. Vati stroked his moustache with two fingers, pondering who knows what, and finally smiled. "Then what you need is a better job, where you can work more regular hours and still earn enough to support your bride!"

Hans stared at his father. "Now? With the streets full of men who've lost their jobs, some of them with far more skills and experience than I have, you want me to quit my job and try to get a better one?"

The smile broadened. "Ah, but they don't have a father who knows the right people! You know, I hope, that the bonds soldiers form are unlike any others. There was a man I served with on the Western Front, a man I helped when he was wounded. I practically carried him to a safe place where the medics could get at him. And now — well, let's say he's done well for himself. I'll set up a meeting with him."

Hans could have resented Vati's taking charge in such a way, but it would be good for his father to feel helpful and hopeful for a change. Hans thanked him as earnestly as if he believed anything would come of his father's scheme.

The following Sunday morning, Hans came to the kitchen to find Vati pressing his good suit. "Do you have something presentable to wear? Does it need pressing? We must look our best today." Were they going to church? If so, did they really have to dress up more than usual? Hans resisted the urge to shrug and went to search his closet.

But Vati soon explained that they were going somewhere more exciting than church. He had actually reached his wartime friend, and they had a meeting with him that very afternoon.

On their way to the trolley, Vati expanded on the story of rescuing the man they were going to meet, going on about the man's gratitude and his vow to repay Vati's heroism when the chance arose. As they got closer and Hans' attention wandered, Vati switched topics to their destination. Apparently this mysterious army companion had connections in high places — specifically, among the former nobility. They would be meeting in a building where none of them, strictly speaking, belonged: the *Deutsche Adelsgenossenschaft*, headquarters of an association of such former nobility. Hans started looking more closely at the taller and more ornate buildings he saw, wondering which of them might be this headquarters, or whether the building would be even grander.

The building they finally approached after getting off the trolley was three stories tall, pink-red brick with domes at the corners, its windows framed in elaborate scrolls. They got off the trolley into a drizzle, the brownish-gray sky muddying the colors of the buildings around them. They mounted steps to an imposing bronze door and announced themselves with the heavy knocker. A servant in an impractical-looking costume opened the door and led them to a study or library, furnished with leather armchairs and wall-covering shelves whose books were bound in older-looking leather. The actual walls, where they showed around the shelves, were covered in dark red fabric. Polished round tables, wood with brass trim, were scattered among the armchairs so that whoever sat in one of the chairs would have a place to set down a drink.

With all these elaborate furnishings, it took Hans a moment to notice the small man in a business suit sitting in an armchair in the furthest corner of the room. He sprang to his feet as they approached, revealing that the suit was well tailored of the best materials. He and Vati clasped each other's shoulders and then shook hands for almost a minute. Then the man turned to Hans, beamed, and said heartily, "And this must be my new distributions manager!"

When Hans just stood there like a particularly feeble-minded statue, Vati stepped back and said, "Herr Richter, my friend, this is my son Hans of whom we spoke." Hans shook off his confusion and offered his hand, receiving a firm, if slightly sweaty, handshake in return.

Herr Richter chuckled and said, "Your father has told me about your experience and your current occupation. I own quite a few shops, selling everything from fine foods to grooming products to — well, you'll learn all about them. I have room for a new distributions manager to keep track of which shop needs more of what and to make sure they get it. You'll spend time in the shops and in my warehouses. Sometimes you may be lending a hand with the actual loading and unloading, and sometimes it'll be a desk job. Your salary will be — " And he named a figure that made Hans' eyes widen as he pictured being able to rent a small flat right away and furnish it suitably, if modestly, for a bride. "And as your father tells me you wish to devote some time to boxing, your hours will make that feasible."

Hans hadn't got to the point of picking a particular sport, but it was no time to quibble over such details. "That would be wonderful. I would work very hard and justify your faith in me!"

Herr Richter rocked back and forth, his thumbs tucked in his waistband, the picture of benevolence. "Yes, yes, I'm sure you will. That's settled, then! Now, Walther, tell me what you've been up to, and how your family is doing."

Mercifully, a knock sounded at the door. Herr Richter called out, "Come!" and sat down again with an air of anticipation. "This will be our drinks, to toast the occasion!" And indeed, another costumed servant entered with a silver tray holding a bottle of Schnaps and three glasses. He set the tray on the table nearest their host, bowed, and exited. Herr Richter waved toward two nearby chairs. "Sit, sit, and let us drink!" He picked up the bottle. "But I am remiss! My friend Walther tells me that you are soon to be married! Tell me, who's the lucky girl, and what are your plans?"

More Schnaps, a toast to Klara, and a few minutes' cheerful conversation later, he and Vati were out the door, a little drunk, to find a sunny day better suiting the occasion than the bleak weather in which they had entered. "A brighter future," he murmured as they made their way toward the trolley. "Let's ride on the upper level and feel the wind in our hair!"

As they climbed aboard, he had a moment of dismay over the difference between his new career and the one he had always dreamed of. He would not even be wearing a uniform. . . . He pushed the thought aside and reminded himself to be grateful for a paying job.

Hans had assumed that now his prospects were so improved, he and Klara would marry soon, within weeks. Klara gently explained to him that weddings didn't work that way. Klara needed time to have a tailor make a dress, as her mother lacked the necessary skill to do justice to the occasion. Hans should be measured for a suit, and obtain the necessary accessories. Family members who lived out of town had to be told, and given time to arrange a visit to Berlin, and found places to stay. They needed to plan the menu for the reception. And so on.

Seeing Hans' obvious frustration, Vati clapped him on the shoulder, grinned slyly, and said, "Time to get started on boxing, the sooner the better! You have some . . . *energy* to work off."

Somehow, the sports associations had stayed active despite the Depression. Hans had been good at tennis in his school days, but he doubted the police would be all that impressed by tennis as a preparation for police work. Boxing, though — boxing would not only build his endurance and teach him how to hold his own in a fight, it would harden him. If he could learn not to care about being hurt, he would be more worthy of not only the police, but whatever struggles might come. And more worthy of Klara.

Klara, however, objected, at least to the timing of his decision. "If you show up with a black eye and bruises on your face, what will the wedding guests think? Some of them will assume you've been brawling, or are in one of those horrible street gangs!"

Hans did his best to remember how his father would fly into a temper, and to act differently. He clenched his teeth, unclenched them, and said, "If I'd gotten into the police and we'd waited to get married until I joined a precinct, I might be bringing a black eye or worse to our wedding. Would you have been ashamed of me on our wedding day?" And as her eyebrows flew up and she shook her head, he asked, softly so as not to shout: "Are you less proud of me because I didn't make it? Would you be so easily ashamed, the way things have turned out?"

Klara looked away from him and chewed her lip. Then she turned to face him again and said, "I understand now. To marry a brave man, I have to be brave too."

Hans found out where an inexperienced boxer needed to go to get started. And he went to every sports event the police sponsored, if he didn't have to be at work. He studied the boxers' form and the sneaky tricks some of them used to win, and practiced them in the vacant lot behind their building. When he and Klara started searching for the flat they would live in together, he made sure to look around the outside for a private place to box, by himself or with other association members.

Klara, of course, had other priorities. She wanted the latest oven, even though he had never seen her in the kitchen except to help her mother carry dishes or to thank her for a meal. He hadn't given much thought to the question of cooking, somehow assuming that getting married would turn Klara into a cook, but now he tried to think of a tactful way to ask her about it. He settled on, "What do you most look forward to making in the new oven?"

Klara opened her eyes wide and then blushed. "I somehow hadn't thought about cooking. How stupid of me! But my mother always did the cooking. I suppose . . . I hope it isn't too hard to learn."

Hans wondered why her mother hadn't raised the subject before, and searched for something tactful to say. He was rather proud of himself when he came up with, "How would it be if the two of us, ah, learned to cook together, from your mother and my father? Then it'll be something we can do together."

Klara looked somewhere between nervous and lost, but she gamely promised to give it a try.

What with a wedding bearing down on him, and fellow boxers pounding on him regularly, and a job he absolutely had to do well, Hans was busier than he had ever been, and quite content to be so.

When Herr Richter, his employer, stopped by the leather goods store where Hans was doing inventory, and Hans' father walked in right behind him, Hans' first thought was that he'd made some horrific mistake, or been accused of a crime, and the two of them had come to confront him. Herr Richter smiled warmly, just as if Hans hadn't leaped to his feet and wasn't standing there with his face frozen in terror. But Vati, for once sensitive to Hans' mood, hurried to put him at ease. "All is well! I know you've been busy learning the job, getting in shape, and getting in your bride's way as she prepares for the wedding." He chuckled, winking at

Hans. "But there's something else we need your help with. You know about the election, of course?"

Hans had heard something about the chaos in the government: the new chancellor had claimed the only way to shed the burden of war debt was to tighten credit and reverse wage and salary increases. When the Reichstag rejected this scheme, the chancellor went forward with it in spite of them, until the various factions in the Reichstag, including the National Socialists, came together to stop him. The chancellor, hoping for a weaker and more obedient Reichstag, had persuaded President Hindenburg to dissolve the Reichstag altogether and schedule an election for new members, sometime in September. Hans had passed some of his few idle moments reading about the candidates, now that he would be old enough to vote.

Herr Richter took over. "I knew my friend Walther here had done me a good turn, introducing me to his son! You've done a wonderful job for me, so hardworking and well organized, and the people in the stores and the warehouses all like you." (Did they? He'd thought, rather, that they paid as little attention to him as they could get away with.) "And now that the most important election since the war is upon us, and people are realizing that this government has led us into economic catastrophe, we must make the most of our opportunity! And that's where you come in! You know about the SA, of course?"

It'd been years since Hans thought of that triumphant march into Nuremberg and the proud brown-shirted men taking part in it. But he'd heard about them from time to time, Herr Hitler's SA, though whether they were stalwart defenders of the German people against foreign influences like the Communists or, on the other hand, trouble-making rabble rousers depended who was talking about them. "Yes, sir. Of course I have."

Herr Richter beamed benignly at him. "Well, did you ever think you'd have the chance to join them? Your chance has come! I have, shall we say, influence in the organization. Your father has your uniform all ready for you!" Vati, on cue, held out a neatly folded pile of brown clothing: shirt, jodhpurs, jacket, cap. A bit of red peeked out: collar tabs? Hans wordlessly took the pile and held it while together, taking turns and sometimes stepping on each other's sentences, Herr Richter and Vati explained the part they intended Hans to play.

Before the election, Hans would be organizing campaign workers, putting up signs, leading marches; on Election Day, he would fend off attempts by Communists and socialists to lure away likely voters, run the information on who had already voted to campaign headquarters, knock on the doors of those who hadn't voted yet. . . .

When he could interrupt without rudeness, Hans asked, "But how will I have time to do all this, with all my other work to be done?"

Herr Richter looked him in the eye, the jovial manner falling away. "Until September 14th, my boy, this *is* your work. Oh, you'll keep track of the essentials, but I expect you to spend at least a few hours every day on a job more important than my business." He stopped to shake his head and laugh. "And I wouldn't say that lightly!"

Hans should be glad, and proud, to be asked, to be invited into an organization so important to the Party, to be trusted with such a task. He had little choice but to be glad. And if he'd had some dim notion that becoming a voter would be another step in growing up, a time for making his own decisions, that was looking like another childhood idea to be outgrown.

Klara was thrilled. "I knew you'd become an important man, but not so soon! You'll be serving not only your employer and your father but the *Vaterland*, helping steer the country where we need to go! Oh, I have the most wonderful idea." Her face glowed all the brighter as she said, "I know we were going to be married in August, but if we wait until the Sunday after the election, one week after it, it'll be a double celebration! And who knows what important friends Herr Richter would bring with him? We'll have to rent a bigger hall . . . ."

Hans put his hands on her shoulders before she could run further into fantasies. "We don't know how the election will turn out. Herr Richter and my father and their friends could all be glumly drinking their sorrows away."

Klara lifted her chin. "I absolutely refuse to believe it! And . . . even if that were to happen, at least we'd still have a reason to celebrate, no matter what."

He couldn't bring himself to try harder to discourage her. And after all, as busy as he would apparently be, he'd have little time to prepare for the wedding. If Klara was so keen on his electioneering, he could leave most of the preparations to her. He'd rather do that anyway.

And he could do his utmost to give her a National Socialist victory as a wedding present.

When it came time for Hans to provide security for a march, It was Vati who gave him his instructions: where to meet the marchers, the number to expect, what groups they came from, the route to be taken, the songs Hans should make sure they sang, and what to do if they were obstructed in any way.

Halfway through, he made his father pause while he got paper and pen for taking notes, not that he would have much chance to consult them. Vati finished his recital, and Hans prepared to ask follow-up questions, but Vati nodded in satisfaction at making it through the list and bustled out of the room.

And Hans only had an hour to get to where the first march was assembling.

He scrambled into his uniform, ran to the trolley stop, saw a trolley that must have just passed by the stop, and chased it down, grateful for how his boxer training had increased his wind. He had enough time to straighten his hair and settle himself into the appropriate attitude: confident, sure of himself, in charge. By the time he got off, he knew he offered onlookers an example to inspire them, to lead them toward the future they would reclaim with their energy and devotion.

He walked quickly through the crowd awaiting him to what would be the head of the procession, once they started along the approved route, and commanded their attention. "We march toward the first step to a better government, a government that represents true Germans and wants a re-vived Germany, not a shattered remnant of our former great-ness kept down by our enemies! We march toward victory!" Their cheers warmed his heart and gave him strength for whatever might lie ahead. And that was before the band at the back of the crowd started playing "The Flag High," the Horst Wessel song, and the people surrounding them sang lustily along. In between songs, he led them in chants of "Restore the Country Betrayed!", "Support Our Farmers!," "NSDAP For Our Future!," and "Freedom and Bread!" When a small group within the crowd started chanting, "Down with the Jews, Down with the Communists!" he hesitated and then joined in for a few minutes before letting them chant on their own. As they passed, a boy standing on the sidewalk selling lemonade from a tank on his back, a canister of cups tucked under his arm, stared wide-eyed at the men parading past.

It was only when they were halfway to Hermann Square that the trouble started. A mob of Communists, with their own signs and chants and some in their own uniforms, came toward their route. Clearly, they meant to intersect it.

Hans halted the marchers and called out, "Who has brought the means to repel attackers? Show them." As the crowd obeyed, brandishing sticks, poles, rusty farm tools, their signs, and even police truncheons, Hans told them, "Keep these things handy, and use them to defend yourselves and to clear our path! But if any of you have brought guns, keep them holstered except in the utmost extremity." He gulped, took a deep breath, and shouted, "Now, forward!"

The Communists howled in eagerness and charged to meet them. The lemonade seller scrambled out of the way, his cups slipping from his grasp and spilling into the street. Hans lengthened his stride to stay in front of his own eager warriors. At the front of the mob, a man with tangled dark hair and a straggly beard, carrying a sign that read "Smash the Fascists," swung it straight at Hans' head. Hans ducked under it and punched the man in the nose and then in the belly, dropping him in a tangle of sign and arms and legs at Hans' feet. All around, Hans heard the sounds of a battle joined, grunts and cries of pain and shouts of anger and cheers for one side or the other.

And then he heard the shrill, piercing sound of police whistles coming at them from one side, where another cross-street fed into the boulevard on which they had been marching.

In moments, what had been a battle between two groups of marchers became a three-way brawl as some of his marchers continued fighting the Communists and others turned to push back the police. Hans froze for what seemed like an eternity before he came to himself and pushed toward the latter group, shouting, "No! The police are not the enemy! Let them arrest the Communists, let them stop the traitors!"

A policeman on his left, truncheon raised, laughed and said, "We're here to stop all of you, you simpleton! All of you need to stop fighting in the streets and go home!" Hans stood staring at him, mouth open, before he went back to trying to restrain his own forces. If they stopped fighting, the police would turn their attention to the true ruffians and take care of them better than he and his men could. But some of them defied him, yelling, "If they're protecting the government and the Communists, they're the enemy and we shouldn't just slink away from them!"

By now the police were clubbing people to the ground, people on both sides. The NSDAP supporters would be needed for other marches, and to spread the word about their candidates. As would he.

Many of the marchers refused to listen to him. But he was able to lead some of them away from the fighting and onto another route. He could count that as something of a success.

Vati did not. "You backed away from the fight! What have I taught you, how have I raised you, to make you do such a thing when we were counting on you! Are you still idolizing policemen the way you did when you were a child? You must learn to be more realistic."

To Hans' surprise and relief, Herr Richter, present for the postmortem, stepped in and said, "Now, Walther, I think you're being short-sighted. The lad has good political instincts. There are already many police who sympathize with our cause. If we encourage them to see us as different from the lawless hooligans the Communists are sending into the streets, that can only be good for us. In the short term, they may be less inclined to interfere with us. And our reasonable example may incline some of them to our side. After all, policemen vote too."

Hans relaxed, nodding as if all this described just what he had been thinking. But Vati had been closer to the truth. He did not want to think of himself as the sort of criminal the police were there to put down. Even though they had turned him away . . . maybe he should resent them for it. Maybe it was weak or unmanly of him to instead want their respect. But he had already had to give up so much of what he cared about as a child. He was not ready to give up any more.

And Klara, his darling Klara, thought he might still be able to be a policeman someday. What if the day should come, and that dream would have been within his reach if not for the things he had done to support the Party? No, there must be a way to serve both dreams, the old and the new.

Hans waited for the election results in a bar about halfway between his flat and Klara's, one where he knew many NS-DAP supporters would have gathered. Depending on how things went, he could decide at the last minute whether to go home, where Vati might be even more drunk than Hans, or to Klara's, where things would at least be quiet. The bar had a radio, and officials were periodically announcing election updates, which the customers greeted with either cheers and toasts or with curses and a thrown glass or two. Hans made a point of not getting too drunk to keep track of who was winning how many seats. By the end of the night, he gave up on that and just downed one beer after another. The Socialist party would still have the most seats, after all their work and struggle.

Seeing Hans' doleful expression, the burly trolley car driver on the stool next to him elbowed him, almost making him spill his beer, and said, "Why so glum, lad? We've done wonderfully well! And this is just the beginning!"

Hans blinked and tried to focus on the man's blurry features. "But the Social'sts won again! Got the mos' seats!"

Seeing the man getting ready to slap him on the back, Hans managed to put his glass down in time not to have it spill all over the counter. He clutched the glass as the driver shouted, "Weren't you listening? We came in second! We got *ten times* as many seats as before! . . . Well, almost ten." He waved away the question of arithmetic, almost hitting the man on the other side of him in the face.

Hans looked around the room. Most of the men were acting as if they agreed with the trolley driver, grinning and toasting the results. One thin fellow with a gray moustache was quarreling with the rest of the men at his table, saying stubbornly, "But what if the Social Democrats and the Communists work together? They'd have almost forty percent of the seats, and then we're all in deep shit!" But the others hooted him down, and one of them exclaimed loudly that the two parties would never agree on sitting in a puddle if their asses were on fire.

It seemed likely enough that Vati would also be celebrating. And Klara might not appreciate having her husband-to-be show up this drunk, and this late. So he wobbled his way home.

Chapter 17

Autumn 1930

Hans hadn't spent much time with Klara's mother, other than as a guest at meals. But with the wedding upon them, Klara and her mother descended on him to tell him all about what they'd been planning and what last-minute tasks he'd been assigned. They talked over each other and finished each other's sentences, beaming at each other and at him, laughing when their eager chatter became unintelligible. This was a side of Klara he had never seen, and it delighted him — at the same time as it made his heart ache for what Lotte was missing and would miss. Who would help Lotte plan her wedding? What woman would be so close to Lotte, listen to her every hope and fear, comfort her when things went wrong, rejoice with her when things went right?

As for all the details the women were attempting to drown him in, he just let them wash over him, speaking up now and then to repeat, "Just tell me what to do, and I'll do it." He made a list, asked the occasional question, and hoped he'd avoid making too much of a fool of himself. Vati had little to do before the wedding day, but he did delve into closets, cabinets, and the building's storage units collecting stoneware and even porcelain, so they wouldn't be smashing up only contributions from Klara's family for *Polterabend* the night before the wedding. It made Hans wonder, for the first time, whether Vati had ever thought of marrying again. Did he just never meet women, spending his spare time either out with his fellow Party members or sitting at home with a newspaper and a beer? Did he despair of finding a woman like Mutti?

There were times when Klara's family made him feel too strongly what was lacking in his own. Herr Bauer somehow combined strength and kindness, and should really have had a son to raise. And at one time or another, Klara and both of her parents had asked him what Otto should do at the wedding, obviously having no doubt that Hans would want his only brother involved. The answer he would have liked to give was "stay out of the way and not show up with any of his wild friends." He found other ways to answer, or avoid, the question.

Klara asked, blushing, if Hans wanted to have a friend "abduct" her before the wedding and leave hints Hans would follow to retrieve her. But while Hans had friendly interactions with various men through his work, there were none he felt he could call on for that task, or knew well enough to trust with his bride's security and feelings. Nor did the idea of calling on his cousin Rudolf, let alone Otto, appeal to him. And he hadn't kept up with many boys from his school days. (The thought of Samuel, wherever he had gone, tried to come into Hans' mind, but he pushed it away.)

As if conspiring with his future in-laws, Otto appeared out of the shadows a few days before the wedding when Hans was walking home. He took Hans' arm as he said, "Come have a drink with me, little brother! Celebrate getting yourself shackled! I know just the place."

It was only appropriate, he supposed. He should probably have reached out to Otto before this. "All right. But I'll pick the place."

He chose a pub with clean tables, plenty of light, and little tolerance for drunken scenes. Otto rolled his eyes, but followed him in and ordered beers for them both. When they were settled at a table, Otto raised his glass and said, "To the bride and groom! You look happy, Hansi." Hans gritted his teeth at the childhood nickname, but clinked glasses and drank.

Otto drained a third of his glass in one gulp. "Seeing you so pleased with life could almost make me think about getting married myself." He paused long enough for Hans to smile before adding, "Not that I'd want the sweet little *Hausfrau* type you picked. I'd want a girl with some spice in her, who'd know adventure if it came up and introduced itself. But each to his own, *ja*?"

Hans put down his glass, sloshing the beer inside, and got up and left without another word. By the time he could see the front steps of his flat, he regretted having walked out. He could have just absorbed Otto's teasing, or turned the joke on him. But it was too late to change that now.

Both Klara and her mother emphatically made it clear that he would not be allowed to see Klara's dress before the wedding, that she would wear nothing more elaborate than a good suit to the registry office the day before. That left him free to imagine just how closely the wedding dress might fit, and what it would cover and what leave showing. He even indulged in some fantasies, late at night, about how he would take it off her. . . . He had already gone for the fittings for his suit, somehow making the time before the election. Klara had presented him with a top hat and made him model it, clapping her hands at how "distinguished" he looked. The day before he and Klara went to the registry office, he brought the suit home and modeled suit and hat for Vati and Lotte. Lotte clapped her hands and kissed his cheek. Vati just stood there, clearing his throat, and finally said, "What a man you've become, my son."

Nothing had made him feel so glad, so proud, so whole, in longer than he could tell.

As they left the registry office the next day, Hans practically walking on air at having completed the first essential step, Klara told him her father wanted to see him. "After the *Polterabend*, Mutti and I, along with Lotte, will be up late hosting the veil dance with all the female wedding guests. Maybe he just wants someone to keep him company."

Hans doubted it.

Herr Richter had given him the day off, so he had the rest of the afternoon in which to fret. He and Klara settled at an outdoor café, and Klara politely ignored her future husband being as jumpy as if sitting on needles, but she soon excused herself and went off on some unnamed remaining errand.

When Hans arrived at the Bauer flat, Herr Bauer — Christoph, he had been instructed to call him, but could not yet think of him that way — was sitting at the kitchen table with a bottle of Schnaps and two glasses, one showing traces of having been filled and emptied. He had never seen Klara's father drunk and was curious how drink would take him, and he was more than ready for a drink himself. He bowed and sat down, filling his host's glass and then his own. He had picked up his glass and was wondering what toast to give when Herr Bauer raised his own glass and said quietly, "To my daughter's future."

Hans gulped, recovered, clicked Herr Bauer's glass, took a modest sip, and said as earnestly as he could, "It will be my life's work to make it a good one."

Herr Bauer's stare felt as if it was drilling holes in him. "We seem to be moving into challenging times. And you associate with people who are eager, not just to meet those challenges, but to stir up more. What matters more to you, your political affiliations or the family you and Klara will make?"

Hans sat up straighter and lifted his chin as he answered, "There might be times when those two bonds pull in different directions, but on the whole, I believe they support each other. Klara and our children will be safer and better off in a revived Germany, a peaceful and strong Germany, a united Germany. I'm willing to work for that goal."

Herr Bauer gave a slow nod and took a drink of his Schnaps. "I can hardly expect a man your age to be a cynical pessimist. I can only ask you to keep your eyes open, and to consider the ways in which things may go wrong. And if you see that things are going wrong, for my daughter's sake, figure out how your affiliations and behavior may need to change."

Hans nodded back, finished his drink as quickly as was polite, and got up, saying, "I'll see you tomorrow, then. Thank you." But Herr Bauer waved him back into his chair, saying, "No, stay a little. The women won't be back for hours yet. I won't get you drunk." He gave a wry smile. "But you can tell me more about yourself, and in exchange, I'll talk about my daughter."

By the time Hans left, he had a collection of stories to cherish about Klara as a mischievous toddler and a loving and lovely young girl. He stumbled toward the flat that had been his home for so long, knowing he would leave it forever in the morning, a little sad that the knowledge didn't sadden him more.

Klara's family had chosen the church, and as Hans stood in the doorway looking in, he was glad he'd consented to their choice. Delicate stone arches flanked intricate stained glass windows leading up to one grand window at the front, red and blue and yellow and even purple light pouring in from all around. Someone had chosen yellow and purple flowers to put in brass vases along the walls.

Hans had never regarded himself as a chatty fellow, overflowing with talk. But the sight of Klara in her white lacy dress, holding a bouquet of delicate white and pink and yellow flowers, left him utterly speechless. When it came time to say his vows, he had to force the first words past his constricted throat.

Then it was off to the reception, where the crowd that had been quiet and attentive at the ceremony was now boisterous and loud, full of congratulations and in some cases bawdy cheers and suggestions for the wedding night. He glared at a couple of fellows, his cousin and one man from work, who went too far, and tried to direct Klara's attention to the less embarrassing guests. There were more guests than he'd expected, some of whom he'd never seen before, and he now understood why Klara's family had rented a hall rather than holding the festivities in their flat. The food was plentiful enough, if barely, for all, but it would have to wait: the crowd was calling for the dancing. The hired musicians launched into a familiar, but newly appropriate, waltz tune, "Two Hearts in Waltz Time." Hans hurried to push back his chair and take Klara's hand, leading her to the clear space on the floor. Was that happiness shining in her eyes, or triumph? He would take either.

After the couple's first dance came the waltz for Klara and her father, who clutched her so tight that Hans wondered if it hurt. She had tears in her eyes, but not, he thought, from pain.

Then came the moment that brought a drop of bitter to the day's sweetness. If his mother had lived, he would be waltzing with her, savoring her joy, trying to convey his love and his promise to remain her devoted son. But now, it was his aunt who approached him, her smile mixed with sadness and understanding. He must have been too slow, for her to have to come to him when he should have gone to her instead. But as much as he could, he put regrets and wishes and unanswered prayers behind him, and took her in his arms to sweep her through the dance before handing her off to Klara's father. Once again, she would take the dance that Mutti could not.

Then, finally, they could eat. And while people made their way through the food, Vati and Klara's father rose to give their toasts, each of them praising the other's child and wishing them all good fortune. Vati would have liked to use beer, saying plaintively that he had always imagined bellowing "*Prost!*" with all his might — but Hans had persuaded him to accept Klara's family preference for wine, and he gamely joined Herr Bauer in shouting "*Zum Wohl!*"

Then came the shoe auction, with the guests, many of them at least half drunk, bidding for one of Klara's shoes, which a friend of Klara's passed from one bidder to the next. When the shoe was almost full of cash, she brought it to Hans and winked. He panicked for a moment, thinking he might have forgotten the necessary bills, but there they were in his pocket, and he crammed most of them into the shoe before seizing it and waving it in victory. Then he brought it back to Klara, kneeling to present it (feeling oddly like the prince in *Aschenputtel*) and waiting for her to take the money and tuck it away before slipping the shoe on her foot. As soon as she had both shoes on, she sprang to her feet, took his hands, and dragged him back to the dance floor.

Tradition required the couple to stay until the last guest left. But Klara, clever as always, had made a point of getting all the female guests to promise they would drag any men who came with them to the door before it got very late. That left unaccompanied male guests for Hans to deal with. He had kept back a few bills for the purpose, and now made the rounds among the men, offering — with what he hoped was a sufficiently clear look — to pay for their first drink at a local bar of their choice. They grinned at him and accepted the money, though his cousin briefly played dumb and said he might go to a bar eventually. The woman started filing out, Lotte stopping to give him a fierce hug on her way, and the men followed.

Only Vati and Klara's parents were left. More hugs from Klara's mother and handshakes from the fathers, and then he and Klara were alone except for the musicians packing up their instruments. Hans took Klara's hands and whispered, "Ready to go home?"

Klara beamed at him, though tears glimmered in her eyes. "Yes, yes! To our new home!"

They had arranged for a taxi ahead of time, to make sure they didn't waste any time after the reception standing on the street and trying to hail one. As they rode to their new flat, Klara snuggled up next to him, closer than she had ever done before. Just as they turned onto their street, she put a delicate hand on his thigh.

The taxi pulled up in front of the building, and the driver hopped out and came around to open the door for them, saying heartily, "*Alles gute*, Herr Schäfer, Frau Schäfer!" Hans heard a quiet gasp from Klara at this first use of her new name, and he vowed at that moment that he would never give her reason to be ashamed of it. As soon as they both stood on the sidewalk, he hoisted Klara in his arms. Grinning, the driver ran to the front door and held it open for Hans to pass through. Their flat was four flights up, but he had practiced after his boxing, carrying the heavy bag around the room and up and down the exercise steps. He knew he could make it to their own threshold. Klara made little "ooh" noises and called him her strong husband as they reached the door. He balanced her in one arm as he reached for the key.

And then it was time to enjoy the fruits of marriage. He'd been nervous about fumbling around or getting things wrong, about hurting Klara or disappointing her. But now, all he could think about was the warm bundle of woman in his arms.

Chapter 18

Late Winter 1932 – Winter 1933

Hans' experience before the 1930 election had left him leery of wading into politics any deeper. Over the next year and a half, he was happy to spend as much time and attention as he could get away with on setting up his and Klara's new flat, working with her on her cooking to the point where he could stop helping cook, enjoying their evenings and their nights, and working hard enough to please his employer. Sometimes, on Sundays, he and Klara took long walks for Hans to show Klara parts of the city she hadn't already seen, like the new, massive concrete buildings going up, severe in their tall straight lines or curving like a woman's body.

Still, as the March 1932 presidential elections approached, he did attend rallies and the occasional march, usually wearing the SA uniform Vati was so proud to have given him. Herr Richter, who had claimed to approve of Hans' approach to confrontations with police, was occupied with other matters, and Vati made no attempt to maneuver Hans into leading the marches. If a march or rally looked to be descending into violence, Hans managed to talk Vati into leaving. It wasn't as difficult as he'd feared: Vati was hardly in physical shape for such confrontations, and may have realized it.

Herr Hitler was one of three candidates, arousing fever-ish excitement in such Party faithful as Hans' father, but he was defeated in the second round by the too-familiar Hindenburg. A few months later, the chancellor infuriated Vati up to the boiling point by outlawing the SA. But then President Hindenburg switched chancellors to a fellow with no real support, encumbered by a cabinet who supported none of the parties and naturally, in turn, had no support from any of them. The arrangement was such an obvious failure that in June Hindenburg, reaching into his old bag of tricks, dissolved the Reichstag and called new elections for the end of July.

The ban on the SA was lifted. Back went Hans to attending meetings, handing out pamphlets on street corners, and knocking on doors. Most of the SA's members were as eager to face the Communists' troops as those thugs were to face them. When Vati asked whether Hans "finally had the stomach to lead a march," Hans excused himself. "Klara's afraid to have me do it, and I mustn't worry her at this special time."

Vati scowled. "Your mother was expecting your sister when I went off to war — should I have stayed home, warming her feet and feeding her bread and milk, instead of fighting?" But as soon as he said it, his face clouded with memories, maybe wondering whether those months of worry had weakened Mutti and set her on the path to her grave. He said nothing more, burying his face in his paper, and Hans went on home to Klara, wondering whether she would like some bread and milk.

When the National Socialists finally won more seats in the Reichstag than any other party, Hans expected his father to be wildly excited, but things proved not so simple. The Nazis were able to select their member Göring as the president, but beyond that, having the most seats made little difference: they lacked a majority and couldn't find anyone who would work with them to form one. The same hated government stayed in power, and yet another election was set for the sixth of November.

"All this politics," Klara sighed as she tried to knit a baby blanket. "Are they going to make you spend a lot of time on it again?"

"It's not like that, darling," Hans said as he looked at the blanket and hoped Klara's mother would come over soon to fix it. "I know how important it is for the National Socialists to get some real power. I just wish . . . I wish there were more hours in the day." He smiled down at her. "I want to sit and watch you knit, and wait for your feet to swell so I can rub them, and keep learning my job so I can get more responsibility, *and* help with the election. But that's life, I guess."

Klara freed a hand from her knitting, grabbed his sleeve, and pulled him down for a kiss. When he reluctantly straightened up again, she smiled at him and said, "Well, you'd better be done with all this election work before my feet need rubbing!"

He laid his hand on his heart. "I promise." And hoped he could keep his word.

As the election neared, all the Party members Hans knew seemed sure of the outcome. "The tide is running our way!" cried Vati, dropping in on Hans and Klara without warning or invitation, too excited to be tired despite an evening spent haranguing passers-by. "Our time has come at last!"

Tides turn, Hans thought as he made Vati some coffee. *That's the one thing I know about them.*

On the night of November 6th, when it was clear the Nazis had actually lost seats, he looked at the indignant and furious faces filling Vati's living room and imagined he heard water, sucking at pebbles as it drained away down the beach toward the sea.

Klara had been planning to cook for the Feast of Saint Nicholas with no help from Hans, her mother, anyone, but she was so near her time that Hans took on the cooking himself.

Herr Richter gave his employees time off before Christmas, and Hans took the train into the country, where he cut a small but well-shaped tree and carried it home again, the conductor chuckling and allowing it. After he got home, Vati showed up at the door with a big box. He set it down under the tree and said heavily, "Your mother and I had these ornaments before you were born. She left them with a neighbor when she moved into the smaller flat. I didn't know, but I thought she might have done that, and I was right. . . . Otto might remember them." It was the first time Vati had mentioned Otto in months, maybe years. "You probably don't, but you were there, and you were so excited to see the tree! You wanted to help decorate it." He laughed. "We found a few you'd have trouble breaking and let you handle them. You were so proud. . . ."

Klara, in her armchair, gestured Vati toward the most comfortable remaining chair. "Thank you so much! You sit here while we decorate, and I'll bring you a drink." She started to hoist herself upright.

Vati winked at her and opened the box. "What, you think I'm as breakable as the ornaments? No, I'll help. And then we'll all have a drink together."

Once Lotte had found a job teaching in her old primary school, she had finally moved out of Vati's flat into one of her own, or rather one she shared with a friend. Hans looked around the room and sighed; Klara, who sometimes seemed able to read his mind, immediately telephoned Lotte and asked her to come over. Luckily she was free, and as soon as she arrived they decorated the tree from the fullest boughs at the bottom to the branch standing up proudly at the top. Lotte chattered cheerfully and made a point of circling the tree, making sure there were ornaments on every side, while Klara gamely hung a few ornaments before she had to sit down again. As they relaxed afterward with their drinks, Vati suddenly put his glass down and reached in his pocket, pulling out a small packet wrapped in tissue paper. "I almost forgot! Here, Klara, little mother, this is for you. That is — it's for the little one when he comes, for his first Christmas."

Klara got back up to take it and unwrapped it carefully to show a multi-pointed glass star, clear except for threads of gold color twined around its heart. Her eyes filled with tears, and she wrapped it back up with even more care and laid it in the corner of the empty box before she went to Vati and kissed his cheek.

It was the best Christmas Hans could remember, better than when the country relatives surprised them so many years ago. And from first to last, Vati had not breathed a word about the Party, or Herr Hitler, or the future of Germany. For this one night, it seemed, he was content to plan for their own future, for their family, and put the rest aside.

And just before the New Year dawned, Walther Hans Schäfer came into the world to share that future with them. They called him Hansi.

After the election, Hans had stopped paying attention to politics, though he did hear that there was still no functioning majority coalition in the Reichstag. He did not learn until later that back in November, major figures in all branches of German society, from banking to industry to agriculture, had written to President Hindenburg asking him to name Adolf

Hitler as chancellor. Nothing else, they urged, could end the cycle of repeated dissolutions of the Reichstag. Nothing else would allow a resurgence of the German economy and deal a final blow to the "state-denying Communist party."

By January, Hindenburg had been persuaded.

On January 30, 1933, in a short ceremony in the president's office, Hitler was sworn in and became Chancellor of Germany.

Chapter 19

Winter - Spring 1933

The first change Hans noticed was the streets filling up with brown-shirted SA troops. They were everywhere, though exactly what they were supposed to be doing wasn't clear. There were also manymore "Heil Hitler!" salutes exchanged between jubilant Nazi supporters, and even some people who seemed more bewildered than enthusiastic. When they visited with Vati, Hans wasn't surprised to find him so energized he seemed years younger. Vati informed him, beaming, that he'd already been allowed to fire two Jewish bank clerks, without the pushback he'd have gotten from upper management just a few weeks before.

Klara was curiously reluctant to talk about the Nazis' success, not only with Vati but even with Hans. When he pressed her for some comment, she said, "I don't give politics much thought. That's how I grew up, I suppose. So many people argue about it, and I don't like arguments."

But it was Klara, one evening, who brought up the idea of applying to the police once more. Sitting in the rocking chair and nursing the baby, she said quietly, so as not to startle Hansi, "You know, darling, the rules for police recruitment may have changed now. Don't you think you should try again? It might be good to check on it soon. If things *have* changed, people will find out soon, and you could lose your chance."

Hans had been relaxing in his favorite armchair, lulled almost to sleep by the rhythmic creak of the rocking chair, but now he sat up. "What will Herr Richter say, if I leave the job he gave me? Here he's worked so hard for the new days to come, and I reward him by quitting?"

Klara picked up little Hansi and set him against her shoulder, patting him until he burped. She kissed the baby's head and said simply, "Ask him."

Hans waited a few days, weighing both the idea and his employer's mood, before he accused himself of cowardice and went ahead. To his relief, Herr Richter immediately supported the idea. "Yes, lad, and hurry up about it! My little finger told me that Hitler will be hiring fifty thousand of our SA troops as auxiliary police, and the force may have less need of new hires after that happens. Go right now! Your work can wait."

Was his work so unimportant? Or was Herr Richter, looking ahead, already determined to do without him? His worries must have shown on his face, because Herr Richter said more soberly, "Don't think I don't value your work. I'd be very happy to have you stay here for a long time. But I know you had your heart set on becoming a policeman. This is a time of dreams coming true, and it'd be ungrateful of me to stand in the way of yours. . . . But wait a moment." He looked on his desk for any stray pieces of paper, found one, and scribbled something on it. "Go see this man. Very useful fellow. Tell him I sent you, and he'll smooth the way for you."

Hans stood very straight and said, "I will never forget your kindness and your assistance." Then he half walked, half ran to the door.

The very useful fellow read the note, looked Hans up and down, and grunted. "Fit enough, especially for a city dweller. Tell me about yourself — what you've been doing, what you can do."

Hans prudently started with the better years, after the money supply had been got under control. He emphasized, or simplified, his stern-but-loving father, who had brought him up to be strong and determined and patriotic. He dwelt on his boxing, and on the heavy lifting his current job often required, and the different ways in which he had been exercising leadership — including where Nazi protests had been concerned. That he had actually led only one march, he decided not to clarify.

He ended where, with a different question, he might have begun. "I have always, since boyhood, respected and admired the police, and longed to be one of their number."

The man harrumphed. "It's all very well being starry-eyed, but it's not a glamorous job, day to day. And one of the most important parts is following orders. Well, with what you say about your father, you'll be used to that."

He looked sharply at Hans for confirmation. Hans nodded vigorously, hoping he hid his mixed feelings about obeying Vati over the years.

"Yes, we'll need discipline in the ranks as we fix so much that's gone wrong! Not so much on the force itself, though there's been some of that, but everywhere. We need good men dedicated to the future Germany has a right to! But Herr Richter knows that, few better." He put out his hand. "Shake on it, Herr Schäfer! And then go get your uniform."

Hans shook hands, his head swimming with the suddenness of how his life had changed, and would change. Finally, finally, he would be enforcing law and order, serving his city and the Vaterland, making Klara proud.

Dressed in his new green uniform, complete with steel helmet, Hans went to Herr Richter's office and resigned, with yet more thanks for his help and encouragement. Warmed by the good wishes of those he'd worked with, he headed home and told Klara. Though he didn't really need to — his face, the lightness in his bearing, the spring in his step all carried the message. She shrieked in delight, startling the baby, who howled accompaniment. Then it was all about soothing Hansi, and hugging each other, and deciding how to celebrate. They ended up going out to dinner at the sort of restaurant they usually avoided as extravagant, with Lotte coming over to babysit. Then they went home, laden with leftovers for Lotte, to pick up Hansi and move on to Vati's flat.

After the initial greetings, sharing the news, and drinking the first toast, Vati pulled Hans aside and said, "Can you stay the night, so we can celebrate properly? This news needs much more Schnaps! And I built a cradle for when my son and his family would visit."

Hans laughed and said, "You told me about the cradle, from the first saw cut to the final varnish. Yes, we'll stay." And if it felt strange to take his wife into his childhood bed, it also seemed right, like completing a circle, except better. This would be a happier night than any he could remember spending in that bed.

Though he had never woken up in that bed with a foul-tasting mouth and a throbbing headache. But every good fortune, he reminded himself, comes with a price.

On the 24th of February, 1933, Chancellor Hitler ordered a raid on the Communists' headquarters. In the same speech in which he announced that the raid had taken place, he revealed what it had found: diabolical plans to attack public buildings.

The Communists furiously denied the accusations, and the public argued for days about whether such a raid had been justified. Hans imagined how he would have felt if the Communists had gained control and then raided Nazi Party headquarters, and suppressed a certain queasy feeling. Surely the results proved the raid had been necessary!

Maybe all the public discussion slowed down the proper government response, or maybe the Communists' plans were so far along that they needed little time to carry them out. On February 27th, the night sky lit up and the air rumbled with the explosions coming from the Reichstag Building. Even with all the fire engines could do, by the morning of February 28th, much of the building, including the gilded cupola, had been reduced to smoldering ruins. Security forces caught the arsonist, but the damage was done. Hitler immediately took action, invoking Article 48's emergency powers and abolishing such dangerous freedoms as freedom of speech, of assembly, and of the press. The government could also tap phones and intervene in the decisions of the various states.

Vati added the newspaper to the collection he had started the day Hitler was sworn in. "When I'm old and looking back at my life, I'll have these to help me remember when things turned around. They'll comfort me as I breathe my last."

Hans' first weeks on the police force had been as much training as anything else, though nothing like the rigorous program that he had tried to join before. But now the day had finally come — he would be the primary officer on an arrest! Two more experienced officers would go with him, but unless some emergency arose, or Hans failed dismally, they would only stand by.

So excited was he that not until they were walking down the street did Hans pay much attention to his companions' moods. Naturally, what was new and thrilling to him would be business as usual to them, but the older of the two looked closer to glum. Hans must seem young and naive to them both — in fact, he realized, he had not even asked on what charge he would be arresting someone. He did so now. The older policeman gave him a look that as much as said, *Now you're curious?* He said dryly, "Newspaper publisher's been printing whatever he likes. And what he likes isn't liked so much higher up. So into the slammer he goes." He paused, looking toward Hans and away again. "My little brother reads that paper. Guess he'll have to find another."

Hans found that his own eager march down the street had slowed a little. The publisher was probably a Communist or something of that sort. The Communists and Socialists must not be allowed to regroup and gain strength. Hans would not only be doing his duty as a policeman, but playing an important part in reclaiming his country. . . . But when, as a child, he had imagined his adult self in a policeman's uniform, making the streets safe for women and children, he had not had such tasks as these in mind.

But of course, what did a child know about what protecting his fellow citizens was all about?

The publisher, a plump red-cheeked man about twenty years older than Hans, looked as if he should be bouncing a grandson on his knee or smoking a pipe in front of a fire, not standing defiantly in front of a printing press with ink-stained fingers. He glared at the three of them and said, "I sent the others home, though they wanted to stand with me. I didn't want them to get hurt. I'd have sent the printing press with them, if I could. Do you plan to smash it and finish us properly?"

No one had said anything to Hans about destroying the press. But then, he hadn't even known his mission until a few minutes ago. He waited for one of the others to answer, and when they didn't, said, "We don't have any orders of that kind. Not today. Now come with us." One of the older men glanced at the handcuffs hanging on Hans' belt, but he said nothing, and Hans chose to interpret his silence as saying Hans could leave the cuffs where they were.

The man had nothing else to say as they took his arms and led him away. But as the door clicked shut behind them, he let out a sudden sob. It took Hans by surprise, after his relative composure up to that moment. It seemed to surprise the man as well, who gritted his teeth and allowed no second sob to follow it. Instead, he muttered something through his closed teeth that might have been "Nazi bastards!" If the words had been clearly spoken, Hans would have had to take some notice of them — slap the man, maybe, or add some appropriate charge when they got back to the station. But as it was, doing either might exceed his assigned duties. *Just as well*, he thought, and then scolded himself for insufficient zeal.

Chapter 20

Spring 1933

Now that Hans was a policeman, he could take part in the police sports programs. Bidding farewell to his sparring companions, he showed up, almost as excited as he was nervous, to a practice session and introduced himself to the coach. The coach, however, was grumbling about two boxers he'd been ordered to drop from the program. It took him a while to get around to mentioning their names, but one of them, Hans realized, had been the man who had made the nastiest comments about how the police were letting in any old rabble these days, even Nazis. He swallowed his discomfort and said, "I'm sorry to hear that you had to lose such good boxers — "

"Had to? *Blödsinn!* If they'd have told me those boys were in trouble, I'd have told them to shut their mouths, and they'd have done it!" He leaned forward and glared at Hans. "If I tell you to do something, will you do it? Or will you go mixing in things that aren't your business? I'm not going to bother turning you into a real boxer and then have my time and effort wasted."

Hans shook his head so hard his neck popped. "I'll mind my own business. All I want is to be a good policeman and to get better at boxing."

The man grunted, stroked his chin, and finally said, "All right, let's see how you do. You'll train for an hour before work, five days a week." He paused as if waiting for Hans to argue with him.

Hans would have liked to protest — he'd either need to go to sleep early, leaving him less time with Klara, or give up an hour of sleep just when Hansi was starting to sleep through the night. But he said only, "I will. When do we start?"

Heading home, hoping Klara would be happy for him more than she'd be upset about the early morning practice, he thought about how close he'd come to being kept out of the boxing program and gave thanks for his narrow escape. Everywhere he turned, it seemed, politics was playing some role in his life — getting him a job, then risking a confrontation with the police or even an arrest, then easing his way into the police, then making his days easier but at the same time putting his next dream in danger. How had his life gotten so complicated?

Hans naturally hadn't seen as much of Herr Richter since he joined the police force, but his former employer made a point of showing that he hadn't forgotten Hans altogether, inviting him to join him and his friends for dinners at fancy restaurants and picking up the bill. When Herr Richter dropped by the station toward the end of March, inviting Hans to the favorite Party bar after work, Hans assumed it would be a similar gathering — until Herr Richter told him to be sure and wear his SA uniform. When he arrived, he found only Herr Richter and one other man, the latter also in SA uniform. And neither of them was already drunk.

Herr Richter had a glass waiting for him, and a pitcher of beer. As he poured Hans' glass, filling it so the foam just passed the rim, he lowered his voice and said confidentially, "I'm in a particularly good mood tonight. Would you like to know why?"

Yes, Hans would. And he decided to drink his beer slowly enough to keep his wits about him. Something in Herr Richter's manner suggested he had a favor in mind, and might try to present it as something Hans would be eager to do.

"Well, I'll tell you." Herr Richter took a swig of his own beer, wiped foam off his moustache, and leaned forward as he said, "There's going to be a boycott! And we have signs ready to post, all over town!"

Hans must have looked confused. The SA officer shook his head at Hans' being so slow on the uptake and said, "Of Jewish shops, of course. Here's one of the signs." He reached into a sack next to his chair and pulled out a sign painted in black letters on thin wood painted white. It read, *Germans defend yourselves against Jewish atrocity propaganda! Buy only at German stores!*

"Our stout SA troops will be posting these next to all my shops," Herr Richter added, "and near all the Jewish shops we can find. And that's where you come in, my good lad!"

The SA man muttered something Hans couldn't catch. He didn't seem to like Herr Richter's bringing this unfamiliar fellow into the operation. Suppressing the urge to shift about in his chair, Hans said, "I'd be glad to, of course, if I can be of use . . . ."

"But of course you can!" Herr Richter boomed, apparently forgetting to keep his voice down. "Don't you see? You know where all my shops are! And I'll wager you've noticed where our Jewish competition is, too."

Hans had noticed some Jewish-looking shops, now and then, but he'd probably forgotten where they were and what they sold, especially since he left that job behind. But after all, he owed that better fortune to the man in front of him. By now, he hoped he'd given his superiors on the force satisfaction . . . but if he was wrong about how well he was doing, it would be prudent to oblige Herr Richter when possible. And he remembered most of Herr Richter's shops, if not all. He put on a smile and said, "Of course I can give it a try."

As instructed, Hans showed up at Herr Richter's printing shop after work on Friday, March 31st, ready to spend hours hustling around the city posting signs. Herr Richter was there, along with ten or twelve SA troops, but the troops were muttering angrily to each other and Herr Richter looked decidedly glum. "They've chickened out," he spat. "The boycott is only going to be tomorrow, and then it's over! They've let the Jews and their allies persuade them with wails about the poor Aryan workers in the shops and how the boycott will affect them. As if any good Aryan would be working in a Jewish shop to begin with!"

It would hardly please Herr Richter for Hans to say that some of the workers might not have had a choice. He looked at the stacks of signs, enough to take dozens of men many hours to post, and asked, "Are we still putting up signs, then?"

Herr Richter sighed. "Yes, yes, we must do what we can. If I'd known sooner, we could have been posting them for days. Ah, well — many good Germans will keep the boycott going, even if we aren't allowed to keep talking about it. Let's see . . . Hans, it'll be most efficient if you post as many as you can in the next hour near my own shops. The SA can handle the Jewish shops. They already know in what rat holes the Jews hide."

Hans hoisted an armful of signs, as many as he could carry without dropping some, and headed out on his errand. Klara knew to wait dinner, but if he hurried, he could have a drink first.

Hans hadn't said as much to Klara or to his father, but he had thought joining the police force might be like starting at a new school. He would know almost no one there, and would have to find a way to make friends, to identify people who felt and thought about things as he did. But it turned out to be easy. Few of the others were actual Nazi Party members, but most of them were sick of all the street violence and hoped Hitler would soon show the value of a firm hand. And so it proved. Street battles were becoming a thing of the past, and criminal gangs were laying low. Some of the men held grudges about how the Party members who had been stirring things up were suddenly in charge of restoring order, but even they acknowledged that order was being restored.

Here and there were men not so easily won over, men who had voted or even marched against the Nazis. For his part, Hans was willing to leave politics in the street when he came in the door — up to a point, anyway. If these policemen were doing their jobs, they were helping, whether they wanted to see it that way or not. He ignored the sneers and comments as best he could.

And then, less than halfway through April, those men were gone, as if a helpful wind had blown them out of his path.

At first he thought they might all have left town to attend some rally with others of their ilk. But as two days went by, and three, and four, and a week, that seemed less and less likely. When Constable Volker, a quiet and competent man almost Hans' height, came by to talk about the following week's schedule, Hans made so bold as to ask him where those men had gone. Had they been transferred to another station?

Volker cocked his head and looked at Hans quizzically. "I'd have thought you would know, with your connections. Are we keeping you too busy to follow the news? There's been a new law passed, the Law for the Restoration of the Professional Civil Service. It lets your friends in the government get rid of Jews and political undesirables. I don't know that any of those men were Jewish, but they certainly didn't have the sort of opinions Herr Hitler wants in his police!"

Hans sat through the rest of the schedule assignments, hoping he'd remember his own in spite of the other thoughts crowding his head. If a man was fired for getting mixed up in the wrong politics, could he get another job, something further from government work? Had these policemen known they were in trouble, maybe had a chance to quit politicking so they could keep their jobs? If they were Jews, of course, there was no changing that.

Chapter 21

Autumn 1933 – Spring 1934

Hans didn't spend much time reading the paper. Reading the paper reminded him of his father, and while he and Vati got along fairly well nowadays, he still didn't make a point of imitating him and generally preferred to err in the opposite direction. But as he and Klara took a stroll one Sunday in mid-October, taking turns pushing Hansi's carriage, a headline at the news stand caught his eye. At first, he looked away so as not to be irritated by mention of the League of Nations. But a moment later the rest of the headline sank in, and he stopped in his tracks, fishing out money to buy a copy. Klara, curious at this sudden interest, stood close to him so she could read beside him as he opened the paper.

He gripped the paper tighter as he read, and before he'd even finished the article. he said excitedly, "Do you see, Klara? Chancellor Hitler has withdrawn us from the League of Nations! That's showing them!"

Klara wrinkled her forehead and asked, "What are we showing them, exactly?"

Hans had no ready answer. He had never paid much attention to the League of Nations. But all their enemies from the war were in it, and they all seemed to think it was important . . . . He made do by reading what Herr Hitler had said about the move. "Our adversaries the French have not let even the wishes of its allies move them to disarm themselves and leave themselves defenseless. Why, then, should we subject ourselves to an agreement that never served our needs, and which our enemies themselves disclaim?"

Klara nodded decisively and said, "Of course! They can hardly blame us for doing what the French are doing, can they?"

At that moment, Hans didn't care who might blame them, or for what. Herr Hitler was showing the world that Germany was now governed by men, not sheep! The news filled him with such vigor that Klara had to ask him twice, on their way home, to slow down. And when he forgot again, she ran with the stroller, which bounced along to Hansi's loud delight.

Hans and Klara tried to have his father and sister over for dinner once a week, usually for Sunday dinner. Klara suggested now and then that they invite Otto to join them, but Hans doubted Otto would enjoy such a family get-together anymore than Vati would. As for himself, it was hard enough for him to be at ease with Otto. With Vati present, or in a different way with Klara present, it would be next to impossible.

On this particular Sunday, Vati was getting together with those Party friends who didn't have families of their own. But Lotte was happy to come. While they waited for her arrival, Klara giving the final touches to the roast lamb and cabbage while Hans set the table and Hansi played on the floor of the living room, Klara fretted about Lotte. "She's more than old enough to be married, Hans. Isn't that what all your Party friends say, that a woman should keep busy with a husband and children?"

Hans could only hope Klara didn't go from trying to mother Lotte to trying to mother him. "Have you talked to her about it?"

"Oh, she always acts like everything is fine. And she does have a happy temperament, so she's good at making the best of things. But she deserves better. And she's so attractive, with that lush figure. She'd make some man a wonderful wife. Do you know someone from work, or in the Party, who might do?"

Hans preferred not to think about his little sister's "lush figure." But Klara might be right about Lotte needing a husband for her life to be complete. He finished smoothing out the napkins, inspected the table, and stepped back. "Give me a minute to see if I know someone." And he could fix himself a drink to help.

By the time Lotte showed up, carrying a basket of *Lebkuchen*, he had run through and dismissed the men at work. Of the unmarried policemen, two of them had rough manners and talked about women in a way that would oblige him to punch them if it was Lotte's name in their mouths. The third would be better, if Lotte could only take to him, but he was homely enough, with deep acne scars and a red face, that some of the others called him *Hackfresse*, mincemeat.

But there was a shop owner he'd met when he was working for Herr Rechter, still single the last time they'd met, hard-working, and nice-looking as far as Hans could tell. The shop sold children's clothes and toys, which should appeal to a young woman's maternal side, and was doing well. He could do a good man a favor and help his sister at the same time. Satisfied with his solution, he welcomed Lotte with a big smile when she arrived. Taking the basket of gingerbread, he lifted the napkin covering it, sniffed deeply, and grinned. "What a baker you've become! Any young man will be lucky to get you."

Lotte rolled her eyes. "Not you too! I suppose Klara's been working on you. You can both stop worrying. I have plenty of time to find the *right* man. Now I'm going to help Klara get dinner on the table." And she whisked herself off to the kitchen, stopping to hoist Hansi off the floor, give him a big hug and kiss, and set him back down gurgling with pleasure.

She was back out in a moment, carrying a bib and saying, "Klara wants me to get Hansi ready." She picked up the baby again and got him settled into his high chair, then fastened the bib around his neck. Admiring the domestic picture they made, Hans gave Lotte a warm smile and then went to help Klara carry the food in.

He'd been planning to wait until after dinner to tell Lotte about the shop owner, but the ease with which she'd handled Hansi, and a certain wistful expression he thought he spied as Lotte watched Hansi make mush of his food, encouraged him to speak up sooner. "Lotte, darling, there's a man I used to work with who has a shop selling toys and clothes for children. I've been meaning to stop by there and pick up some things for Hansi, and I thought you could come along and help me."

Lotte looked back and forth between Hans, Klara, and the baby and then back at Hans. "I'm glad you can get things for Hansi. It's so different from how we grew up, isn't it? But wouldn't Klara want to go with you? I'd bet she knows more about what Hansi needs, and what he likes, too." She looked at Klara again, just as Klara stopped looking confused and started looking guilty instead. "Wait a minute. This man you used to work with. Is he married?"

"As a matter of fact," Hans admitted, "no, I don't think he is. I can't think why not — he's a decent fellow, and handsome too."

Lotte put down her fork. "You're serious about this matchmaking business, aren't you? I do wish you wouldn't.

And . . . was it when you worked for that Richter fellow that you knew this man?" At his nod, she huffed and said, "So is he another one of Richter's creatures, his pet Nazis? Do you really think I'd want to marry a Nazi?"

Klara had gone a little pale and was covering her mouth with her napkin. Hans couldn't help raising his voice as he said, "And why not? Would you rather end up with some good-for-nothing from the theatre, the kind of man Otto would introduce you to?"

Lotte had gone red, in a way that made her look more like Vati than Hans had ever seen. "I suppose you've forgotten all about your friend Samuel and his sister, my dear friend Grete. But I haven't." Klara turned and stared at Hans, but Lotte was too caught up in her tirade to notice. "What do you suppose your precious Nazis would like to do to her? Should I marry a Nazi and listen to him talk about the evil, dirty Jews? And how dare you mention Otto! Do you know how long it's been since I saw him, because he doesn't want to come near what you and Vati have turned into? It's your fault that my *big* brother won't come near me!" She grabbed her own napkin and hid her face in it, bursting into sobs.

Hans knew his mouth was hanging open. In case he'd missed it, Hansi dropped his own jaw and pointed at his food-smeared mouth, giggling. Klara got up quietly, wiped Hansi's mouth and hands, and went over to Lotte, bending down to hug her and then urging her to her feet. "Here, love, you come on into the kitchen with me. I have some sherry I keep in the cupboard there. We'll sit at the kitchen table and have a little drink to help you calm down. We can leave Hans to look after the baby for a bit." She threw Hans a glare as she led Lotte out of the room.

Hans grabbed his fork and knife, cut himself a huge wedge of potato, stuffed it in his mouth, and narrowly escaped choking on it. Why was his wife blaming him, when she'd been the one to wind him up about Lotte in the first place? Wasn't that just like a woman! Well, he was damned if he'd have anymore to do with it. If Klara wanted Lotte married off, she could go and find the right man herself.

Was Otto really as opposed to the Nazis as Lotte claimed? How would she know, if he 'wouldn't come near her'? Maybe she was just assuming it, to make herself feel better about Otto being a bad brother. Whether it was true or not, Hans was just glad no one else had been at dinner to hear how Lotte talked. Why couldn't she forget about Samuel and Grete, the way he had? And mouthing off about the Party . . . it was the sort of thing those policemen had done, that had lost them their jobs. What would happen to a woman? He didn't know. But he didn't want Lotte to find out.

Either the sherry or a bit of mothering from Klara soothed Lotte enough that once they emerged from the kitchen, the evening continued without anymore drama. Once Lotte had gone home and Klara had put Hansi to bed, they started on the dishes. Klara washed, Hans dried, and neither of them was saying anything. Finally Hans steeled himself and asked, "Were you, ah, startled by what Lotte said about her friend Grete?"

Klara carefully put down the plate she'd been washing and turned toward him. "And your friend Samuel? Yes. I didn't know what to think. That's how you knew what my family's flat used to look like?"

Hans nodded.

"How did it happen? Did you not know, at first, that they were Jews?"

Standing in the kitchen, holding a dish towel, Hans pulled the memories out of the past: how he had gone looking for Jews at school, and everything that followed. While he talked, Klara went back to washing the dishes, if slowly, and handed them to Hans to dry. Hans finished the tale just before all the dishes were done.

Klara stood there studying his face, maybe looking for signs she had missed, signs of unreliable morals or outright treachery. She asked quietly, "Did you try to stay friends – to write to him? Did you know where they'd gone?"

All he could think of to say was, "I didn't ask."

That night, Hans dreamed he was a boy again, visiting a friend and the friend's sister. He knew them, and he knew he knew them, but he couldn't remember their names. It didn't really matter for anything they were doing, the games they were playing, the way they talked to each other, but still, he should know their names. He woke up before he'd decided whether to ask. He must have made some unhappy sound, or twitched, because Klara stirred in her sleep and reached for him. He moved closer against her, and retreated into sleep as soon as he could. He was lucky this time, and didn't dream.

Lotte had quit her teaching job. She hadn't told him why, but Hans guessed the school was now teaching subjects and lessons the Nazis favored, and Lotte was too stubborn to go along. Hans would have asked the man with the toy shop whether he needed a helper, but Lotte might turn that job down too. He waited and worried for weeks until she told him she'd found work in a dress shop, helping women choose flattering dresses and learning sewing when business was slow.

As for Otto, Hans had no idea how he was earning his keep these days. It wasn't likely Vati would support him, given what Vati thought of his lifestyle, and the kind of parts he'd had in the theatre wouldn't bring in enough to pay for food between parts, let alone lodging. He might be imposing on friends, probably one after another as people got sick of it.

He might be doing worse. Hans could only hope whatever Otto was doing wasn't actually illegal, or that if it was, Hans wouldn't be called upon to arrest him.

But a couple of weeks before Easter 1934, for the first time in his life, Hans received a letter from his brother. Or rather, an envelope, in which he found an announcement: a theatre company he'd actually heard of would be presenting a play by British playwright Oscar Wilde (presumably translated), opening night to be three days from now. The announcement included a partial cast list, including the four most important roles, and the part of Lord Windermere, a husband accused of infidelity, would be played by Otto Schäfer. Hans looked in the envelope again in case tickets were enclosed, but found nothing.

He could easily enough buy tickets for himself and Klara. And for Lotte — surely she'd want to go. He had better hurry and invite her. He and Klara and Lotte could go together . . . and Hans could make sure Otto didn't try to introduce their sister to anyone of dubious character.

As the three of them stood in the lobby waiting for the house to open, snatches of conversation from the crowd around them drifted over. Hans had no special desire to eavesdrop, but neither did he find Klara's and Lotte's discussion of the best shop for inexpensive shoes, and the desirability of something called a "pillbox" hat, of much interest, so he sampled what he heard around him. He noticed one exchange between two young men, both dressed in somewhat shabby clothes that appeared to date from the mid-twenties, because one of the men was airing his opinion more loudly and the other was trying to hush him. The louder one was saying that some other actor had been better in the part of — he almost turned toward the men when he recognized the name "Lord Windermere." The other man was soothing him, saying that directors had their notions about what mattered, and this director must have had some reason or other. The complaining man snorted and said, "You know damn well why they dropped him! And what proof did they have that he was Jewish, anyway? His name isn't, is it!"

Now it was the other man's turn to scoff. "You know how actors are, changing names to change their fortunes. A few months ago, it might've been Abramowitz."

The loud man got louder. Hans wasn't the only one listening now. "And you call yourself a lover of theatre! I've been following him for years!"

This was becoming a disturbance. And if Otto didn't already know who'd had the part before him, this wouldn't be the time to find out, right before he had to go on stage. Hans moved closer to the two men and said quietly, "Pardon me for intruding. But you're becoming disruptive." Both of them turned on him, their quarrel forgotten, and he made haste to say, "I am a member of the *Schutzpolizei*. I would prefer not to spoil the occasion for the other patrons by arresting you, nor to miss the performance myself in order to take you to the station. Please control yourselves."

The two men drew closer together like nervous children and stared up at him. He'd expected them to argue with him, and had just hoped they wouldn't start a fight, but they had no fight in them, after all. He returned to Klara and Lotte, Klara beaming proudly at him. Lotte looked at him as if she had never properly seen him before.

Call Otto her *big* brother, would she, and Hans something less? Now she could see more clearly. Between her brother the actor, when he was that, and her brother the policeman, she could know where respect was due.

Otto did a fine job, better than when Hans had seen him before. After the curtain calls, while most people were leaving, the three of them and other similar groups made their way backstage. A party was going on, with Schnaps and cheap wine and what looked like day-old biscuits, several of the men and two of the women smoking hand-rolled cigarettes. In spite of all the trappings of celebration, some of the actors seemed less than comfortable with each other, though Otto was grinning and drinking as two of the others slapped him on the back and congratulated him. Hans and Klara and Lotte joined this little circle, praising his performance and in Hans' case, taking a swig from the bottle they were passing around. Lotte, as if trying to make up for having let Hans impress her, made a point of gushing on and on about his skill and stage presence. Hans was thinking about pulling the women away and heading home when Klara asked, "It's your biggest part so far, isn't it? How did you get it?"

The chatter and laughter in the room didn't stop all at once, but most of it did, and then the few oblivious actors and guests still carrying on realized that everyone else had stopped, and so did they. If Hans had thought Klara heard the gossiping men outside and knew what she was saying, her wide eyes and the sudden tension in her shoulders told him otherwise.

Lotte was looking down at the floor. She must have heard what Hans had. Maybe the way she'd been flattering Otto had been her way of saying it didn't matter, that it wasn't his fault, that she was still happy for him.

Otto glared at Klara, who shrank back and half hid behind Hans. He snarled, "What difference does it make! Do you think I get so many good parts that I can just say 'No, thanks all the same' when one comes along?"

Hans whispered in Klara's ear, "I'll explain it all once we get out of here." Turning back to Otto, he said stiffly, "Thank you for inviting us. You did a good job. We'll be going now."

Lotte hung back long enough to dart at Otto and give him a hug before they headed for the front of the house. As they neared the door, Hans heard the talk, and then the laughter, gradually resume behind them.

Chapter 22

Summer – Late Autumn 1934

When Hans got to work on the first Monday in July, he found three of his fellow policemen huddled over a newspaper. His height let him look over their shoulders without crowding them, though he couldn't see the entire page. But he saw enough to send him stumbling to the nearest bench in dismay. Dozens of people in the SA — at high levels of the SA — had been killed, shot or stabbed, by members of the Party, Hitler's elite SS, under Hitler's orders! And hundreds had been arrested!

He got back up and stood again behind the three men, reading further. What came next gave him a different kind of shock. There had been socialists, Communists, and degenerates in the SA? This group to which he belonged, whose uniform he kept clean and pressed in his closet, had been rotten at the core?

If all this were true, such a purge had been long overdue, and he could only give thanks that it had come at last. But where he had longed to find certainty he now saw confusion, fog and swamps where he had thought he stood on firm ground.

He'd expected Vati to be just as shocked as he was, but Vati now claimed he'd known all along. "It's a grand new beginning, my boy! All the traitors are getting what's coming to them, and now we can march forward united into the great era to come."

Hans could only hope things were that straightforward and simple. "I can always use the brown shirt for any dirty jobs around the house," he muttered, more to himself than to Vati. But Vati snapped, "Don't talk nonsense! The SA will be better than ever! You keep that shirt as clean and tidy as you always have, and don't let me hear talk like that again."

All the same, though Hans still received invitations from Herr Richter from time to time, or saw the man at the Party bar when he condescended to go there, he no longer passed along any SA assignments. After a few weeks, Hans moved his SA uniform to the back of his closet. He had a better uniform these days, and he would wear it with pride.

Hans was pleased to hear, one gray day in November, that the season would be enlivened by a "Day of the German Police," actually spread over two days that coming December. He was, however, stunned and embarrassed to be ordered to report to a photographer, who would use him as a model for one of the posters to be displayed before and during the event.

The photographer had several poses in mind for Hans and the other two policemen who showed up for this duty. One would be directing traffic amid converging cars aiming in his direction; one would be racing after a masked robber, a hooked nose visible despite the mask, holding a bulging bag out of which a diamond necklace peeked; and one would be holding a child's hand on the front step of a modest flat, smiling at a relieved mother wearing an apron. Hans must have startled when the photographer got to that part of the list, because the man looked at him with an eyebrow lifted. "That one appeals to you?"

Actually, Hans would rather have been the athletic policeman about to lay hands on the robber. But he could hardly deny the way things had come full circle. He said meekly, "If you think best, sir."

Hans had had hopes of taking part in one of the boxing exhibitions, and had only learned otherwise the day before. He was still nursing his disappointment and resentment when he reported for duty on December 18th and was assigned his red and white collection can. Apparently all the policemen taking part would be competing to bring in the highest amount of donations for the Winter Relief Fund, and those organizing the Day would not be pleased by any but the most diligent effort. The man distributing the cans took pains to point out to each policeman the small hole toward the top, labeled *Papiergeld*, for rolled-up bills. "If a child drops a coin in one of the coin slots, look happy and thank them. If an adult holds a coin ready to do the same, say something like, 'Sir, Ma'am, can't you find it in your heart to give a little more for the children who will be cold this winter?" and point to the hole for paper."

Like beggars, Hans thought in disgust. He was all for helping children get through the winter — he hadn't forgotten their own flat, not much better than being on the street on the coldest days with no coal — but surely there were plenty of civilians, plenty of women, who could do the begging. As he stomped toward his assigned street corner, something tugged on his coat, and a child's voice said, "What's wrong, Herr Policeman? You looked so much happier in the picture!"

He looked down and saw a boy about five or six, a woman who must be his mother running up behind and looking flustered. The boy glanced over his shoulder, sidled closer to Hans, and said in a rush, "I want to be a policeman just like you when I grow up! Can I put something in your collecting can?"

Hans stood very straight, but still felt more relaxed than he had since arriving. He smiled at the boy and said, "I felt just the same when I was your age — and here I am! I hope the same happens for you. Do you have a coin for me?" He bent over to make it easier for the boy, who reached a grubby hand into his pocket, brought out a ten Pfennig coin, and proudly dropped it in.

"Thank you so much! The children who might have been cold and hungry this winter thank you!" Hans saluted the boy, whose eyes went wide. As Hans walked away, he could hear the boy say, "Mama! Mama, did you see? The policeman saluted me! I'm going to be just like him someday."

Hans moved on with a spring in his step, smiling at the people he passed, pausing every few steps to wave his can around and call, "Donations, donations? Help your fellow citizens! Help keep Berlin warm this winter!" He'd collected more coins and a couple of bills by the time he reached the corner where he would spend the rest of the morning.

It got harder to stay upbeat when he heard the cheers for whoever had just won one of the sports competitions. But he perked up when one of the policemen on horseback rode up, reined his horse in, and saluted, saying, "I see how busy you are, how many donations you're getting! Your station is sure to win the competition for the most money collected."

Hans grinned at him. "I'll do my best to make sure of it!"

At midday, another policeman relieved him and helpfully told him where the best sandwich cart had set up and where the speeches were being given. Hans treated himself to two *Fischbrötchen* sandwiches and, one in each hand, went to hear what was being said to fire up the crowd. As he walked up, a sergeant was proclaiming, " . . . like our brothers in decades past! Like them, it is our joyful duty to fight the Communists who would undermine our leaders, sap our willpower, and divide our citizens! And all of you defy them in your turn, as you sacrifice to ensure that your fellows will not suffer from the season that bears down upon us . . . ."

Hans' mood improved further when he passed a pretty young girl kneeling on the ground between two tall dogs around whose necks someone had placed collection cans. She was charming the passing crowd by speaking for the dogs in her version of a dog's voice, asking them to help keep their masters warm, or pleading on behalf of all the dogs who might suffer from the cold if not for their generosity. As he walked by, she interrupted her performance and cried out happily, "And there's the policeman on the poster! How fine you looked, helping that poor child. Have you helped many such children?"

He would have preferred another question. He had never had occasion to do that. But he vowed then and there to seek out any children who appeared lost or confused, in order to live up to his new reputation.

When he resumed his place on the corner, he was soon rewarded with the sight of Klara, pushing Hansi in his pram. He would have liked to greet her properly, but his duty prevented it. It did not, however, prevent her from joining the small group surrounding him, giving Hansi a coin, and lifting him out of the pram so he could drop it in the can and laugh in delight. Hans took off his helmet and bowed to Klara, saying solemnly, "Thank you, madam, for your generosity and that of your son."

Klara gave him a dazzling smile. "You're most welcome, Officer. What lovely manners you have! Your wife must be a very lucky woman." And with that, she tucked Hansi back in his carriage and walked on, leaving Hans struggling to suppress his laughter.

The visit from Klara and Hansi, the inspiring speech emphasizing the continuity of the police force, and the comments from people who had seen his poster had him so cheerful, for the rest of that afternoon, that people seemed to flock to him to share in his feeling. By the time he returned to the station with his collection can, it was so full, heavy with coins and with a bill sticking out of the *Papiergeld* hole, that he doubted any other policeman could match it.

His earlier disappointment at his assigned role had been premature and short-sighted. It should be a lesson, he told himself, to have more faith in those in authority above him.

Chapter 23

Late Winter 1935 – Winter 1936

In the middle of March, 1935, Vati stopped by in the evening brimming with news. Hans had only to start asking what it was about for Vati to spill out his excitement. "Herr Goebbels will be making a major announcement at the Sports Palace tomorrow! This is a day that will finally begin to undo the terrible injustices inflicted on Germany by that cursed Treaty. Will you come with me to hear him?"

The next day was a Saturday. "How can I go hear a speech on a working day?"

Vati laughed. "You can be sure that the police will be allowed to attend!"

Klara, bouncing Hansi in her arms and crooning to him, interrupted herself to say, "It may be a very . . . *lively* crowd. Hansi and I will stay at home, and you can tell me all about it later."

Saturday proved how accurate Klara's prediction had been. The stomping, cheering crowd could not contain itself; even though Herr Goebbels' deep, resonant voice seemed to come from a far larger man, they sometimes drowned him out. But straining to his utmost, Hans did hear him explain that Germany was introducing military conscription and would create an army almost five times the size the Versailles Treaty had decreed. He exclaimed,

Whereas Germany completely fulfilled her obligations under the Treaty, other powers had one-sidedly released themselves from their obligations, leaving Germany exposed . . . . Indeed, far from even remaining at a standstill, the armaments of a number of countries had increased. Countries were perfecting machinery of destruction . . . . Germany . . . is defenselessly exposed to every threat and menace . . . . Henceforth defense will be entrusted to Germany's own power! . . . Thus the dead are honored and the living guaranteed security. In this hour we bow before the Fatherland's greatness. Long live the Führer!

Hans could not have resisted the crowd's excitement if he'd tried, and he had no mind to try. At last the great betrayal would be undone! Vati, cheering himself hoarse, had tears in his eyes. When the proclamation ended and people started streaming out, Vati pulled him aside and seized him in the tightest embrace Hans could remember. When he let go, he seemed at a loss for words, and even a little disoriented, as if he could hardly tell whether he was awake or dreaming. Hans gently led him home.

Later, telling Klara about it, he confessed to her that his feelings were mixed, his rejoicing tempered by shame that as a policeman, he would apparently not be among those called upon to serve. Klara planted her hands on her hips and scolded him for such thoughts, reminding him, "You men of the Police have been serving the Reich right along! You're even part of the army now, aren't you?"

"Well, yes," Hans admitted. But — "

"But nothing! You should be just as proud as any new recruit stumbling around in too-big boots!"

Hans had to laugh at the image. Hansi clapped his hands in glee.

Hans had naturally made friends on the force. He sometimes went out with them to a bar after work, though not as often as he would have if not for Klara waiting at home with dinner and a kiss, and Hansi eager to play with his "Vati" after a long day without seeing him. Now and then they would invite one of these work companions over, or be invited to their flats. It was beginning to look like Gerhard, one of their newest recruits who'd come from somewhere in Austria, might become a friend. Gerhard was a boxer, and better than Hans, with a special coach and the goal of making it to that summer's Olympics. His training regimen, stricter than Hans was willing to live by, kept him from spending time at bars, but they had started grabbing coffee together on some of their midday breaks.

One Saturday a few weeks into 1936, Gerhard passed by Hans in the hallway and muttered, "Join me for a beer after work? I think I'm due one. It's been a rough week."

As Gerhard didn't seem inclined to stop and talk, Hans turned and walked with him, saying, "I could do with a beer, but I won't have time for more than one. At the beer hall down the street?"

Gerhard just barely shook his head, and named a bar Hans hadn't heard of. "It's in Wörtherplatz. I'll meet you there." And then he sped up and walked away, leaving Hans wondering just what was going on, and whether he should think of Gerhard as a future friend after all.

The bar was somewhere between crowded and full. If Hans had been much shorter, he'd have had trouble spotting Gerhard at a table in the farthest corner from the door, with a pitcher and two glasses already in front of him. Hans pushed his way through to join him, saying apologetically, "I'd buy the next pitcher, but I shouldn't stay that long. The wife at home, you know." He half expected Gerhard to make some comment about apron strings, but the man only nodded and waited for Hans to sit down.

Hans poured his beer, drank, and leaned across the table to be heard above the noise. "What do you think of this place? Is it a favorite of yours?"

Gerhard shrugged. "A neighbor suggested it. A bit loud, but the beer's good." Hans hadn't noticed until that comment, but Gerhard had already drunk half his beer. He must have been quite a drinker before his coach reined him in.

Gerhard took another swig and said, "A tough week. I hope they're not all like that here." He paused, picked up the pitcher, and refilled his glass to the brim.

At this rate, Hans might not get the whole story before he had to leave. "I haven't found them so. What made this one such a trial?"

Gerhard looked up at him, his glance suddenly keen. "You know about all sorts of Jewish professionals having to stop practicing their professions?"

"Well, yes. But how would you get mixed up in that? Don't they go quietly?"

Gerhard slurped the foam off his glass and drank before answering. "I guess most of them do. One didn't. He'd been the head of his tax consulting practice. He should have stepped down, but he wouldn't go. He said he'd hired most of the others and worked for big, important companies, and how dare some jumped-up bureaucrats try to take his profession away from him, and so on. So they called us, and I got the job of prying him out of his office like a fox from his hole."

Hans shook his head and took a small sip. "You'd think a professional man would have more dignity. But I suppose Jews don't value dignity so much."

Gerhard forced a chuckle. "I should have known a tax consultant would talk my ear off — they're almost like lawyers, aren't they? He kept going on about how his family had lived in 'this very city' for centuries — 'longer than yours, my lad!', he must have noticed my accent — and how he'd served in the War. He claimed he'd even won a medal, not that he could show it to me when I asked . . . why did you jump?"

Hans had indeed started enough to slosh his beer in the glass. "You just reminded me of something I heard long ago. Do you think he'd really been given a medal?"

"I don't know what to think. And that reminds me. He kept going on about how he'd always been a true and loyal German, and his father before him, and *his* father before that. Was he simply lying, do you think?"

Hans' beer was almost gone. He nodded sagely and said, "People can convince themselves of almost anything. He might think he was a good German. Or he could have been lying . . . ." A thought struck him, suddenly enough that he put his glass down with a clunk. "Or he could, ever since the Army even, have been working with enemies of the Reich. It could have been such an enemy who gave him his medal, to poison the ranks of those who received honors."

Gerhard had been studying the bottom of his glass, but now he looked up at Hans, relieved. "That could be it. It just goes to show how dangerous it would be to leave Jews in influential positions. Our leaders are wise."

Hans drained his glass and stood up to go, bidding Gerhard farewell. As he hurried home to Klara, he felt edgy and unsettled. There was no reason to feel that way. He had come up with a good explanation, one that satisfied Gerhard. It should satisfy him as well. And if not, he'd be better off not thinking about it too much. Thinking wasn't his job, after all.

But he would have been glad of a boxing match to work off his inconvenient attack of nerves. He walked faster instead.

Chapter 24

Early Spring 1936 – Early Spring 1937

The news came in March that Chancellor Hitler had taken the daring move of sending armed troops into the Rhineland, pried from Germany's possession after the war. Vati, of course, crowed about Hitler's manly determination to restore Germany's standing in the world. Not everyone took the matter so well: Klara fretted and even dissolved in tears, recalling every story Hans had told her about the city's wartime hardships. Throughout Berlin, there was an air of people holding their breath, waiting to see what might befall them.

But in the end, nothing much happened. Apparently the past few years of firm policies had intimidated their enemies enough, or the war had drained their energy and resources enough, that they had no mind to make trouble. The only response, mainly in the United States but in Great Britain and a few other countries as well, was to talk of refusing to attend the 1936 Olympics. Hans was inclined to think this would be their loss and nothing to worry about, but Herr Richter, in one of their now-rare encounters, disagreed. "These Games are a great opportunity to show the world what Germany has already achieved, how great it is becoming! We're the ones who will look like fools if this boycott movement grows. There's even talk of rival Olympic Games in Spain. That must not happen!"

In the end, however, opposition to the Berlin Games collapsed. Spain, of all places, started fighting a civil war between those supporting a fascist government and communist-led rebels. No one could keep pretending it was the place to gather the world's athletes for the vigorous but peaceful competition of sport. All could go on as planned.

In mid-June, all the men in the precinct were called together to hear the announcement that Herr Himmler had been appointed Chief of Police. The new chief had a plan: all the police precincts would be controlled by a central office and would be divided into two forces, the Order Police and the Security Police. The former would concentrate on many tasks, from controlling traffic to finding and arresting ordinary criminals. Only the Security Police would have the greater function — here Constable Volker, reading from the announcement, raised an eyebrow — of finding and hunting down the greater enemies of the Reich, such as Jews.

A man standing next to Hans asked eagerly, "Will we be in the Security Police, fighting such enemies?"

The constable seemed less than pleased with the question, but answered, "For now, all of you have plenty to do, doing what we have always done. But I will inquire how you can apply to the Security Police, if you like."

The man turned to Hans, elbowed him, and said, "Want to apply with me? We could go on working together!" But he was not one of Hans' favorite members of the force, so Hans said something noncommittal and turned away.

Enthusiasm for the coming Olympic Games swept the city as summer came. A gigantic new sports center was under construction, complete with a stadium and a luxurious village for the athletes soon to converge on Berlin from all over the world. Hotels were being remodeled and new ones built. Anyone who could bear to be away from Berlin during the Games was spreading the word that their flat — always, according to them, comfortable and ideally situated — could be rented for August 1st through 16th. Hans considered taking the family to the country and earning perhaps twice what the trip would cost — but Hansi was so excited about all the athletes and competitions that Hans couldn't think of tearing him away. Not that Hans would be able to afford tickets, even just for Klara and Hansi since he'd almost certainly be on duty. It was vital that the city be at its best, its cleanest and safest as well as its most impressive, for the athletes and journalists and dignitaries and the rest.

Walking his beat one day in mid-July, he noticed a man in working clothes roughly tearing down a poster that looked to be in perfectly good condition. Was the poster obsolete, announcing some past event, despite looking new? Or was the man vandalizing it? He came closer, wishing for a moment that he wore the police uniform of his boyhood, complete with truncheon, instead of the military-style uniform adopted since. He would have enjoyed twirling a truncheon as he faced potential criminals.

The man snapped to attention and said, "Good day, *Offizier!*" He didn't shuffle his feet, look over his shoulder, or otherwise show any signs of guilt. Instead, he looked somewhere between puzzled and intrigued.

"Why are you tearing down that poster?"

The man started to sneer, then apparently changed his mind at the wisdom of doing so. "Orders. The highers-up don't want the visitors seeing any signs or posters about the

Jews. We have to act like we're fine with Jews running all over the place like rats, until all the foreigners go away again."

Hans had been too busy studying the man to note the contents of the poster. Not all of it remained on the wall, but he could still make out the words "Jewish Enemies of the Reich Not Welcome!"

"Very well. You may continue your work." Hans continued his circuit of the block. As he walked, he looked for any signs or posters like the one the man had been tearing down. He saw none, on that block or the next, or anywhere downtown.

The walls looked a little bare, compared to what he was used to. But the Party had greater goals than decorating walls. Other countries must be placated while Germany continued to grow in strength.

That must be why he felt more at ease with the signs gone. There could be no other reason a good German would feel any such relief.

The Games would begin in just a few days. New posters had replaced the prohibited ones, showing muscular men and women, mostly blond with blue eyes, posed as if they were ancient Athenians throwing the javelin or the discus or running a race. He had not been chosen, this time, to model for a poster. It was just as well — the men had only just gotten tired of teasing him about the last time.

Now it was time for Hans and the other police to receive their assignments. Volker pointed to each of them, calling out their tasks for the next two weeks. "Koch — patrolling the Olympic Village. Jäger — stadium security. Schäfer — traffic control."

Hans went home that night prepared to grumble to Klara about it. "Directing traffic!" he announced as he walked in the door. "The most important event for years to come, where it's absolutely essential to keep all the athletes and visitors safe, and they've got me impersonating a traffic light!"

Klara came to him and gave him a hug. "But darling, that means you'll be right there, in the thick of it. Who knows what famous people you may see? And you'll see the new buildings and stadiums and all, right up close."

Hans' spirits lifted considerably when he learned that one of his duties would be to hold back the crowds while a runner carried a torch, the torch brought by one runner after another all the way from Greece, to light the Olympic flame. No Olympics had conceived such a grand project, ever in history!

His assigned stretch of street was along Heerstraße. The runner, a tall blond man about Hans' age, somehow managed to run while holding his body as straight as if he were standing at attention. The torch flamed and smoked, and the crowd pressed toward the front, cheering and waving. Hans planted himself in place, resisting the push from behind. What if he fell in front of the runner, and the runner tripped, and the torch went out! But he held firm as he drank in the sight of the runner, moving steadily down the street, tall and proud. Hans caught just a glance of his face, exalted as if gazing at some glory beyond, as he passed by.

A little while later, Hans heard the distant roar as the crowd in the stadium welcomed first the athletes marching in and then — at least for the Germans attending — Chancellor Hitler. He could hear more cheers about once a minute as Hitler gave his speech. Hans couldn't help being curious, though he knew the speech would be in the papers later. And after all, he'd heard Hitler speak before . . . though, if the removal of the anti-Jewish posters provided any clue, this speech would have some important differences from what Hitler would have said on some other occasion.

Klara was thrilled, and a little envious, to hear about his day, especially the torch runner. She oohed and aahed over Hans' white coat, issued specially for those handling Olympic traffic. "How fine you look!"

Hans could just imagine what his fellows on the force would have to say about it. "What sort of police uniform has to be kept clean? I look like a china doll."

The other policemen made the sort of comments he'd predicted. He took it with good humor at first, even offering up the china-doll comparison. When a couple of them kept needling him, however, he growled, "Try me, and you'll find I don't break as easily. Do you want to see?"

He went home still worked up, and with plenty of pent-up energy. Klara managed to soothe his temper without wasting the energy. It could well have been that night, he later calculated, that he gave Klara their second child.

Overseeing the traffic between the different competition areas, Hans had plenty of opportunity to catch glimpses of visitors. Some came in their national costume; others dressed in what looked very much like high fashion in Berlin. They all looked wealthy, naturally, or they could not have afforded tickets, let alone travel. Hans also saw the sort of shocking behavior that had been common during the years of the Weimar Republic, but thankfully rare since. When he commented on it in the squad room one evening, another man rolled his eyes and said, "It's more of this coddling of foreigners. Can't upset the deviants, apparently. Keep them comfortable, let them think there's nothing about Germany that's really any different from whatever cesspit they came from."

Throughout the games and afterward, whenever Hans saw Vati or, once, Herr Richter, they overflowed with triumph and glee. "We've shown the world!" Herr Richter exulted. "They're all seeing a strong, reborn, united Germany! They'll know better now than to think they can walk all over us, grind us under, treat us as a nation of rabble and sheep!" If they were showing the world a somewhat unreal version of the new Germany, hiding some aspects of its rebirth, Herr Richter seemed untroubled by it.

When Hans relayed those comments to Vati, Vati agreed completely. He added, with a sly wink, "And when all these weak-minded tender-hearted foreigners depart, we can go back to dealing with the Jews."

The government waited a week after the Olympics ended, possibly for all the foreign reporters to leave town. And then, as Vati had predicted, the signs and posters went back up, more than before.

In March of 1937, Constable Volker called them together to tell them about a major operation. Thousands of criminals who had been convicted, but, for whatever reason, not yet imprisoned, were to be cleaned off the streets and sent to a series of camps in other parts of Germany, relieving the citizens of Berlin of the burden of supporting them. "You'll need to be on your toes, men. Some of these miscreants will not go quietly. You'll be well armed. We begin tomorrow morning, so stay out of the bars tonight and show up bright and early!"

The next day was the most exciting Hans had spent in years. He raced after and caught three different criminals and singlehandedly wrestled one would-be escapee to the ground, collecting a black eye and almost-sprained wrist in the process. He felt as if his work and his boxing pastime had come together in heaven-sent union, and boasted happily to Klara afterward, while she sponged at his eye with oil of comfrey dissolved in water and checked the bandage on his wrist, taking it off and putting it back on to be sure it was just the right tightness. Her response to him that night made him think of heroes welcomed back from battle.

When the operation ended, it took a while for all of them to be content with the usual routine. Volker tried to amuse them by describing the stark conditions of the camps to which the criminals had been sent. He added with a laugh that the criminals would now have jobs perfectly suited to them. "They'll be set up as guards on new criminals and other undesirables. No coddling those!"

"Undesirables?" asked one of the newer recruits. Hans had wondered, but he rather thought he knew.

Sure enough, Volker said with a poker face, "Gypsies, Jews, Communists, sexual deviants. Undesirables."

A few weeks later, Herr Richter invited Hans and Klara to one of his social evenings. There would be a string quartet, the finest wines, and massive quantities of food. Hans expected Klara to stay home, big as she'd become, but she insisted on coming along, saying, "With a baby at home, who knows when I'll get a chance to go *anywhere*, let alone a party like this?" Lotte agreed to babysit in exchange for any leftovers they could carry away with them.

Herr Richter seemed particularly elated as he welcomed them in. "Come in, my boy, my dear Klara! Come and share my good fortune! What are good times for, if not to share with friends?"

Klara accepted two glasses of champagne from a waiter navigating the crowd, handed one to Hans, and toasted the prince with the other. "To your good fortune, then! Is it anything you can tell us, or is it some complicated business secret?"

Herr Richter called the waiter back to get himself a fresh glass and make sure Hans' glass wasn't yet empty. "I can certainly tell you! No one better than our Hans to appreciate it. After all, my lad, you knew all about all my different shops and other establishments back before the police lured you away. Thought I had plenty of them, didn't you? But now I've added half again as many!"

Hans remembered not only the various shops, but the books kept by most of them. The overall collection had been profitable, but something new must have happened for Herr Richter to be able to afford such an expansion. He paused to find the best wording and then said, "That must have taken plenty of planning. How long have you been getting ready?"

Herr Richter gestured as if waving away the very thought of long-range plans. "Not a bit of it! I just kept my ear to the ground. You know how many friends I have, in all sorts of useful places. They kept me up to date on which Jewish businesses would be confiscated, before the word got around more generally. I could be first in line to scoop them up! Bargain rates, of course — beggars and Jews, I say, can't be choosers."

Hans gulped down the rest of his glass. He hadn't made much time for prayer in years, but as he looked around at the party and the guests eating their fill, Herr Richter urging them to heap dainties on their plates, he gave thanks that neither he nor his father owned one of those shops. Or was, of course, a Jew.

Chapter 25

Spring - Summer 1937

It was hard for Hans to believe, when he and Hansi played silly games or went for walks, or when Hansi asked him all sorts of questions about his police work, that Hans might have had games and walks and conversations like this with his own father when he was little. He remembered almost nothing about Vati from before the war, and yet Vati must have all sorts of memories of that time, just as Hans would. Unless Vati had ignored him and left it up to Mutti to talk to him, play with him, care for him.

Had anyone held his hand and walked with him to a candy shop, as he was walking with Hansi to the ice cream store? During the war, the thought of candy, ice cream, anything with sugar had become an impossible dream. Did Hansi realize he was growing up in a better time, a better Germany?

Hans must once have asked someone — Vati, Mutti, Otto, Aunt Gertrud — about the baby Mutti was carrying, the baby who would be Lotte. But he couldn't remember what he had asked or what they had answered, and now it was his turn. Even the thought of their destination wasn't enough to distract Hansi from the strange, mysterious change coming to the family. The question he asked most often, probably because he didn't like the answer, was, "Will I have a brother or a sister?"

Tired of explaining that he didn't know, that no one knew, that no one could find out ahead of time, Hans tried a different tack. "Whichever it is, we'll be counting on you to be a good big brother. I've been a big brother, so I can help you."

Hansi wrinkled his forehead. "You were Aunt Lotte's big brother?"

"That's right." He almost said that Hansi could ask Lotte whether Hans had been a good big brother, but then thought better of it.

Hansi started skipping as they approached the ice cream store. Hans gripped his hand tighter to make sure he didn't get loose. Hansi squeezed back and asked, "If I have a sister, will she be like Aunt Lotte?"

Hans thought back to Lotte as a little girl, all wild curls and busy arms and legs, and found he was smiling. "She might be. Or like Mutti." Klara was sturdy and strong. Her daughter should be also.

Hansi giggled and said, "Maybe she'll be like Uncle Otto!"

Hans opened his mouth and closed it again. A girl who insisted on defying conventions, mingling with riff-raff? A girl who listened to nobody, who cared nothing for having a home and family? What a nightmare! But he could hardly say that to Hansi. Instead, he asked, "Will you have chocolate again? Or try something new, like . . . herring ice cream?"

There, now. That was a better reason for giggles.

It was a strange time, waiting for their family to change. His work required him to be strong, firm in the face of turmoil, but without realizing it, he had grown used to coming home and relying on Klara for reassurance and support. Now, he needed to be the strong family anchor, with Klara so close to her time, and with Hansi needing so much explanation and reassurance. When Hansi held up his arms to be carried and Klara had to explain that she could no longer pick him up, he would cry as if his heart was broken unless Hans quickly swooped down to hoist him high in the air. There were times he wanted to scold Hansi, to tell him he needed to be a big boy now. But deep down, he understood.

And then, one night in early May, Klara was crying out in the darkness, and Hans and Hansi were running to fetch the midwife. And then Hans was pacing the floor, with Hansi crying again because of the terrible noises coming from the bed where Klara lay. And then, finally, Klara was propped up on all their pillows, exhausted but beaming, holding the tiny bundle that was their daughter, and Hansi was staring agog at his new little sister.

They named her Emma, after his mother. Klara generously agreed that as she still had her own mother in her life, they could name their first daughter after his mother instead. Telling Hansi where the baby's name came from, he found himself remembering stories he'd forgotten, stories from the better times, and of his mother's kindness in the bad times. He had never told even Klara those stories, and she was glad to hear them, and he to honor his Mutti's memory in the telling.

This new world in which he found himself stayed steady, or somehow gave him the gift of being so. On those days when his work got under his skin, it was easier to remember what he owed not just to his fellow policemen and his city, but to the woman and little boy and baby girl awaiting him at home.

Years ago, as soon as there were plenty of trains and enough coal to fuel them, their relatives in the country had invited Lotte to come visit and see all the people she'd lived with during the war. She had had such a warm welcome and such a satisfying visit that she went back every year, if she could make it happen. This time, she wanted Klara to go with her. "Hans and his father, and the upstairs relatives, and my parents, can look after Hansi. Emma is healthy enough to travel, don't you think? Who knows when you'll get another chance to meet this part of Hans' family? They're such lovely people. And the country is beautiful, and the air so fresh — wonderful for Emma! — and we can finally spend some real time together. And I hear the Strength Through Joy program is putting on theater performances on buses in different country villages, so we might get to see one with the family. Do come!"

Lotte didn't seem to consider it necessary to ask Hans how he felt about this plan, let alone get his permission. But Klara did ask, promising to accept his decision while making plain that she wanted the chance to know his sister better.

So off the two of them went, baby Emma in tow, telling Hans they would miss him while bubbling with excitement over the trip they had chosen to make. Hans saw them off on a Sunday morning, delivered Hansi to Klara's parents, took a long and unsatisfying walk, and spent the evening in a bar. The bar had a radio, playing light music frequently interrupted by government announcements and slogans. It took another two evenings spent the same way to convince him that it wasn't worth having to work with a hangover the next day, and didn't make the flat less empty when he stumbled home. After that, he picked Hansi up after work each night and filled the time playing with him, reading to him, chatting with him — and, of course, making their dinner, cleaning their dishes, getting Hansi to bed and trying to keep him there. And comforting him when he cried for his

Mutti, reassuring him that Mutti would be home soon, that she hadn't gone away forever. Was that a normal thing for a boy to fear? Had someone told him how his grandmother had gone away forever when his father was a boy?

All in all, it was with gratitude as well as relief that two weeks after Lotte and Klara's departure, Hans took Hansi to meet the train. Holding the eager Hansi's hand tight, he breathed deep for what felt like the first time in weeks as he saw Klara and Lotte step down from the train, one after another, Klara cradling Emma. The baby seemed to have grown in just those two weeks, and her rosy cheeks and energy suggested the trip had done her no harm. A man followed them so closely that Hans went on alert, ready to seize the man if he was bothering them or had worse intentions.

But then Lotte grabbed the man's hand and tugged him toward Hans and Hansi, somehow looking happy and defiant at the same time. Klara, following close behind them, looked happy and nervous, searching Hans' face as if for clues as to how she should feel.

Hans had been trained to size people up with a glance. The man Lotte was leading toward him was about Hans' age, muscular from daily labor, stunned to find himself in a busy train station full of machines and people; ready to follow Lotte's lead, and determined to measure up to whatever inspection was coming. Hans sensed no meanness or greed — and he was out of time, the two women standing in front of him before Klara handed him the baby, then scooped up Hansi and hugged him tight, kissing his face all over. She spared Hans a quick smile and kiss before carrying Hansi toward the exit, obviously leaving Lotte and her — swain? — to Hans to deal with.

"Hans, this is Günther Schmidt. He's the blacksmith who always makes the horseshoes for Opa's horses. His father used to do it when I lived there. Though Günther helped him, even then."

Günther put out a hand, and Hans shifted Emma to his left arm and shook it, keeping himself from wincing at the strength of the man's grip. Some men shook hands that way to try to dominate or to show off. Hans had the sense that Günther was, simply, both strong and jumpy, with no thought to spare for whether he was gripping too hard, but Hans still squeezed Günther's hand as hard as he could.

Lotte was looking back and forth between Hans and Günther. She might have been holding her breath. Hans twitched an eyebrow and said, "Welcome, Herr Schmidt. Do you have business in Berlin, or are you just here to see the sights?"

Lotte rolled her eyes, the way she always did when Hans teased her. Though Hans hadn't been teasing her, so much as talking as if things were as simple as he wanted them to be. "Brother, be nice! Günther is here to meet *you*! — and Otto, if we can track him down before . . . before Günther has to go home." Which wasn't what Lotte had started to say, not quite.

Had she started to say "we"?

Klara, now holding Hansi's hand, returned and took charge. "Lotte, Günther, I hope you'll come to our flat! Lotte and I can go shopping for dinner, and Hans and Günther can use the time to get to know each other." Hans hoped he looked less startled than Günther at this suggestion. Apparently he did, but not for the better, as Klara moved close to him to whisper in his ear, "Stop looking like you're planning to eat the boy alive!"

Hans hadn't done much detective work, but he imagined that many a detective interviewed witnesses and unwary suspects over a beer, or two, or three. He stopped on their way home to pick up a few bottles, winking at Günther and earning himself a suspicious look from Klara. Lotte, fortunately, was too busy entertaining Hansi with skipping races and some sort of word game that left the boy laughing himself breathless.

Klara nursed Emma as soon as they got home. Then, after a quick consultation between the two women, Klara laid Emma in her pram and took her along. Hans put Hansi in his room with a new puzzle, promising him time with the visitors later. Then he grabbed two of the beers, opened both, and handed one to Günther while waving him to the straighter and less cushioned of the two armchairs. For a moment he considered taking the rocking chair, normally Klara's. It would make him feel more like an older man sizing up a younger one who wanted to marry his daughter. But Lotte wasn't his daughter, and Klara might want the rocker when she got back. He settled himself in his usual armchair, took a long drink of his beer, and said, "So you wanted to meet me. What did you expect to find?"

Günther had been about to drink some of his beer. Now his eyes widened, and he slowly lowered his beer, resting it on his muscular thigh. And then, surprisingly, he smiled, a smile Hans couldn't help but notice was charming. "I expected to find a protective big brother, ready to warn off a presumptuous country bumpkin. And here he sits, frowning at me."

Hans fought a laugh and then gave in. Frustrated, he went back to the kitchen for two more beers, opening one and putting the other on the side table for Günther to grab when he was ready for it. As he took a gulp, memories of Lotte flooded his mind. The little girl, plump and playful and then thinner, paler, lethargic; Lotte coming home healthy and strong and getting thin again; Lotte sharing in the better times, coming home from school arm and arm with a friend, teasing him, playing games, growing out of games, becoming a young woman . . . .

He put his beer down hard enough that it sloshed inside the bottle. "Tell me about Lotte when she lived in the country. And what she means to you now."

Günther nodded slowly and leaned back in the chair, his weight enough to tip the chair on its back legs. Hans had the fleeting thought that if he and Günther boxed, Günther outweighed him and might use that weight to make up for lack of skill. But he'd better listen instead of woolgathering, because Günther was answering his question. "Lotte was so thrilled with everything she saw, and everything the family asked her to do. Cows, horses, chickens, they were all exciting, and that made anyone around her appreciate them more. She especially loved collecting eggs. She almost never got pecked, and while she might cry when she did, she still wanted to collect eggs again the next day." Günther looked toward his beer and then away from it, as if he didn't want to associate beer with Lotte. "And she thought I was magic for being able to bend metal — to make it glow orange and then bend it. Some horses get edgy when a stranger's around and watching, but Lotte never bothered them."

If Günther was starting to work as a blacksmith back then, he might be older than Hans. "How old are you?"

Günther sat forward again and shifted in his chair. "Two years older than you, from what Lotte told me. When she first came, she said being around me made her miss you more, but also made her feel more at home."

And Lotte had been there for three years . . . . "When she moved back home, did you miss her?"

Günther chuckled and said, "I should probably say yes, I did — but my life was so busy that I didn't, most of the time. Only she'd pop into my head at odd moments. And then she came back to visit, not a little girl anymore, and so pretty, and everything was different."

Hans stroked his chin, feeling the bristles — it was harder to find time to shave with Hansi bouncing all around. "When did she stop thinking of you as a brother — if she did?"

Günther looked Hans in the eye. "When she grew up. She did, you know."

Hans snorted, allowing the point. "Go on and drink your beer."

They drank together for a minute or so before Günther said quietly, "We'll be going to see Lotte's — your father, of course. But she feels closer to you. She wants your blessing most of all."

Hans was out of objections, but he didn't answer right away. He was thinking about all the ways Lotte had brightened his life, not just as a little girl but long after: her warm hugs, her delight in Hansi and in the new baby, her willingness to help Hans or Klara without even being asked. And now, just when Hans was learning to appreciate her, she'd be going off — or would she? "Where do you think of living?"

Günther had the nerve to look sympathetic as he said, "In the village nearest the farm, where I have my smithy. So she can see her grandparents and cousins often."

Far more often than she would see Hans.

It wasn't just Lotte who had grown apart from their father – Hans had as well. And given how rarely he saw Otto, Lotte often felt like the only family Hans had left. Besides Klara and Hansi and Emma, of course, and they mattered more than anything else to him . . . but still . . . .

And at that moment, with his feelings so unsettled and Günther waiting for an answer, Klara and Lotte and the baby came home, the women fresh-faced from outdoors and carrying bags, talking to each other at top speed and Emma in her pram babbling along. Hansi came running in to greet them, and Lotte engaged him in a contest to see which of them could pull the strings off more green beans, while Klara brought Emma to Hans to take care of before rejoining Lotte and Hansi in the kitchen. Günther asked if he could hold Emma and Hans allowed it, watching him closely to see how comfortable Günther was with a baby. When a familiar odor announced that the baby needed changing, Hans considered leaving the task to Günther before some mixture of prudence and mercy prompted him to take the baby back and carry her to Hans' and Klara's bedroom. He glanced back as he reached the doorway and saw Günther gazing at them with a wistful, longing expression.

Hans halted and beckoned Günther. "Here, you may as well see what it's like close up. You'll be needing to know."

Günther shot out of his chair and stared at Hans, his mouth hanging open before he said, "Does that — do you mean . . . ."

Hans beckoned again, and slapped Günther on the back when the man got near enough. "I guess it does. Welcome to the family. Now get ready for what fatherhood means — shit, and plenty of it."

Günther breathed out a long breath, grinned, and said, "I can't wait to tell Lotte! She'll be so relieved, and so happy! Thank you, thank you!"

Hans laughed. "Thank me after the diaper's changed."

All through the mess and the cleanup, he drank in the sight of his daughter. Here was a little girl who wouldn't grow up and leave him, not for many years to come. And his family might be shrinking, but he'd be an uncle soon enough. He was a fool to feel sad, almost robbed, almost as if he were losing Mutti all over again. This was how things were supposed to go, and it was up to him to be a man and accept it.

But he told Günther to wait until dinner was over before he shared the news.

Chapter 26

Late Winter – Summer 1938

As 1938 moved from winter toward spring, there was much to gladden Hans' heart. Lotte was happy with her blacksmith, and Hans' first niece or nephew was expected in two months. Otto had actually bothered to write a letter, probably because he had something like a success to announce, a national tour with a theater company. And Hans had much for which to give thanks beyond such personal concerns. Step by step, Germany was reversing the damage done to it, the territory hacked away. Two years ago, the Rhineland; this year, a far more ambitious project, the claiming of Austria for a Greater Germany! Hitler had been pursuing this goal as far back as the infamous days of his imprisonment, and with dedication and devotion, he had now achieved it. And the Austrians eagerly welcomed the new nation. Or so declared the result of the Austrian referendum on the subject, though Hitler, so skilled at reading the mood of the people — and an Austrian native himself, for all that he now identified so completely with the Reich — sent the army across the border the day before. Apparently, the countries who should have seen Germany's new vigor as a threat still didn't have the sense to do so, perhaps assuming that all German-speaking countries belonged together and the rest of the world need take no notice.

Vati, who had lately acquired the habit of speaking as if he and Hitler were the closest of confidants, told Hans all about Hitler's plans for Austria one night when Hans, Klara, and Hansi had come to dinner. "Hitler knows the Austrians! After all, he used to be one of them. He knows how they've been longing for the grand destiny that only union with Germany can offer. And when it comes to the Jews, the Austrians are as eager as Germans, if not more so, to send the vermin scurrying away."

But away to where? Not to Germany, surely. The rest of the world had better get ready for more Jews. If the Jews were as much a plague as the Party said, he could almost feel sorry for the places they would go.

Hans nevertheless found himself uneasy over the next few weeks, as Vati and his friends gloated over reports that Austrian Jews were being beaten in the streets and subjected to "scrubbing parties" to clean public toilets. Austria passing laws like Germany's to limit the power and influence of Jews, that was one thing, that was only prudent self-defense. But the rest of it — maybe it was the policeman in him that saw even one-sided brawling in the streets and gang-like gatherings as undesirable in a state bound for greater things.

At a midday briefing later that month, Constable Volker studied the paper in front of him and then pointed to Hans and another of the taller and stronger men. "You two, you'll be suited to this one. It's a sort of trespassing case."

The other man, more comfortable with asking questions, did just that. "How can a case be 'sort of' trespassing? Whoever it is either does or doesn't have a right to be on the property."

The constable had a look Hans had seen more and more often on his face, as though he were tasting something sour. "You're right, of course. This property used to be his, but it isn't anymore. The family still owns the house, but there's a garden next to it, and they aren't allowed to have gardens now."

Hans had seen a headline as he passed the newsstand the day before. "They're Jews, aren't they? Jews can't have gardens anymore."

"That's right." Volker produced a stout padlock. "The garden has a gate, so you can lock it up with this. It may have to be destroyed, but that can wait until we see if someone wants it. If the fellow will go into his house, you can leave him there; otherwise, arrest him. Clear?"

As Hans and his fellow policeman approached the address, Hans kept an eye out for the Jew. Would he be one of the scrawny sort, or a fellow with a big belly and plump fingers? Other possibilities drifted into Hans' mind; he pushed them firmly away again.

But when they reached the pretty little garden with the wrought-iron gate, what they saw between the rows of spinach and the beds of yellow tulips was quite unlike what he had guessed. It was a woman, her hair mostly gray, with the beginning of a dowager's hump, dressed in a long gray skirt and black knitted shawl. She carried a basket half full of spinach.

The two policemen paused in the street next to the garden. Hans' companion whispered, "If that isn't her garden anymore, isn't it stealing to pick what it grows? Do we have to add theft to the charge?"

Hans looked at the woman, who so far had taken no notice of them. Was she hard of hearing, or pretending not to see them? Pretending the garden was still her own, and she was simply gathering the products of it on a spring afternoon like any other? Just then, the woman straightened up and turned partway toward them. She didn't meet their eyes, or even give any sign that she saw them standing there. She seemed to be looking past them at something very far away.

It was pure fantasy for Hans to think, at that moment, that she looked like his mother. His mother had never been stooped like that. And she had never lived to grow old, to have the gray start in her hair.

The moment passed. But the memory of his mother wasting away, worn to death by the hardships of a war the Jews had helped to lose, hardened his resolve. He walked forward to the gate, opened it, and threaded the padlock through its door. He opened his mouth to speak — but what was the proper form of address for a Jewess? He should have thought about that ahead of time. For lack of a more appropriate word, he fell back on what he was used to. "Madam," he said, "You must not be here. This garden belongs to the Reich. Go inside, and that will be the end of it."

She looked straight at him for the first time, and her lip trembled. Then she turned her head to look back at the house to which the garden had belonged, and for the first time, she looked frightened. Hans had a guess about what she was thinking. "Go now," he urged, "before your husband comes out. If he resists, he would go to jail, and I doubt he would be treated well on the way." He left unspoken that if she herself refused to leave, she too would be arrested, with treatment he could neither foresee nor guarantee.

She looked back at Hans, then at the other policeman, as if making sure he had no help to offer, and then back at Hans again. Bringing the basket against her breast as if cradling a baby, she spoke for the first time, in a surprisingly cultured voice. "May I take the spinach with me?"

Hans took a step back and beckoned his colleague, saying when the other got within whispering distance, "The garden doesn't belong to anyone else yet. And the spinach would wilt in the meantime. Let's let her take it. She'll go more quietly that way."

The other man nodded dumbly. Hans came toward the woman again. "Yes, you may take the basket and what's in it, if you go inside right away."

Out of the corner of his eye, Hans caught some motion at the door of the house. The woman saw it too, and hurried toward it, faster than Hans would have guessed she could. In a few seconds, she had gone inside and shut the door behind her.

Spring passed, summer came, and Hans was awaiting a new assignment when there came a sudden interruption.

"What a pile of *crap*!"

Constable Volker's voice echoed down the hall. Hans had never gone into the man's office unless summoned there, but then he'd never heard the man shout in anger. Should he go ask what was wrong? While he was dithering, one of the other policemen came up to Hans brandishing a folded map and growled, "Cleaning up Berlin is a grand idea, but do they have to send us running in circles and getting tied up in knots to do it?"

"What's this all about? Is it the same thing the constable is furious about?"

"Probably." The man opened up the map, which had at least a dozen streets circled in red. "What is it that takes the new men longest to get used to? What keeps them from being any good for the first week or two or three? Not knowing their way around! You can tell them the robbery just happened at 15 Hallerstrasse, and they just look at you like an ox. Well, now we can all relive those days! They're changing all these street names."

Hans grabbed the map. "But why would they — oh." Most of the circled street names sounded Jewish, or had "Juden" as a prefix. "They don't want any Jewish street names in Berlin."

"And if we show up too late when there's a break-in, I suppose the householder will be glad that at least he doesn't live on a street with an unsavory name? As if it's worth letting criminals get away!"

Hans quickly looked around to make sure no one else had heard, and said in quiet warning, "I wouldn't talk like that, these days. We'll just have to make it work."

The other man pointed down the hall to the constable's office. "Volker hasn't exactly been holding his tongue, has he?"

Hans made no answer.

When he told Klara that evening, her mind also went to practicalities, though different ones. "How will people get their letters? Will the post office have a list of all the old and new addresses? Oh, dear, I hope nothing goes astray."

He kissed her forehead to comfort her. "I doubt it will. Things are well organized these days. They'll have thought of everything. It'll be fine."

Chapter 27

Summer 1938

Hans had always admired and respected Constable Volker. Looking back, he had no idea how he had been so simple-minded as to assume the man would stay in that job as long as Hans remained there. He should have remembered how Herr Richter had eased Hans' own way into the Force. And then there was the way Volker had objected to some of the recent changes . . . .

He should have expected it, then, when Volker called them all together on a morning in early August and announced that he would be leaving and Constable Bluth would be taking over. But he was still taken aback, though not too much to notice the trace of distaste, even disgust, on Volker's face as he mentioned the new constable's name.

And then an overweight man in a too-tight uniform, its collar open and a button missing around the middle, was coming forward, brushing close to Volker and smiling a wide smile with barely disguised malice beneath it. "You can move along now," said the new arrival. "I'm better at introducing myself anyway."

Volker ignored him long enough to say, "You're a splendid group, and I've been honored to work with you." He glanced over at his replacement and said, with a certain heaviness, "I wish you the best of luck." He saluted and walked quickly out of the room.

Bluth looked around at the gathered policemen, with a different smile just as unpleasant as his first, a sort of conspiratorial leer. "Well, well, aren't you all a fine-looking lot. You could pose for one of those posters I see around town."

Hans stiffened. The man looked his way and cocked his head before going on, in a sneering tone, "Maybe that's what Volker wanted from you, but you'll find I have different ideas. You can shave twice a day and iron your uniforms and look pretty for each other on your own time. And playing cops and robbers won't be your most important job either. The time when the Criminal Police could keep their distance from the Security Police is over. The Security Police have important work to do, and it's your duty to assist in that work. Understood?"

Hans wasn't sure he understood. But he was glumly certain that things had changed, and for the worse.

When he shared the news with Klara, she sympathized at the loss of a good superior, but scolded him gently for the way he described Bluth. "What's so terrible about his being fat? You know what a wonderful man Herr Krauss the butcher is, how often he's been ready to help out with anything anybody needs. You can't tell what someone's like by looking at them."

Hans shook his head, exasperated. "Any policeman can tell plenty about a man by looking at him. And Krauss isn't a policeman! Bluth is supposed to be, but he couldn't chase down a criminal if his life depended on it. I guess that doesn't matter anymore."

Two days later, Hans walked into the locker room to find a familiar and unwelcome sight. The poster he'd modeled for, back at the time of the first Day of Police, had been pasted on his locker, partly over the door. He had to tear the poster to get it open. He heard a guffaw behind him, and turned to see Bluth standing in the doorway, rocking back and forth with his hands folded on his belly. "That was careless of you!" he said when he was done laughing. "Look what you've done, and after I was so generous as to share my poster with you! Well, I've got plenty more. There'll be a new one there tomorrow."

Bluth did not, to Hans' relief, paste up a new poster on his locker the next day. Instead, and to his surprise, the man singled him out to be in charge of two other policemen on an assignment to evict a businessman — "Jewish, of course" — from the premises he was no longer allowed to run.

The building was in good repair, and the flow of people in and out, some looking like workers and the others more affluent, suggested it was doing well. It might keep doing well under proper German management, as long as he managed to remove the Jew without damaging the property or causing a commotion where the customers would see it. He waited at a discreet distance for someone who looked like a worker to go in a back entrance and then took his men in the same way, bypassing the main floor in the hope the staff offices would be higher up.

As they emerged from the stairwell, they almost walked into a young man in the clothes of a clerical worker, carrying an armful of files. He backed against the wall of the hallway, eyes wide. Hans asked him, or rather ordered him, "Please take us to the office of Herr Levin." There was no point in confusing the clerk, or giving him an idea of their mission, by omitting the "Herr."

"This way, officer," said the clerk, staring at them rather than at where he was going, and bumped into an older, stouter man who was just then emerging from one of the doors. "Oh! Excuse me, Herr Levin!" he gasped. "These, ah, gentlemen were looking for you."

Whether or not the clerk had any idea of what the police presence meant, the older man clearly knew. His face set as hard as stone, though he was able to say in something like a normal voice, "Thank you. You can go on with what you were doing." He turned to Hans and said, "Will you kindly come into my office?"

"Your office, you say?" interrupted one of the other policemen. "That's the problem, isn't it?" Hans gave him a stern look, hoping it would serve as a reminder of who was in charge. They followed the Jew into the office in question. Herr Levin lifted his chin and sat down behind the desk with a defiant look just short of a glare.

Should Hans sit down, the better to look the man in the eye, or remain standing in a more commanding position? He picked the latter and planted his hands on his hips. "I believe you know why we're here. The issue is that you're still here, so many months after the State decreed that your role here is not in the interests of the new Germany."

Levin planted his hands on his desk. "Are prosperous businesses in Germany's interest? Satisfied customers? Good jobs for good workers? I provide all of that! And I have for fifteen years! No newcomer could step into my place, without the knowledge and connections and good will I've built up, and do half as well."

Was the man under the impression that Hans made the rules? Or that he was free to ignore them? Even if he'd wanted to let the man keep his company, there was no way that could happen. And Hans would be doing him no kindness to let him keep deluding himself, even if he could get away with doing so.

The man was still talking, as if it would make any difference. "Do they think all my customers are Jewish? Of course not! Go look, go talk to them! I've dealt honorably with them, I've earned their business, and they don't want to see me driven out like — like some sort of, of . . . ." It seemed he had no good comparison at hand. Hans could have supplied a few, but there was no point and no need.

The third policeman, who had said nothing until now, saw it differently. "A foreigner, not a true German! Now that's enough stalling — get out, or we'll haul you out!" He looked disapprovingly at Hans for dragging things out. He would probably have plenty to say on the subject when they got back to the station.

Levin stared at the three of them and then slumped down, as if he were a balloon just punctured and already losing its air. He shoved his chair backward, slowly, the legs dragging on the floor as if in sympathy with his reluctance, and picked up a large black leather briefcase. It looked new, or else well maintained, and expensive. No one in Hans' family had ever owned anything like it. It suddenly occurred to him that he could probably snatch the briefcase away from the man and keep it for his own, as long as he let the other two policemen find their own pickings. He thrust the thought away from him as if it were poisonous, and clasped his hands behind his back for good measure.

He had better regain the initiative, after such an unimpressive showing. "You've had months to prepare. It's time to go. If you hurry up and pack your things, you may leave under your own power. Of course we'll stay close, to make sure you don't attempt any . . . detours."

Levin stared at his desk and then looked slowly around the room. When he looked back at Hans, his eyes were wet. "Every time I've left this office, I've taken some papers with me to work on at home. There's no point in that now, is there?"

Hans took a deep breath and answered, "No, Herr Levin. The papers should stay here anyway, for someone else to deal with."

The man's face twisted into the most bitter of smiles. "Yes, for someone else to deal with. Some true German."

He picked up a framed photograph from the desk and put it in the briefcase, holding it close to his chest so none of the policemen could see what it showed. Then he walked toward the door, but one of the men was in the way. He waited there, looking at none of them, until Hans gestured for the policeman to move aside. Levin walked out of what had been his office, and the three policemen followed close behind, to the staff stairway and down it, out to the street.

Hans hesitated. Should he close the place down? His orders had not gone into that much detail. And it would take a long time to make sure everyone was out of the building. Nor did he have enough men with him to prevent looting. He cleared his throat and asked Levin, "Will your employees take care of things without you?"

The man looked at Hans as if he could hardly believe in his existence. "Now you're concerned about what happens to my company? Now you wonder if it can carry on without me? Let your true German worry about it!" The surge of energy ebbed quickly. "They'll take care of things. As I said, they're good people and they care about their work. About this place." He started walking. "By now they know I've left, and why. I can't promise you they'll be back tomorrow. Some of them may not care to stay."

The policeman who had threatened to haul Levin out turned and spat on the ground. "Good riddance to them, if they'd rather work for a Jew!"

Levin smiled that bitter smile again and said, so softly that Hans could barely hear him, "Your true German will want to find men just as good, no doubt — if he can."

They followed Levin home, to make sure he didn't double back and try to get into the business again. Then they reported to the station. Hans went straight to Bluth, to get his account in first. "We removed Levin from the building without incident." Though of course he couldn't say so, he was rather proud of how efficiently they'd managed it. A short conversation and then out on the street with no disruption, no fuss.

Bluth lowered his eyebrows and stared at Hans under them. "No incident, you say." He laughed. "Nice and clean, just the way you like it. You could've worn your pretty white coat, and not even got it mussed. You didn't rough the Jew up a little, pay him back for squatting there like a toad when he was supposed to make way for his betters? Didn't make him clean up the chair he'd been farting on all that time? Just excuse me, sir, if it wouldn't be too much trouble, would you remove your Jew ass from the premises?"

Hans did his best imitation of a statue. "I considered an orderly removal preferable to a brawl, Constable Bluth."

Bluth scowled. "That's the trouble with you prissy types. Why you think police work should be neat and tidy and leave you without any bruises, I can't imagine. Well, don't expect to be in charge of any more arrests. Not that I'm surprised you couldn't manage it." He held up his hand as Hans opened his mouth to protest. "Yes, yes, you got him out. My three-year-old son could've done that much. Maybe your own five-year-old son could've done the same."

The ugly thought of this man in charge of a son quickly fled before the chilling fact that Bluth knew anything about Hans' own family. Hans gave a crisp salute, turned on his heel and walked quickly to the locker room. Stripping off his uniform, he opened his locker to find the threatened white coat hanging there. He pulled out his street clothes and threw his uniform in, letting it lie in a heap on the floor of the locker, and got dressed as quickly as he ever had. Gerhard came in just then and approached him, but before the man could ask any questions, Hans said hastily, "I've got to go home."

Gerhard's eyes went wide with concern. He hesitated and then asked, "Do you need me to go with you?"

Hans narrowed his eyes. "Do you think Bluth would go so far as to have me attacked in the street, or to ambush me at home?"

"No, no. In fact, if he plans to do you any mischief, I'm more likely to hear about it here. I'll keep my ears open. But what should I say if he asks where you are?"

A great weariness was creeping over Hans. "Whatever you think best. I'm sorry — I've got to get out of here." He left without another word, without responding to the surprised or suspicious looks from the men he passed.

Hansi was delighted to see his father home early. He was well settled in kindergarten by now and started telling Hans all about it, from his teacher to his classmates to the picture he had drawn to the lesson on ethnic types and the destiny of Germany. He garbled some of the details, naturally, coming out with some notion of German noses having been stolen by the big-nose people and Germany having to go to other countries to get them back. Klara finally got him to go into the kitchen for a snack, giving Hans a chance to tell her about his disheartening day. At first, she tried to get him to share her notion that it was just an adjustment period, that Bluth and Hans would get used to each other and learn how to work together. "And if the white coat means you'd spend some time on traffic detail, would that be so bad? You don't like pushing Jews around, and when you direct traffic, you're just helping everyone get where they want to go, without even knowing if it's a Jew in the car."

But as soon as he told her Bluth had mentioned Hansi, she went pale and quiet, and even tiptoed into the kitchen to make sure Hansi was still happily eating his snack. Hans stayed in the front room, but Hansi's "Mutti, can I have some more?" and Klara's murmured reply reassured him that all was as usual. When Klara came back, she was calmer, and her wrinkled forehead showed she was now mulling over the problem. He could see when she thought of something he could do, and then when she realized he might not want to do it. But she went ahead and said, "You could talk to Herr Richter."

Hans held onto his temper. "I don't think he would approve of my going around the chain of command."

Klara tapped her lips a few times. "It wouldn't be like that if you're asking for advice — about the right way to make suggestions, or about how to persuade the man in charge to take advantage of your experience. Or you could ask whether, when you're supervising police yourself, you'll be expected to know all about your men's families. If there's anything unusual with Bluth knowing about Hansi, Herr Richter might know."

Hans had little hope that such a conversation would do any good, and could imagine it making things worse. But it was that, or do nothing and wait for what Bluth would do.

Herr Richter sat back in his favorite club's deep leather armchair and took a sip of his expensive wine. "Bluth is what we could call one of the new men — not military, not police, not one of my set. I believe Chancellor Hitler met him around fourteen years ago. You understand?"

Hans did the arithmetic and kept his face expressionless. Herr Hitler had apparently met the man in prison.

"He's a very dedicated Party member, very reliable. As long as you don't give him any reason to doubt your devotion to the cause, you should get along fine."

And of course, Hans had already given him a reason.

"If I were you, I'd make a point of wearing your brown SA shirt to work. If it isn't too hot out, you could even keep it on under your uniform. Just in case he doesn't know." Herr Richter picked up the wine bottle. "Are you sure I can't pour you a glass? It's an excellent vintage. Do try it."

Hans dumbly held out his glass to be filled.

"Ah, that's better. Now what was it you asked me? Whether it's expected for officers in his position to know all about their men's families? I'm afraid I couldn't say. After all," and he chuckled, "I've never held such a position, now have I? But Herr Bluth is very thorough — rather more meticulous than his appearance would suggest. You could look at his knowledge of his men as something to aspire to." He looked at Hans' untouched glass. Hans made himself pick it up and take a swallow. "I would suggest, Hans, that you try not to disappoint him."

Hans spent the trip home coming up with something to say that might soothe Klara's fears without being an outright lie. He could at least try to hold that line: to remain as honest as Vati had taught him to be, and not to lie to his wife.

When he got to work and found a row of three clean, freshly pressed white coats in his locker, and received his assignment to traffic detail, he was thankful it was nothing worse.

The next day began with another unpleasant confrontation with Bluth. Apparently one of the policemen who had accompanied Hans to evict the Jewish businessman had accused Hans of showing the Jew inappropriate respect. Constable Volker would have disapproved of such tattling, but Bluth had apparently welcomed it.

"I knew it!" shouted Bluth as crumbs of ash fell from his cigar and littered his desk. "Did you feel sorry for him, or were you sucking up to him in hope he'd throw a reward your way? They all have money to burn, and you were hoping for a little of it?"

Hans stood as straight as he could, his chin thrust out and his fists clenched despite the deference due his superior in rank. "I would never consider taking a bribe from a criminal or an object of investigation or — whatever you like to call this man. Neither my personal integrity nor the rules — "

Bluth waved the cigar in Hans' face. "Rules, rules! You've probably got them all in some little book that you take to bed with you at night! Meanwhile, the enemies of the Reich — many of them lawyers — will hide behind rules while they burrow into the heart of Germany and attack it from within! Well, this station may not be part of the Security Police, but the Criminal Police and the Security Police are going to be working together more and more. And you'd better be prepared to do what is necessary!"

"I am, as always, ready to perform my duties," said Hans stiffly. "As I did in removing the Jew from a functioning business without alarming its customers or causing its employees to flee their work."

Bluth wrinkled up his face in disgust and made shooing motions with both hands. "Go on, get out of here! Go direct traffic! At least there, you can't do much harm."

And so it continued, with snide remarks and crude insults and traffic duty and various degrading cleanup tasks, for more than a month.

Chapter 28

As Hans took his place on a quiet, unimportant street corner that October morning, he fumed over Bluth's latest tirade. Would he be dismissed, and if that happened, what would he do to support his family? Maybe Herr Richter was protecting him in some way. But how long could he stand it, having Bluth hovering over him and insulting him and mocking him in front of the other men, finding every unpleasant and demeaning task it was in his power to assign? The thought of such scenes made his tie feel tight against his neck, and he loosened it.

He was deep enough in his gloomy reflections that it took a moment for him to register the metallic sound of one bicycle striking another, and then the gasps and exclamations from pedestrians and people waiting for the bus or the trolley. About ten meters away, an elderly man and his bicycle lay half in the street and half on the center divider, while a boy about ten years old was disentangling himself from his own bicycle and stammering apologies. Standing nearby were two other boys, both holding bicycles: one handsome well–built lad about two years older than the first and one wiry boy with a thin face and black, densely curled hair. Hans' mind flashed back to his father's description of how to identify a Jew. This boy's nose was only a little longer than average, but his overall appearance could have been used to illustrate "Jew" in one of the new school textbooks.

And then Hans heard the different rumbles of two different vehicles: a bus, coming from the same direction as the bicycles must have come, and a trolley approaching on the median, not far behind.

Hans whirled around and threw up his hand toward the bus, which was already screeching to a halt. He turned to the trolley and, to his enormous relief, heard the squeal of it coming to a stop as well. As both vehicles came to rest, their doors opened and a stream of people spilled out of each, all eager to see what had happened and, for some, probably wishing the outcome had been more exciting. As the drivers came out in their turn, Hans assigned them to making sure their passengers stayed out of the street while he thought about how to handle the accident itself.

The youngest boy's bicycle lay near Hans' feet, its shiny handlebars catching Hans' eye. All three bicycles, he noted, looked new and expensive — far newer and more expensive than the bicycle Hans and Otto had owned so briefly. If the boys were brothers, all as Jewish as the thinnest boy, they probably had plenty of money to spare.

What should he do next? The boys should not be let to escape all consequences, not with the old man only now rising to his feet and leaning heavily on the arm of a helpful bystander. If they had been normal German boys . . . or even if Constable Volker had not been forced out, and replaced by the abominable Bluth . . . Hans would have lectured the boys, possibly cuffed them on the ear, and taken their names and address in order to follow up later. He would confiscate the bicycles, at least for some period of time. And if the man proved to be injured, he would discuss with their parents what additional punishment might be sufficient to show them how serious their offense had been. But what would happen now, if he did only that? Bluth would get to hear about it, and nothing of the sort would satisfy him. He would want the boys, yes, and all their family arrested, maybe sent to one of those camps where the criminals Hans had helped to round up were now in charge of the inmates. What would such men, resenting their captivity and eager for someone on whom they could take out that anger, do to these boys?

Hans looked at the three of them. The middle one might be a healthy handsome lad, but on his face was a look of calculation that Hans disliked. He must be trying to come up with some way to minimize their role in the accident, or even, in some shifty Jewish way, blame it on someone else, probably the old man. As for the youngest boy, he was looking toward his bicycle, his face screwed up as if he were trying hard not to cry. Then he felt Hans' eyes on him, and his face went pale and his eyes very wide. He stared at Hans as if at some monster from a children's tale. Klara's past fears about Jews and babies came to mind. Did Jews tell their children tales of the fearsome police who might snatch them and eat them whole?

In all the activity, Hans realized now, the top button of his uniform had come undone. The brown shirt he wore underneath might well be showing. If the boy knew the look of a Nazi brown shirt, no wonder he was terrified. Hans was used to seeing criminals afraid of him, those that were not taking refuge in defiance. But he had never before had the sight of him frighten a child.

If he arrested the boys, it might improve his situation at work, might placate Bluth and even convince the man that Hans was reliable where Jews were concerned. He could imagine Bluth sneering and saying, "Well, at least *today* you've seen fit to serve the Fatherland and your Führer. I hope you can bear up under the strain. Put that white coat back in your locker and get an assignment fit for a *man* to do." . . .

Traffic had backed up along both streets, and drivers were beginning to honk and to call questions and complaints out their windows. Hans growled under his breath. At least he would follow procedure and question the boys. He drew himself up to his most intimidating and faced the boys. He could almost see the handsome boy's mind racing as he asked, "Did you boys have anything to do with this?"

He had paid little attention to the thin boy beyond realizing how Jewish he looked. But now that boy stood up very straight, almost as if saluting, and said loudly, "*Jawohl, Offizier.*"

Of all the things the boy could have said, Hans had not expected this simple admission. Was the boy slow-witted? Did he not realize what Hans was? He might not have been able to see the brown shirt. But there was intelligence in the thin face, and even a sort of solemnity. The boy realized he was speaking to a policeman, and he must know by now, after almost six years of Nazi rule, who policemen were required to serve, who was really in charge . . . men like Bluth.

But the boy had answered without trying to avoid the question, without trying to run away. Without lying. Without breaking into tears. Just answered, and with the truth.

Hans had little hope of getting the right answer to his next question, an answer that would let him fall back into his normal routine with his usual options. But he looked at the thin boy this time, and asked, "Are you boys Jewish?"

A very short pause, and then: "*Jawohl, Offizier.*"

There were so many people standing around. They could see what he saw, recognize what the boy's features meant. But many of them were talking to each other, or offering to help the old man, holding his damaged bicycle for him and asking whether he was injured. However conspicuous Hans felt, there might not be that many people watching him at this moment. And he was in charge. For this moment, it was all up to him.

The two other boys had shuffled closer to the thin boy, the three of them clustered together. Hans leaned toward the boys and spoke quietly, but with all the authority he had learned in these last five years. Gave them an order. "DISAPPEAR."

The youngest boy and the handsome boy gaped, the family resemblance showing clearly. The two of them grabbed the thin boy by the elbows, and they started to walk away, almost to run. Hans stepped into their path and nodded toward the three fallen bicycles. The handsome boy, quickest to understand, grabbed one of them; his brothers hurried to pick up the others. In a moment all three of them were riding down the street as fast as they could, the older two in front, the youngest wobbling behind.

Behind Hans, the voice of a woman rang out. "Wait! Aren't those the boys that ran into the old man?" Hans said nothing. He walked over to the two drivers and instructed them to collect their passengers and clear the road. He gestured to the closest drivers to back up from the bus. When the trolley had rumbled and clanged its way down the median and the bus had driven down the block, he looked for the old man, but he was already being escorted somewhere by helpful, or officious, bystanders. Hans planted himself at the intersection as if nothing had happened, looking this way and that as the cars and pedestrians passed him by.

Aftermath

What happened to the man I have called Hans?
Here are three possibilities.

One

The woman who had confronted Hans in the midst of the chaos had not, as Hans had hoped, given up and gone away. Instead she walked up to him, stood unpleasantly close, and asked impatiently, "Well? What are you going to do about those boys?"

Hans tried to keep his face pleasant and uninformative while his thoughts raced. When she opened her mouth to repeat herself, he said, "Madam, whatever your assumptions, there are some police tasks that are more urgent than others. It is my assigned duty for today to ensure that traffic flows as smoothly as possible, without undue interruptions. I have performed that duty, and must continue to do so." As she tossed her head and glared at him, he added, "That will not prevent me, or possibly another officer, from investigating the recent incident. Did you see the accident?"

The woman hesitated, frowned, and shook her head. Hans would have liked to sigh in relief, but refrained and went on. "No matter. I observed both the boys and their bicycles in detail. The bicycles, you may or may not have noticed, were quite new. If I am indeed the officer assigned the task, I can inquire of the various bicycle shops whether they sold such bicycles and if so, when. One or more of the boys may have been present for that transaction. If not, we may hope that whoever made the purchase looked Jewish or otherwise revealed that status. In fact, I could start with shops previously owned by Jews, which might be more familiar to the family." He allowed himself a knowing smile. "I have connections that would make it easier to pinpoint shops that have recently changed hands in that manner."

The woman had dropped her hostile manner and was starting to nod and smile along. He finished by saying, "Not only would that allow for a thorough investigation at the appropriate time, but it might enable us to find the boys' family as well."

The woman clasped her hands to her breast and breathed, "How fascinating! I do apologize for my presumption. It must take such cleverness to be a policeman." And, finally, she went on her way and left him in peace.

Now he could take a deep breath, and relax as much as was consistent with his role as a policeman alert to his surroundings and in control of them. Now he could think beyond the moment, and his thoughts made him wish he could scowl, or go somewhere and have a drink.

The woman had been only the beginning of the trouble coming his way. Bluth might seem a lazy idler at first glance, but Hans would wager he had plenty of energy when the chance came to be vindictive, or to make extra trouble for some Jews. Hans might end up being forced to do just what he'd outlined to that woman. Or — would it be better or worse if Bluth assigned someone else, someone he considered more reliable, to track down the boys?

Hans' mind drifted back to his recent meeting with Herr Richter. It might be wishful thinking, but Hans had gotten the impression that the man didn't so much like or approve of Bluth as have a wary respect for his dangerous potential. If Hans moved very carefully, he could explore that notion — and see whether Herr Richter might be willing to use his position to undermine Bluth in some way, or get him transferred to another precinct. Hans would undoubtedly owe his former employer a major favor in exchange. But better such a favor than having Bluth looming over him and his future.

Herr Richter had been cordial about another meeting so soon after the first, but not as jovially friendly as usual. After offering food and drink, he dismissed the servant who brought the biscuits and Schnaps and said, "What brings us together tonight? Is it Herr Bluth again?"

Hans' lips tightened. "I'm very sorry to trouble you again, sir."

Herr Richter shook his head and looked serious. "I did warn you to tread carefully where Bluth was concerned. What's happened?"

Hans had spent the walk over wondering how to answer that question. If he explained the encounter with the boys in all its complexity — or, from another point of view, its simplicity — Herr Richter might think less of Hans from that moment on. He might even make sure Bluth heard all about it. Hans fell back on a truth that exposed him less. "Frankly, sir, I think I was doomed from the first. Do you remember that blasted poster? From the Day of Police four years ago?"

The prince fingered his chin and then sat back and laughed. "Oh, my goodness! Yes, there you stood looking so much the ideal Aryan. Bluth dug that up?"

"Indeed he did. Sir, last time we met, you mentioned Bluth's appearance, and that I shouldn't assume his character matched it. I think, though, that his appearance, and, and mine, may be why he took against me from the moment he saw me. And it's only getting worse."

Herr Richter took a modest swallow of his Schnaps and said in a more sympathetic tone, "Well, then. What were you hoping I could do to help?"

When Hans, in a slow halting manner, explained what he'd had in mind, Herr Richter started shaking his head before he could finish. "I'm flattered you think I have that much influence, but Bluth is not someone I could dislodge. I do, however, see a more practical solution within our reach. I could probably get you transferred to another precinct. Wouldn't that serve just as well?"

Hans' spirits had plunged at the first words. The rest came as a most welcome reprieve. "I think so, sir. Thank you for your willingness to assist me."

Herr Richter's face grew grave, and he held up a plump finger. "There's one thing I need to know first. Whatever happened with Bluth that made you decide you had to come to me — and I know you must've been reluctant to make your request — can you assure me that if I recommend you to the man running another precinct, the same issue won't arise again?"

If Hans took too long answering that question, he could lose this chance of rescue. And how could the same circumstances arise again? "Yes, sir. I can promise that."

As Hans walked home, warmed by the combination of relief and Schnaps, he did his best to reassure himself. His spur of the moment decision would no doubt have been different without the spectre of Bluth hanging over him, hanging over the boys. And that thin boy, the one who had answered so bravely, must surely be a most unusual Jew. Nothing of the sort was likely to happen again.

Two

It was over. Hans' dearest dream, once crushed and then, beyond hope, granted, had slipped through his grasp, and by his own doing.

He had given Bluth the perfect lever with which to pry him out of his position. And Bluth had taken full advantage, calling the men together and describing, with a show of outrage failing to disguise his glee, just how Hans had failed in his duty. "An elderly German, entitled to all our respect for his many years of endurance and toil, callously ridden down by three Jewish brats raised on wealth stolen from the Reich, who could have been caught in the act. And what did this poster boy, this self-styled model policeman, do? He let them slither away!"

Hans, his face wooden, had room in his mind for two bitter questions: who among his fellow policemen had carried the tale to Bluth? And who had written this speech for him?

Bluth turned to Hans, his face contorted with disgust. "You will turn in your uniform. I will have it burned, rather than let it taint the better man who replaces you. But you may take with you that pretty white coat, once I make one small addition to it. Give it here."

Hans numbly shrugged off the coat and handed it to Bluth. Bluth took out a thick black grease pencil and scrawled on the back: JEW-LOVING TRAITOR. Then he threw the coat in Hans' face and said, "Change your clothes and get out."

Nothing since his mother's death — not confronting armed murderers, not helping put out a factory fire — had frightened Hans as much as going home and telling Klara what had happened, what he had done. He stopped off at a run-down bar, far from any that policemen used, and downed two quick glasses of cheap Schnaps before taking himself in hand and marching himself to his flat. It seemed all wrong that the front room looked just as usual and smelled of good roast beef and potatoes.

Klara came to meet him with a fond smile that fell away when she saw him. He was still carrying the defaced coat, and his face must have told the tale. She stopped in her tracks and cried, "What's happened? What did that man do to you?"

Her loyalty made him want to cry. He couldn't bear to see what became of it when she knew the truth. "I'll tell you after supper. It smells good."

Hansi must have been playing outside. He ran in just then, yelled, "Vati!" and pelted over to be picked up. Any other day, Hans would have swooped down and hoisted the boy high in the air. Instead, he knelt down, gathered Hansi into a hug, and clutched him tight. Hansi hugged him back and then started wriggling. "Vati, I want to eat, and Mutti won't let me until I wash my hands!"

Hans let go and watched Hansi run off. He might just as well have been carrying Hans' happiness with him.

The beef and potatoes were as good as ever. But halfway through the meal, Hans dropped his fork and hurried to the bathroom to vomit up every bite. Klara appeared in the doorway as he was straightening up from the toilet and wiping his mouth. She put her hands gently on his shoulders and said softly, "It's time to tell me, don't you think? I'll be right back." She kissed his cheek and left him there.

Hans used the time to take some deep breaths, waiting over the toilet in case they would make him sick again. When nothing else came up, he splashed cold water on his face, combed his hair, and looked out the bathroom door to see what was going on. He saw Klara giving Hansi a sweet bun and, to the boy's surprise and confusion, sending him to his room to eat it there. Then she came back to the bathroom, led Hans to their own bedroom, sat him down on the bed, and looked at him with calm expectation.

So he told her everything.

It only made everything worse to see Klara so brave. He held her as if she had broken down, and she finally shed a few tears before pulling herself loose and insisting they talk about the future. "It's too soon for me to cry, when everything may work out for the best. The police force isn't the only good job in the world — and it looks to be getting worse, with worms like Bluth in charge. Could you . . . I know it would feel like going backward, but could you try to get your old job back? You were so good at it, and you didn't seem unhappy then."

Hans had already considered that, and imagined what Herr Richter would think when Hans told him — or when someone else told him — what Hans had done, or rather failed to do. "I doubt he'd have me back. If nothing else, he wouldn't want to make an enemy of Bluth and those like him."

She stroked his hair back off his forehead. "It sounds as if you've already thought about that. What else have you thought of?"

He'd done little real thinking, only enough to beat himself with. But now he thought. What was out there, maybe possibilities that hadn't existed when he first failed to achieve his dream? "There's munitions work, more than there's ever been since the war. I could try to get hired on for that. I don't know how well it pays when you first start out. And I don't know if they'd take me, now."

She turned his face to hers and said, "Tomorrow's Sunday. We'll go to church and pray for guidance. We haven't been throwing money around — we have enough saved for you to take a little time to find your next step."

He moved to kiss her and then remembered what he'd just been doing. She saw him hesitate and laughed a little before pulling him close and kissing him. When she let him go, she laughed again and said, "In good days and bad, darling."

Hans closed his eyes and started his prayers with one of thanks for the great blessing that was his wife.

That night, after only one drink, he lay beside Klara and listened to her breathing. He could certainly try one of the munitions factories. It would be cowardly to give up without that test. But if they wouldn't have him . . . what about the army?

As a policeman, he'd technically been in the army already. He was fit and strong, these days. He could travel to an army post outside Berlin, and hope word of his shame wouldn't have spread that far. He was still a member of the Party, unless Bluth had already acted to get him expelled. And he could truthfully tell them how his father was one of the honored veterans and had raised him to long for the return of a strong Germany, and taken him to hear Herr Hitler way back in 1927, when so few had faith in him.

To be a soldier! How thrilled he'd have been, in those dark days after the war, after the terrible treaty, even to think that Germany would have so many soldiers again, let alone that he could be one of them. And if war came, as people were starting to predict, he could fight for Lebensraum, for Greater Germany, for the Reich. It wouldn't be all about the Jews, whatever men like Bluth seemed to think.

And after they'd fought and won, when they were marching toward the glorious future, who, after all, would remember or care about the Jews? In such company, with such a grand task before him, maybe he too could forget.

Three

Hans avoided the station for the rest of the day. At the end of his shift, he went straight home instead of changing out of his coat and uniform first. Klara's eyebrows went up when he opened the door, but she smiled and walked around him, saying, "How fine you look! Hansi, come see your father in his uniform!"

Little Emma was sitting on the floor, playing with the wooden farm animals Lotte had sent her for Christmas. Hansi came running from his room. He looked up at Hans with his eyes shining, and said, "Can I be a policeman when I grow up? I want to be a policeman and look just like that!"

Hans forced a smile. Out of the corner of his eye, he saw Klara frown before she smoothed out her expression and said, "Supper will be just a little late tonight. Hansi, you can get *one* biscuit out of the cupboard to help you wait, and then play in your room until I call you. I want to talk to Vati about something."

Hans just stood where he'd halted until Hansi had gone into and out of the kitchen and closed his bedroom door. He stood there until Klara came up and took his hand, saying, "Come sit in your chair, and tell me what happened."

When he was sitting, and trying to figure out where to begin, she went to the kitchen herself and got him a glass of beer. Handing it to him and sitting in her own favorite chair, she said gently, "Start with what was usual, and go from there."

So he did.

Klara looked startled and then concerned when he described the accident, her mouth dropping open when he got to the oncoming trolley and bus. She sighed in relief when he said they had both stopped in time. And then she sat very still as he told her the rest. He thought she would speak when he described the boys riding away on their shiny new bicycles. But she just sat there and waited, knowing there was more. That he would try to somehow explain.

So he tried. "Klara, I wish you could've seen him, the oldest boy. He must have been terrified, but he stood there and told me the truth."

Klara nodded and said, so softly he could hardly hear her, "I know how much truth matters to you."

"And — I can't believe I'm saying this, but I'd have been proud to have a boy like that. I hope Hansi grows up to be so brave."

Hansi stuck his head out of his bedroom. "Did you call me, Mutti? Is it supper yet? I'm hungry!"

Over the cold ham and carrots, Hansi chattered about his day at kindergarten, Klara reminding him frequently not to talk with his mouth full, Emma sometimes trying out a word here and there. About halfway through the meal, when Hansi's stream of talk had slowed down a little, he said, "Vati, I have a question. You'll know the answer! Do all the Jews look like the pictures, and are they all as bad as my teacher says?"

Hans slowly laid down his fork. He glanced at Klara, who held her fork as if she'd forgotten it, and took a deep breath. Finally he said, "No, Hansi, they don't all look like that. There was a Jewish boy when I was in school who didn't have a very big nose or especially dark hair. And he was my friend."

Hansi's eyes got very wide. He gulped and said, "Vati, how could you be friends with a Jew?"

"It was easier then. I saw pictures like what you saw, and heard the same sort of things, from your grandfather, but not in school. Many people didn't care so much about Jews then. And no, they aren't all bad people." His throat had gone dry, and he took a sip of his water. "And it turns out even the ones who look like the pictures can be good people. You'd better not say anything like this in school." Klara nodded anxiously, and Hans wondered, too late, whether the children were being taught to report family members for such opinions. "But you asked me, and that's what I think."

Hansi took another forkful of ham, chewed, swallowed, and said, "I wondered. Thank you for telling me. Mutti, can I have some more ham? Almost all I've got left is carrots."

Klara's smile trembled as she said, "Eat some more carrots first. Then, if you still want it, you may have some ham. But leave room for the plum tart I have for dessert."

Hansi beamed. "I'll stop right now, while I have room!"

Klara chuckled and said firmly, "After some more carrots." Hans looked on, his heart feeling full to bursting.

After Emma was sleeping soundly in her crib, and after Hansi was tucked into bed and had tried getting up again and been herded back, Hans and Klara sat together over glasses of sweet white wine. At first they talked about small things, how fast Hansi was growing, how soon the winter weather would start. But finally, Klara put down her glass, looked in Hans' eyes, and said, "What are we going to do?"

Hans wasn't sure whether she meant about his job, or Bluth, or Hansi's school, or something more fundamental. But no matter which of those, his answer was the same. "I don't know."

Epilogue — The Boys

Hans never knew what happened to the boys and their family. And their subsequent story — which led to my existence, and all the stories I have told and may ever tell — is perhaps more incredible than anything in Hans' past or future.

At the time, Germany had a strict quota system for allowing Jews to leave. That portion of the quota reserved for those of German birth was continually full. However, the boys' father had been born while his mother was visiting friends in Russia, and so the family officially counted as Russian and were allowed out. The father had been a wealthy businessman, and a friend (either a member of the Nazi Party or with connections there) helped him retain some fraction of what the business was worth. He then spent almost every penny on their exit. Those expenses included buying tickets and then buying more when the seller resold the tickets to someone else.

The family was one of the few Jewish families given British permission to enter the Palestine Mandate. They spent some months there waiting for their American visa to come through. By the time they sailed past the Statue of Liberty, they were close to penniless. Karl, the oldest boy, the obsessively truthful one, was sixteen years old by then and worked to support the family of eight while his father found his feet. When the United States entered the war, Karl and the next youngest brother, Berthold, tried to enlist, but were refused because, in the view of the military bureaucracy, they were "German" and "enemy aliens." Karl found a way for them to "volunteer to be drafted" instead.

Karl was in the infantry. He served in the 42nd ("Rainbow") Division of the Third Army, eventually led by General George S. Patton. He fought in the Battle of the Bulge, and was in the unit that liberated the Dachau concentration camp. In early 1945, this 5'6" young man, 130 pounds soaking wet, and two buddies stumbled on a company of Germans (about 100 men). His buddies wanted to open fire, but Karl restrained them and instead shouted — in his fluent German with its upper-crust Berlin accent — that the Germans were utterly surrounded, and that their only hope of surviving this day was to lay down their arms at once. They believed him.

So at least once in his life, Karl deliberately told a lie.

After the war, he went to college on the G.I. bill. Bronislawa Zarkoweruvnar, the woman he would marry, worked to put him through graduate school in engineering. He had a long and varied career as an engineer and, eventually, a businessman. He had two children. I'm one. He had two grandchildren when he died at age ninety-four.

Berthold served in the 82nd Airborne Division as an Army medic. His unit entered a smaller concentration camp, Woblein, near the town of Ludwigslust, and set up a temporary hospital for the surviving inmates. As the only member of the unit fluent in German, he was in charge of conveying orders to the Germans who were required to staff the hospital. After the Army, he attended NYU and Harvard Business School, then made a career in product research, developing more effective methods for large corporations. He had two children. As of this writing, he has four grandchildren and three great-grandchildren, and recently celebrated his 100th birthday.

Siegfried, the youngest, was too young to serve in World War II. Poor eyesight made it difficult for him to join the military, but he finally managed it and served as a gun mechanic in the Occupation Army in Japan. He eventually graduated from Harvard Law School and became a highly successful attorney who at one point represented playwright Arthur Miller before the House Un-American Activities Committee. In addition, he served in the Kennedy and Johnson Administrations, attaining the rank of Deputy Assistant Scretary of Defense in the latter. He opposed the Multilateral Forces Treaty, which would have given Germany a key role in the mutual defense of the United States and Europe against the Soviet Union. The plan for that treaty was eventually abandoned. Siegfried lived to age eighty, and had three children and three grandchildren.

Would Hans, if he had come to know all this, have regretted making these futures possible – or would he, sooner or later, have been proud? Who can say?

Acknowledgments

I've been shameless about begging various historians for help in getting my details right, or at least plausible. These historians include George S. Williamson, Associate Professor at Florida State University, and Pamela Swett, Assistant Professor at McMaster University, who kindly responded to emails from a stranger. Professor Swett recommended several books I found invaluable: Hsi-Huey Lang's *The Berlin Police Force in the Weimar Republic*, Belinda Davis's *Home Fires Burning: Food, Politics, and Everyday Life in World War I Berlin*, and Richard Bessel's *Germany After the First World War*. Bill Davies, Associate Professor at American University, Volker Berghahn, Professor at Columbia University, and David G. Blackbourn, Professor at Vanderbilt University, went way above and beyond by actually reading a draft of the book and flagging historical inaccuracies. Professors Berghahn and Blackbourn and Thomas Kohut, Professor at Williams College, also answered a host of historical and cultural questions. Isabel Virginia Hull, Professor at Cornell University, did the same and gave me a long list of German museum sites to check.

Following Professor Hull's pointers led me to Michalina Cieslicki at the Stadtmuseum Berlin, who in turn suggested some museums with Berlin police collections.

Josh Whitacre, Reference Librarian at Indiana University's Herman B. Wells Library, provided some useful sources about the Berlin Police during and after the Weimar Republic and about the Great Police Exhibition of 1926.

I cannot realistically hope to have avoided all outright historical errors.

As always, I also owe a deep debt of gratitude to my beta readers. This time, they were (in alphabetical order) Jill Franclemont, Danusha Goska, Otto Gross, Steven Karel, Sara Macri, Lynn Paniz, Wendy Teller, and Bert Wyle — aka the handsome boy in the pivotal scene. Wendy Teller also lent me her copy of Margaret Macmillan's *Paris 1919: Six Months That Changed the World*. My husband Paul Hager, an autodidact with an interest in military history (as well as degrees in sociology and computer science), answered the many questions I threw at him during the initial writing of this book. (He's also good company.)

I consulted innumerable online sources not just on the relevant political and historical events, but concerning, among many other topics, varieties of cakes, German names, the history of bibs, anti-Jewish graffiti, police uniforms, food adulteration, various aspects of the school system, and typical marriage proposals. There are so many that it would make this book noticeably longer and at least a little more expensive if I were to list them all. Any reader interested in the source for a particular detail should feel free to contact me and ask on what source(s) I relied.

Author's Note

This is a fictional biography of a very real man — about whom I know almost nothing, in spite of the fact that for a few brief minutes, he played a critical role in my family's life and future.

I originally planned for this book to be more complex in structure. After doing National Novel Writing Month (aka NaNoWriMo or NaNo) every November since 2010, usually "writing into the dark" with only a few character and scene notes on November 1st, I decided it was time to save myself the ten-or-so months of wrestling with a very messy rough draft from January on. Instead, I would plan the book ahead of time — which, for historical fiction, meant doing most of the research ahead of time as well. And to take full advantage of this new process, as well as to respect how little my family and I actually knew about the main character, I would create three different plot lines leading up to his crucial decision, and then three different plot lines showing the results of that decision.

But it turned out one thing hadn't changed about how I approached a novel: it wanted to write itself, without too much interference from my conscious mind.

As I researched the conditions in which my character Hans would have grown up, and the various transformations of the Berlin police force, I came up with scenes that flowed from that factual background. And as I worked, I became dissatisfied with the idea of separating out all the ideas I had for the story — at least, that part of the story answering the crucial question of "why" — into separate threads. It would mean less immersive detail, I felt, and thus distance the reader from the story. It felt like a structure more appropriate for a short story than a novel.

So, as you've seen, I ditched that idea.

What about the three "what happened afterward" plot lines? Somehow, doing three full-blown explorations of that question felt . . . I'm not certain what the right word is, but perhaps "unnecessary." Or "distracting."

In the end, we — my family, my father and uncles, the reader — can't know who the man I've named Hans really was, or what form of grace touched him and led him to spare those three Jewish boys. I've presented one version of his formative years and emotions and personality. I hope it helps all of us honor his decision. In addition, the extent to which Hans is something of an Everyman may make it easier for readers to feel capable of emulating him.

Here, for the heck of it, are some ideas I had at the start about the possible alternate paths toward the crucial scene.

— Hans could fall for, and fall in with, a girl who turned out to be in the resistance. I abandoned this idea because (a) there were very few resistance fighters in the early 1930s, which would have required me to leave Hans unattached until quite late in the story or else add infidelity to the plot, and (b) it struck me as too easy, too obvious an approach, and lacking in the sort of narrative tension I strove for.

— A variant: Hans could be troubled or even disgusted by much of what the Nazis are doing and fantasize about being in the resistance. When the crucial moment comes, he could feel as if he's suddenly living his fantasies. I found this idea unsatisfying as straying too far from the Everyman aspect of the story.

— Hans' love interest could be not an opponent of the Nazis, but an ardent supporter of them. He could become a

Party member to please either her or her father. As you'll see, I went for a more subtle approach to her attitudes.

I also did some picking and choosing when it came to what incidents from my family's past to include. More difficult was deciding how many interesting historical details were worth mentioning. I struggled, for example, over whether to feature the celebrations of Hitler's birthday, or of the anniversary of Hitler's becoming Chancellor of Germany. In the end, I decided I had already hung enough baubles on the Christmas tree of my story.

I also didn't include every historical event possible. For example, I have Hans' father work in a bank, but didn't directly address the fact that many banks failed in 1931.

Authors of historical fiction must find their own point of balance between the demands of accuracy and those of narrative. (One complication is the frequency with which research sources and experts disagree.) Unlike some, I avoid moving historical dates to more convenient points in a story, though where there is uncertainty as to a date, I pick the possibility more useful to me. For example, I have soldiers marching to war singing *"Deutschland, Deutschland Über Alles"* based on a single account of soldiers singing that song in November 1914, though it didn't become the national anthem until sometime in the 1920s. The photograph that inspired me to include a boy selling lemonade from a tank on his back is dated 1931, but after confirming that such tanks existed in other countries far earlier, I included a lemonade seller so equipped in a scene set in 1930.

Nor do I move geographical locations around, though I'll toss in possible locations (streets, neighborhoods) both for purely fictional scenes and when I can't readily discover where a historical scene occurred. Similarly, where I can't find the name of, e.g., a school, I'll make up a plausible one.

When it comes to including fictional characters, I try to limit that practice to characters whose existence would have left few obvious ripples. If I include a historical character and give that character words and behaviors of my own invention, I aim at plausibility. I hope I've achieved it.

About the Author

Karen A. Wyle was born a Connecticut Yankee, but eventually settled in Bloomington, Indiana, home of Indiana University. She now considers herself a Hoosier. She and her husband have two wildly creative adult offspring.

In addition to writing novels (science fiction, afterlife fantasy, general fantasy, and historical fiction including historical romance) and picture books, Wyle is an appellate attorney (though quasi-retired) and photographer. Her voice is the product of almost five decades of reading both literary and genre fiction. It is no doubt also influenced, although she hopes not fatally tainted, by her years of law practice. Her personal history has led her to focus on often-intertwined themes of family, communication, personal identity, the impossibility of controlling events, and the persistence of unfinished business.

Connect With
the Author

Learn more about Karen A. Wyle by looking her up on
her author website (http://www.KarenAWyle.com),
Twitter (@KarenAWyle),
Facebook (https://www.facebook.com/KarenAWyle),
Goodreads (https://www.goodreads.com/kawyle),
or her blog Looking Around (https://looking-around.
blogspot.com/).

You can also follow the author on BookBub (https://
www.bookbub.com/authors/karen-a-wyle), which will send
you alerts about new releases.

Like the book? Please tell readers! Online book reviews
are enormously helpful – and old-fashioned word of mouth
is terrific as well!

You can sign up for Wyle's monthly newsletter, including news of upcoming releases as well as looks at her writing process and extras like excerpts and cover reveals, at the newsletter signup link on her website.